One of My Sons by Anna Katharine Green

Anna Katharine Green was born in Brooklyn, New York on November 11th, 1846.

Anna's initial ambition was to be a poet. However that path failed to ignite any significant interest and she turned to fiction writing. She published her first—and most famous work in 1878—'The Leavenworth Case'. Wilkie Collins praised it and it sold extremely well.

It led to Anna writing 40 novels and to becoming known as 'the mother of the detective novel.'

In helping to shape the genre she brought many other innovations including a series detective: her main character was detective Ebenezer Gryce of the New York Metropolitan Police Force, but in three novels he is assisted by the nosy society spinster Amelia Butterworth, another innovation and a prototype for Miss Marple, Miss Silver and others.

She also invented the 'girl detective': in the character of Violet Strange, a debutante with a secret life as a sleuth. Anna's other innovations included the now familiar dead bodies in libraries, newspaper clippings as "clews," the coroner's inquest, and expert witnesses. Yale Law School once used her books to demonstrate how damaging it can be to rely on circumstantial evidence.

Her career was now well advanced and she was much admired.

On November 25, 1884, Green married the actor and stove designer, and later noted furniture maker, Charles Rohlfs, who was seven years her junior. They had three children; Rosamund, Roland and Sterling.

Although Anna was a progressive she did not approve of many of her feminist contemporaries, and was opposed to women's suffrage.

On November 25, 1884, Anna married the actor and noted furniture maker, Charles Rohlfs, who was seven years her junior. They had three children; Rosamund, Roland and Sterling.

Anna Katharine Green died on April 11, 1935 in Buffalo, New York, at the age of 88.

Index of Contents

BOOK I

THE SHADOW

CHAPTER I

THE CHILD, AND WHAT SHE LED ME INTO

I was walking at a rapid pace up the avenue one raw, fall evening, when somewhere near the corner of Fifty—Street I was brought to a sudden stand-still by the sound of a child's voice accosting me from the stoop of one of the handsome houses I was then passing.

"O sir!" it cried, "please come in. Please come to grandpa. He's sick and wants you."

Surprised, for I knew no one on the block, I glanced up and saw bending from the open doorway the trembling figure of a little girl, with a wealth of curly hair blowing about her sweet, excited face.

"You have made a mistake," I called up to her. "I am not the person you suppose. I am a stranger. Tell me whom you know about here and I will see that someone comes to your grandpa."

But this did not satisfy her. Running down the stoop, she seized me by the arm with childish impetuosity, crying: "No, no. There isn't time. Grandpa told me to bring in the first man I saw going by. You are the first man. Come!"

There was urgency in her tones, and unconsciously I began to yield to her insistence, and allow myself to be drawn towards the stoop.

"Who is your grandpa?" I asked, satisfied from the imposing look of the house that he must be a man of some prominence. "If he is sick there are the servants"—But here her little foot came down in infantile impatience.

"Grandpa never waits!" she cried, dragging me with her small hands up the stoop and into the open door. "If you don't hurry he'll think I didn't do as he told me."

What man would not have yielded? The hall, as seen from the entrance, was wide and unusually rich. Indeed, an air of the highest respectability, as well as of unbounded wealth, characterised the whole establishment; and however odd the adventure appeared, it certainly offered nothing calculated to awaken distrust. Entering with her, I shut the door behind me. In an instant she was half-way down the hall.

"Here! here!" she cried, pausing before a door near its end.

The confidence with which she summoned me (I sometimes wonder if my countenance conveys more than the ordinary amount of good nature) and the pretty picture she made, standing in the flood of light which poured from the unseen apartment toward which she beckoned me, lured me on till I reached her side, and stood in full view of a scene which certainly justified her fear if not the demand she made upon a passing stranger.

In the midst of a small room, plain as any office, I saw an elderly gentleman standing who, even to my unaccustomed eyes, seemed to be not simply ill, but in the throes of actual dissolution.

Greatly disturbed, for I had anticipated nothing so serious, I turned to fly for assistance, when the little child, rushing by me, caught her grandfather by the knees and gave me such a look, I had not the heart to leave her.

Indeed it would have been cruel to do so. The appearance and attitude of the sick man were startling even to me. Though in a state bordering on death, he was, as I have said, standing, not lying, and his tall figure swaying against the large table to which he clung, formed a picture of mental and physical suffering such as I had never before seen, and can never in all my life to come, forget. One hand was pressed against his heart, but the other, outspread in a desperate attempt to support his weight, had fallen on some half-dozen sheets or so of typewritten paper, which, slipping under the pressure put upon them, kept him tottering, though he did not fall. He was looking my way, and as I advanced into the room, his collapsing frame shook with sudden feeling, and the hand which he held clenched over his heart opened slightly, revealing a scrap of paper crushed between his fingers.

Struck with compassion, for the contrast was pitiful between his naturally imposing appearance and his present helplessness, I murmured some words of sympathy and encouragement, and then supposing him to be alone in the house with his grandchild, inquired what I could do to serve him.

He cast a meaning glance down at his hand, then seeing that I did not understand him, made a super-human effort and held that member out, uttering some inarticulate words which I was able to construe into a prayer to take from him the paper which his stiffening clutch made it difficult for him to release.

Touched by his extremity, and anxious to afford him all the solace his desperate case demanded, I drew the paper from between his fingers. As I did so I noted, first, that it was a portion of one of the sheets I saw scattered about on every side, and, secondly, that it was folded together as if intended for someone's private perusal.

"What shall I do with this?" I asked, consulting his eye over which a glaze was fast forming.

He let his own glance wander eagerly till it fell upon some envelopes, then it became fixed, and I understood.

Drawing out one, I placed the slip in it, and fastening the envelope, consulted his face with a smile.

He answered with a look so full of thanks, appreciation, and confidence that I felt abashed. Something of more than ordinary significance was conveyed by that look, and I was about to ask what name I should write on the envelope, when the faint sounds with which he had been trying to express his secret wishes became articulate, and I heard these words:

"To no one—no one else! To—to—"

Alas! at this critical moment and just as the name was faltering on his lips, his utterance failed. He strove for expression, but no words would come.

In a desperation, which was but the faint reflection of his own, I tried to help him.

"Is it for your lawyer?" I suggested; then, as he made no sign, I hastily added: "For your doctor? For your wife? For anyone in the house?"

He gave me one supreme look, raised his eyes, and for an instant stood in an attitude so expressive of joy and indefinable expectancy that I was astonished beyond words and forgot that I was in the presence of death. But only for a moment. While I was still marvelling at this sudden change in him, the child who was clinging to him uttered a terrified scream and unloosed her arms. Then I saw him sink, gasp, and fall forward, and, springing, caught him in my arms before his head could touch the floor. Alas! it was the last service I could render him. By the time I had laid him down he had expired, and I found myself, in no other company than that of a trembling child, bending above the dead body of a man who with his last breath had charged me with a commission of whose purport I understood nothing, save that under no circumstances and upon no pretext was I to deliver the letter he had entrusted to me, to anyone but the person for whom it was intended.

But who was this person? Ah, that was the question! Certainly my position in this house of strangers was a most extraordinary one.

CHAPTER II

THE YOUNG DOCTOR AND THE OLD

Meanwhile the child had started down the hall, and up the stairs, calling:

"Papa! Papa!"

Startled by this intimation of another person's presence in a house I had supposed to hold no one but ourselves, I hastily followed her till she reached the floor above and paused before a shut door. Here something seemed to restrain her.

"Papa's inside," she whispered.

If this was so, he was not alone. Laughter, quick exclamations, and the clink of glasses could plainly be heard through the door; and shocked at the contrast offered by this scene of mirth to the solemn occurrence which had just taken place below, I hesitated to enter, and looked about for some means of communicating with the servants who I now felt must be below. But here the terrified child, who was clinging to my knee, interposed:

"I do not think papa is there. Papa does not like cards. Uncle George does. Come, let's look for papa."

She dragged me toward the front of the house, entered another room, and seemed surprised to find the light turned down and her papa gone.

"Perhaps he is with Uncle Alph," she faltered, and, bounding up another flight of stairs, turned around to see if I was behind her.

There seemed no alternative left but to follow her till I came upon someone; so I hastened up this second staircase. She had already entered a room.

"O Uncle Alph!" I heard her cry. "Grandpa's lying on the floor downstairs. I cannot find papa. I'm so frightened," and she ran sobbing towards the young man, who rose to receive her in an abstraction which even these startling words failed to break.

For this and other reasons I noticed him particularly notwithstanding the embarrassment of my own position. He was a handsome man of the luxury-loving type, whose characteristics it would be useless to describe, since they were of a nature to suggest, rather than explain the extent of his attractions. I afterwards heard from such of my friends as were in the habit of walking the avenue with him, that he never failed to draw the attention of passers-by; something in his features, his carriage, or the turn of his head and shoulders stamping him as a man worth looking at, not only once, but twice. At this moment, however, I was not so much impressed by his good looks, as by his uneasy and feverish expression.

He had caught up a letter which he had been engaged in writing at our entrance, and as the child's appeal rang out, he crumpled it nervously in his hand, and dropped it into the waste-paper basket. As a certain furtive haste characterised this action, my attention was caught by it, and I found myself wondering whether it was a letter or memorandum he thus sacrificed to his surprise.

Meanwhile he seemed to be trying to take in what the little one wanted. Evidently he had not as yet noticed me standing in the doorway, and I thought it best to introduce myself.

"I beg your pardon," said I, "I am Arthur Outhwaite of the firm of Robinson & Outhwaite, lawyers. I was passing by the house when this child called me in to the assistance of her grandfather whom, I am sorry to say, I found in a very precarious condition in his study downstairs. If he is your father, you have my sympathy for his sudden demise. He died in my arms a moment ago; and having been the witness of his last moments, I could not leave the house without explaining my position to his relatives."

"Dead! Father?"

It was not grief, it was hardly astonishment which gave force to this brief and involuntary exclamation. It was something quite different, something which it shocked me to hear in his tones and see sparkle in his eye. But this expression, whatever it betokened, lasted but a moment. Catching up the child in his arms, he hid his face behind her and rushed towards the door. Me he hardly noticed.

"Where is he?" he asked, ignoring or forgetting what I had told him.

It was the child who answered.

"In the den, Uncle Alph. Don't take me there; I'm afraid. Set me down; I want to find Hope."

He hastily obeyed her, and the child ran away. Then, and only then, he seemed to take in my presence.

"You were called in from the street?" he wonderingly observed; "I don't understand it. Where were my brothers? They were near enough to render him assistance. Why should a stranger be called in?"

This was a question for which I had no answer, so I made none. He did not seem to be struck by the omission.

"Let us go down," said he.

I opened the door which the little one had closed behind her, and proceeded toward the stair-head. From certain indistinct noises which I had heard during the foregoing short interchange of words, I expected to find the house in a state of alarm and everyone alert. But the card-players were still at their game on the floor below, and I was not surprised to see my companion pause and give an admonitory kick to the door through which such incongruous noises issued.

"Father's ill!" he shouted in a voice hoarse with many passions; and waiting for no reply, he rushed ahead of me downstairs, followed by some half-dozen partially sobered men.

Among these latter I noticed one whom I took to be the elder brother of him whom the little one had addressed as Uncle Alph. He had the same commanding appearance, the same abstracted air, and woke, when he did wake, to the same curious condition of conflicting emotions. But I did not have time to dwell long upon this feature of the extraordinary affair in which I had become thus curiously involved.

The alarm which had been so slow in spreading above, had passed like wildfire through the lower part of the house, and we found some half-dozen servants standing in and about the small room where the master of the house lay stretched. Some were wringing their hands, some were crying, and some, rigid with terror, stared at the face they had so lately seen with the hue of health upon it.

At our approach they naturally withdrew to the hall, and I presently found myself standing between the group thus formed and the three or four young gentlemen visitors who had not followed the brothers into the room. Amongst the latter I saw one whose face was not altogether unfamiliar, and it was from him that I gained my first information concerning the man to whose dying passion I had been witness, and from whom I had received the strange commission which, unknown to those about me, made my continued presence in this house a necessity from which the embarrassment of the occasion could not release me.

The dead man was Archibald Gillespie, the well-known stockbroker and railroad magnate, whose name, as well as those of his three spendthrift sons, was in every man's mouth since that big deal by which he had made two millions in less than two months.

Meanwhile one of the gentlemen who had accompanied the two Gillespies into the room where their father lay, came out looking very pale. He was a doctor, though to all appearance not the family physician.

"Will one of you go for Dr. Bennett?" he asked. "Bring him at once and at any cost; Mr. Gillespie cannot be moved till he comes."

Dr. Bennett evidently was the family physician.

"Why can't he be moved?" called out a voice near me. "Is there anything wrong? Mr. Gillespie was violently sick a month ago. I suppose he got around too quickly."

But the young doctor, without replying, stepped back into the room, leaving us all agog, though few of us ventured upon open remonstrance.

In another minute one of the men near me slipped out in obedience to the request just made.

"Is Mrs. Gillespie living?" I asked, after a moment spent in more or less indecision.

"Where have you come from?" was the answer given, seasoned by a stare I bore with what equanimity I could. "Mrs. Gillespie has been dead these fifteen years."

So! the letter was not meant for his wife.

Here I caught an eye fixed on mine. It was that of one of the servants who stood huddled about the doorway of what appeared to be a large dining-room on the opposite side of the hall. When this man, for it was a male servant, saw that he had attracted my attention, he made me an imperceptible sign. As he was old and grey-haired, I heeded the sign he made and stepped towards him. Instantly he greeted me with the whisper:

"You seem to be the only sober man here. Don't let them do anything till Mr. Leighton comes in. He is the saint of the family, sir."

"Is he the little girl's father?" I asked.

The man nodded. "And a good man, too," he insisted. "A very good man."

Was this honest judgment or sarcasm? I had heard that each of Mr. Gillespie's sons had given his father no end of trouble.

Meantime a silence deeper than that of awe had spread throughout the house. Feeling myself out of place and yet strangely in place, I drew aside into as inconspicuous a corner as I could find, and waited as all the others did, for the family physician.

While doing so I caught stray glimpses of my first acquaintance, Alfred Gillespie, who, fretted by some anxiety he could not altogether conceal, came more than once into the hall and threw furtive glances up the stairway. Was it the little girl he was concerned about? If so, I shared his anxiety.

At last the bell rang. Instantly, so great was the strain upon us, we all moved, and one or two bounded towards the door. But it was opened by the butler with that mechanical habitude such old servants acquire, and, though nothing could shake the calm deference of this trained domestic, there was something in the bow with which he greeted the newcomer which assured us that the man we so anxiously expected had arrived.

I had seen Dr. Bennett more than once, but never before showing so much anxiety. Whether from shock or some secret cause not to be communicated to us, this old and capable physician seemed to be in a condition of as much agitation as ourselves, and obeyed the summons of the young doctor who stood beckoning to him from the threshold of the little den, with an appearance of alacrity that nevertheless had an odd element of hesitation in it. I might not have noticed this under other circumstances, and am quite sure that no one else detected any peculiarity in his manner, but to me, everything was important which offered anything like a clue to the proper understanding of a situation in which I found myself so deeply, yet so secretly involved.

Mr. Gillespie's physician remained for some minutes closeted with the sons of the deceased and their young medical friend; then he came out. Instantly I saw from his expression that our fears or rather, those of the young doctor, were not without foundation. Yet he was careful not to raise an alarm, and in addressing us, spoke in strictly professional tones:

"A sad case, gentlemen! Mr. Gillespie has taken an overdose of chloral. We will have to leave him where he is till the coroner can be called."

A gasp followed by the clink of breaking glass came from the dining-room behind me. The old butler had dropped a glass he had just lifted off the mantel-shelf of the dining-room.

The doctor was at his side in a moment.

"What is that?" he demanded.

The butler stooped for the pieces.

"Only the glass Mr. Gillespie drank out of. He asked for wine a half hour ago. Your words frightened me, sir."

He did not look frightened; but old servants of his stamp possess a strange immobility.

"I will pick up these pieces," said the doctor, stooping beside the man.

The butler drew back. Dr. Bennett picked up the pieces. They were all dry. Evidently the glass had been drained.

As he came out he cast a keen but not unkindly glance at the group of young men drawn up in the doorway.

"Which of you was the witness of Mr. Gillespie's death?" he asked.

I bowed. I dreaded his questions, yet saw no way of evading them. If only Mr. Gillespie had been able to articulate the one word which would have relieved me of all further responsibility in this matter!

"You are the person who was called into the house by Mr. Gillespie's grandchild?" the doctor now asked, meeting my eye with the same expression of instantaneous and complete confidence I had seen on the features of his unhappy patient.

"I am," I replied; and proceeded to relate the circumstances with all the simplicity the occasion required. Only I said nothing about the letter which had been entrusted to me for delivery to some unknown person. How could I? There had been no encouragement in Mr. Gillespie's expression when I asked him if the note I had taken from him was meant for his doctor.

The account I was able to give of the deceased broker's last moments seemed to deepen the impression which had been made upon the physician by the condition in which he found him. Taking up the pieces of glass he had collected from the dining-room hearth, he sniffed them carefully, during which act the two sons of Mr. Gillespie watched him with starting eyes. When he laid them down again, we could none of us conceal our curiosity.

"You have something dreadful to communicate," murmured the elder son.

The doctor hesitated; then he glanced from one to the other of the two handsome faces before him, and remarked:

"Your brother is not here. Do you know if he is likely to return soon?"

"Where is Mr. Leighton?" inquired Alfred, turning towards the servants. "I thought he meant to remain home to-night."

The butler respectfully advanced.

"Mr. Leighton went out an hour ago," said he. "He and Mr. Gillespie had a few words in the den, sir, after which he put on his hat and coat and went out."

"Did you see your master at that time?"

"No, sir, I only heard his voice."

"Did that sound natural?"

The old servant seemed loath to reply, but feeling the doctor's eye resting imperatively upon him, he hesitatingly admitted:

"It wasn't quiet, sir, if you mean that. Mr. Gillespie seemed to be angry or very much displeased. He spoke quite loud."

"Where were you?"

"In the dining-room, sir, putting away the last of the dinner dishes."

"Did you hear what your master said?"

"No, sir; it was something about religion; too much religion."

"My brother attends too many mission services to please my father," explained Alfred in a low tone.

The doctor heard, but did not take his eye from the old servant.

"Was this before he took the glass of wine you have just told us he asked for?"

"Yes, sir, just before. It was Mr. Leighton who came for it. He said his father looked tired."

"Ah, and how came the glass to be back then on the dining-room mantel-shelf?"

"I don't know, sir. Perhaps Mr. Gillespie put it there himself. He never liked any litter on his study table, sir."

At this statement the older brother opened his lips, but I noticed he did not speak. There were no traces of intoxication about him now.

"I wish you would show me the bottle from which you poured the wine."

The butler, whose name I afterwards learned to be Hewson, led the way to a large buffet extending half across the dining-room wall. From where I stood in the hall-way I could see him pointing out a bottle of what looked like sherry. Suddenly he gave a start.

"That isn't the one," he cried, loud enough for me to hear. "The bottle I took out for Mr. Leighton was half-empty. This is quite full."

Again I saw the lips of the elder brother move, and again he refrained from speaking.

"I should like to have that bottle found," said the physician; "but no one need look for it now. Indeed, it would be better for us to wait for Leighton's return before making any further movement. George, Alfred, may I ask you to leave me alone with your father for a few minutes. And let the dining-room be cleared. I don't want to have to make any excuses to the coroner when he arrives. Your father has not died a natural death."

It was an announcement for which we had been in a measure prepared by the serious manner of the young doctor, yet it seemed to me it ought to have occasioned a greater, or at least a different display of feeling on the part of the two most intimately concerned. I looked for an exchange of glances between them or at least some hurried words of sorrow or dismay. But though all evinced strong emotion, no looks passed between them, nor did they make the least attempt at mutual sympathy or encouragement. Were they not on confidential terms? The moment certainly was one to call out whatever brotherly feeling they possessed.

"I shall have to make use of the telephone," Dr. Bennett now announced. "You must pardon my seeming disrespect to the dead. The occasion demands it."

And with one hurried look to see that his commands had been obeyed, and that the dining-room had been cleared of the huddling servants, he stepped back into the so-called den and closed the door behind him.

Next moment we heard his voice rise in the inevitable "Hallo!"

"I don't understand Dr. Bennett's strange demeanour," I now heard uttered in remark near me. It was George speaking in a low tone to his brother.

But that brother, with one of his anxious looks up the stairs, failed to answer.

"Father was in the habit of taking chloral, but I thought he always waited until he got to his own room. I never knew him to take it downstairs before," George went on in a low tone between a whisper and a grumble.

This time Alfred answered.

"He made an exception to-night," said he. "When I ran down to your door at half-past eight, I met Claire coming out of father's room with a bottle in her hand. She had been sent up after the chloral, and was taking it down to him."

George gave his brother a suspicious look.

"Did she say so?" he asked.

"Yes."

"Poor child! She will miss her grandfather. I wonder if she knows?"

I felt that I had no right to listen. But I was standing where the doctor had left me, and hardly knew how to withdraw till I had received my dismissal from someone in authority. Yet I was thinking of going farther front when the doctor came out again and, approaching me, remarked:

"This delay is probably causing you great inconvenience. But I must ask you to remain a short time longer. I presume you can find a seat in the drawing-room."

With a glance at the young gentlemen, I expressed my obligations for his courtesy, but did not make a move towards the room he had indicated.

Instantly, and with an understanding of my feelings which surprised me, George took the hint I had given him, and stepping forward, raised a heavy plush curtain at the left and begged me to be seated in the richly appointed room within. But I had hardly taken a step towards it when a diversion was created by the entrance into the house of a gentleman whom I at once took to be the third brother for whose presence all waited with more or less suspense.

He was sufficiently prepossessing in appearance to awaken admiration, but he bore no resemblance to his brothers. He seemed to have more character and less—well, I find it difficult to say just what impression he made upon me at this moment. Enough that with my first glimpse of him I felt confident that no ordinary person had entered upon the scene, though just what special characteristic of his personality or disposition would prove the emphatic one it was not easy to judge, at a moment's notice.

He had a downcast air, and to my eyes looked weary to the point of collapse, but he roused at the sight of a stranger, and cast an inquiring look at the doctor and then at the servants crowding in the passage beyond.

He evidently took me for one of his brothers' boon companions.

"What's amiss?" he demanded in some irritation—an irritation I was fain to construe into a total lack of preparation for the fatal news awaiting him. "What's the matter, George? What's the matter, Alph?"

"The worst!" came in simultaneous reply.

"Father is dead!" cried George.

"Took too much chloral," added Alfred.

Leighton Gillespie stood stock-still for a moment, then threw off his hat and rushed down the hall. But at the door of what now might be called the chamber of death, he found the doctor standing in an attitude which compelled him to come to a sudden stop.

"Wait a moment," said that gentleman. "I have to correct an impression. Your father has not died from an overdose of chloral as I had at first supposed, but from a deadly dose of prussic acid. You have only to smell his lips to be certain of this fact. Now, Leighton, you may enter."

CHAPTER III

WHAT A DOOR HID

It was a startling declaration, and the horror it called up was visible on every face. But the surprise which should have accompanied it was lacking, and however quickly the three nearest the deceased man's heart strove to cover up their first instinctive acceptance of a fact so suggestive of hidden troubles, I could not but see that the prosperous stockbroker had had griefs, anxieties, or hopes to which this sudden end seemed to those who knew him best, a natural sequence.

I began to regret the chance which had brought me into such close relations with this family, and felt the closed envelope in my pocket weighing on my breast like lead.

Meanwhile, he whom they called Leighton was saying in a highly strained tone, which he vainly endeavoured to make natural:

"May not Dr. Bennett be mistaken? There is the chloral bottle on the shelf over the fireplace. We are not in the habit of seeing it here. Does not its presence in this room argue that father felt the need of it. Prussic acid can only be obtained through a doctor, and I am confident you never prescribed him such a dangerous drug, Dr. Bennett."

"No, for it is totally inapplicable to his case. But you will find that he died from taking it, Leighton; all his symptoms show it, and we have only to determine now whether he took it in the chloral, in the glass of wine he drank, or by means of some other agency not yet discovered. I regret to speak so unequivocally, but I never mince matters where my profession is concerned. And, besides, the coroner would not show you this consideration even if I did. The fact is too patent."

They were now inside the study and I did not hear Leighton's reply, but when they all came out again, I saw that the latter had not only accepted the situation, but that he had been informed of the part I had been called upon to play in this matter. This was apparent from the way he greeted me, and the questions he put concerning his child's conduct during the last terrible moments of her grandfather's life.

As he did this I had a fuller opportunity for studying his face. It was the most melancholy one I had ever seen, and what struck me as being worthy of remark was that this melancholy seemed a settled one and quite apart from the present grief and disturbance. Yet he had been heavily shaken by his father's sudden if not inexplicable death, or appeared to be, which possibly is not quite the same thing.

"I do not understand why my father should have called anyone in from the street to witness his sufferings while he had sons in the house," he courteously remarked; "but having felt this necessity and having succeeded in obtaining such help, I am glad that chance favoured him and us with a person of such apparent good feeling as yourself."

I scarcely heeded him. I was pondering over the letter and whether I should pass it over to this man. But instinct withheld me, or rather my lawyer-like habits which happily acted as a restraint upon my natural impulse. I had received no intimation as yet that it was intended for any of Mr. Gillespie's sons.

"You will oblige us by waiting for the coroner?" he now went on. "He has telephoned that he will be here immediately."

"I shall wait," I said. And it was by his invitation I now stepped into the parlour.

A quarter of an hour, a half-hour, passed before the front door bell rang again. From the hubbub which ensued, I knew that the man we wished for had arrived, but it was a long while before he entered the room in which I sat, during which tedious interim I had to possess my soul in patience. But at last I heard his step on the threshold, and looking up, I beheld a spare, earnest man who approached me with great seriousness, and sat down near enough to indulge in confidential talk without running the risk of being heard by anyone.

"You are Mr. Outhwaite," he began. "I have heard of your firm and have more than once seen Mr. Robinson. Had you any acquaintance with Mr. Gillespie or his family before to-night?"

"No, sir; Mr. Gillespie was known to me only by reputation."

"Then it was pure chance which led you to be a witness of his final moments?"

"Pure chance, if we do not believe in Providence," I returned.

He surveyed me quite intently.

"Relate what passed."

Now here was a dilemma. Did my duty exact a revelation of the facts which I had hitherto felt obliged to keep even from the deceased man's sons? It was a question not to be decided in a moment, so I made up my mind to be guided by developments, and confined my narration to a recapitulation of my former plain account of Mr. Gillespie's last moments. This narrative I made as simple as I could. When I had finished he asked if Mr. Gillespie's grandchild had been present at the moment her grandfather expired.

I answered that she had been clinging to him all the time he remained erect, but shrank back and ran out of the room the moment he gave signs of falling to the floor.

"Did he speak to her?"

"Not that I heard."

"Did he say anything?"

"A few inarticulate words, no names."

"He did not ask for his sons?"

"No."

"For none of them?"

"No."

"How came the alarm to be spread?"

"I went up with the child and called the young men down."

Coroner Frisbie stroked his chin, still looking at me intently.

"Was there an empty phial or a piece of paper lying about on the study-table or on the floor when you went in?"

I started.

"Paper?" I repeated. "What kind of paper?"

"Such as is used by druggists and physicians in rolling up their prescriptions. The prussic acid which Mr. Gillespie has evidently taken must have been bought in liquid form. The bottle which held it should be lying about and possibly the paper in which it was wrapped. That is, if this poison was swallowed intentionally by Mr. Gillespie."

I recalled the exact look of the scrap of paper I had put into an envelope at this gentleman's request. It was not such a one as is used by druggists in wrapping up parcels, and I felt my breast grow lighter by a degree.

"I did not see any such paper."

"Where is the little girl?" he now queried. "I must see her."

I had made up my mind to one thing. If the child said that I had been given a paper by her grandfather I would acknowledge it and produce the envelope. But if she had forgotten the fact or had been too frightened to notice it, I would preserve silence in regard to it a little longer, in the hope of being shown a way out of my difficulty.

I was therefore not sorry to hear him ask for the little girl.

"I take it that you are not anxious to remain here," he now remarked. "If you will give me your address and hold yourself in readiness to obey my summons, I can excuse you for the night."

For answer I held out my card, and seeing that I had no further excuse for lingering, was moving toward the door, when Dr. Bennett came hurriedly in.

"I have found something—" he began, and then paused with a quick glance in my direction, as if questioning the propriety of proceeding further with his discovery in my presence.

The coroner showed no such hesitation. Hastening to meet the old family physician, he said:

"You have found the bottle or only the paper in which the bottle was wrapped?"

Dr. Bennett drew him aside, and I saw what looked like a small cork pass between them.

"Was it in Mr. Gillespie's study you found this?" queried the coroner. "I thought I had thoroughly searched the study."

The answer was uttered in the lowest of low tones, but I had no difficulty in catching the gist of what he said.

"It was on the dining-room floor, under the edge of the rug. A very suspicious fact, don't you think so? Mr. Gillespie would never have thrust it there. Some other person—don't know who—not say anything yet—shrink from seeing the police in this house."

The two doctors interchanged a look which I surprised in the large mirror opposite. But I gave no sign of having seen anything extraordinary. I felt too keenly the delicacy of my own position. Next minute we were all walking towards the hall.

"Silence!" came in admonitory tones from the coroner as we paused for a moment on the threshold. "Let us not disturb the young men any further than is necessary to-night."

At that moment we heard the cry:

"Where is Miss Meredith? Has anyone seen Miss Meredith? I cannot find her in any of the rooms upstairs."

"Hope! Hope! Where are you, Hope?" called out another voice, charged with feeling.

Hope! Did my heart beat faster as this name, destined to play such a part in my future life, was sounded in my ears? I cannot say. That heart has beat often enough since at the utterance of this sweet monosyllable, but at that time—well, I think I was too interested in the alarm which this cry instantly raised, to note my personal sensations. From one end of the house to the other, men and women rushed from room to room, and I heard not only this name called out, but that of the child, which it seems was Claire.

"Cannot the child be found either?" I inquired impetuously of the coroner who still lingered in the lower hall.

"It seems not. Who is Miss Meredith?"

It was the old butler who answered him.

"She is the young gentlemen's cousin," said he. "She was a great favourite with Mr. Gillespie, and lived here like a daughter. They will find her somewhere upstairs."

But the prophecy proved to be a false one. Slowly the servants came creeping down whispering among themselves and looking very much frightened. Then we saw George descend shaking his head impatiently, and then Leighton, wild with an anxiety for which he had no name.

"She must be here!" he cried, thinking only of his child. "Claire! Claire!" And he began running through the great drawing-room where we knew she could not be.

Alfred had remained above.

Suddenly I recalled a fact connected with my own visit upstairs.

"Have they been up to the fourth floor?" I inquired of Dr. Bennett. "When I was in Mr. Alfred Gillespie's room on the third floor, I remember hearing someone rush through the hall. I supposed at that time it was someone going below. But it may have been someone going higher up."

"Let us go see!" the doctor suggested.

I followed him without a thought. As we passed Alfred's door, we could see him standing in the middle of the room in a state of rage which made him oblivious of our approach. He was tearing into morsels a piece of paper which had the same appearance as the one he had formerly thrust into the waste-paper basket, and as he tore, he muttered words amongst which I caught the following:

"Why should I write? If she loved me she would wait. She would not run away now, unless he—"

Dr. Bennett, with his finger on his lip, slid by. I hastened after him, and together we mounted the last flight.

We were now in a portion of the building as new to the doctor as to myself. When we reached the top of the stairs we found the whole place dark save for a little glimmer towards the front which proved to be a gas-jet burning low in one of the attic rooms.

Turning this up we looked around, opened a closet-door or two, then walked into the back, where the doctor struck a match. Two closed doors met our eyes. One of these upon being opened disclosed a well-furnished room, similar in appearance to those in front, the other an unfinished garret half filled with trunks and boxes.

"Well!" he ejaculated, as the match went out upon this scene. "This is a mystery."

"Hark!" I urged; "our ears rather than our eyes must do service in this emergency."

He took the hint, and together we listened till some sound—was it the breathing of a person concealed near us?—caused us both to start and the doctor to light another match.

This time we saw something, but the match went out before we could determine what.

Annoyed by these momentary flashes of light, I dashed back into one of the rooms we had left, and catching up a candle I had previously noted there, lit it at the gas-jet, and proceeded back with it to this garret room.

Instantly a sight full of the strangest interest revealed itself.

Crouched against the farther wall, with wide-extended eyes fixed full upon us, we perceived a woman, upon whose pallid face and risen locks terror or some other equally emphatic passion had so fixed its impress that she looked like some affrighted creature balked in flight by some dreadful, some unprecedented sight which held her spell-bound. That she was beautiful, in that touching, feminine way which goes to the heart, did not lessen the effect of her appearance, nor were we unmoved by the fact that the child for whom the house had just been ransacked lay curled up and asleep at her feet.

"Who is it?" I asked. "Miss Meredith?"

The doctor pressed my hand. "We must be careful," he whispered. "She seems on the verge of delirium."

"The child shows no fear," I murmured.

Meanwhile the doctor was approaching the new object of his care.

"Why choose so cold a place?" he asked, smiling on the young girl who still clung, as if fastened, to the wall against which she had drawn herself. "Claire will catch cold; had you not better come downstairs?"

With a start she looked down at the little one resting at her feet, and her eyes showed a sudden intelligence.

"How did she come here?" she asked. "I did not call her."

"And how came you to be here?" he smiled. "Your white dress looks out of place in this garret."

She lifted herself straight up, with her back to the wall. Claire, who was thus dislodged from the place at her feet woke, and began to cry.

"I heard that Mr. Gillespie was dead," came from lips so stiff with fright or some other deep emotion that I wondered they could form the words. "I loved Mr. Gillespie, and I brought my grief here."

She was still standing pressed against the wall, her hands behind her; and disguise the fact as I would, I could see that her teeth were chattering with something more than cold, or even such fear as might follow the sudden death of a near friend and benefactor.

"Will you not come below?" urged the doctor, taking up Claire to his fatherly breast.

"Never!" her lips seemed to cry; but I heard no sound, and when the doctor, giving me the child, threw his arm about her and drew her away, she yielded pliantly enough, though with a steady look into his face I did not understand then nor for a long time afterwards.

At the stair-head we met Alfred. Perhaps he had heard us go up, perhaps he had simply thought of searching the attic himself. His recoil and the exclamation he made were simultaneous.

"You have found her!" was his cry, a cry which did not refer to the child. Then in reproachful tones: "Hope, why should you give us such a scare? Had we not enough to face without having our hearts wrung with terror for you?"

Her answer was a murmur. With the first moment of encounter with this man her face had become a mask.

CHAPTER IV

"HE DRANK IT ALONE"

In making this statement it is not my wish to create any special prejudice against Alfred. Indeed, I have no right to do so, for when a few minutes later his brother Leighton came running up the stairs at sound of his child's voice, I noticed the same recoil on her part, followed by the same impassibility. Nor did she show a different feeling when in the hall below George came forward with the inquiries her surprising absence had naturally provoked. From one and all she involuntarily shrank, but not without suffering to herself and an obvious attempt to hide this natural impulse under a demeanour more in accordance with her near relationship to these three men. In Alfred this chilling conduct awakened emotions only too easy to read; in Leighton, surprise, and in George, a distrust bordering upon a passion so fierce that he turned from white to red and from red to white in an instant. Evanescent expressions all of them, but important as showing the feelings entertained towards her by these men among whom she had been living for more or less time as a sister.

But of my personal sensations you have already heard too much, especially at this period of my story. Happily, I was able to hide them from other eyes, and simply showed a natural curiosity when Dr. Bennett, with a sly look in her direction, whispered in my ear:

"How came she to know of her uncle's death so soon after its occurrence? You say you heard her rush upstairs while you were in Alfred's room. That was very soon after you laid the old gentleman out of your arms. Is it possible that you had already met Miss Meredith? Did she share that first alarm with you?"

"Not to my knowledge," I returned. "My first view of her was in the attic with you. Yet she may have been somewhere in this great hall, or in some of the many rooms I see about us."

Meanwhile I was taking in her beauty, or what I must call beauty from the lack of any other adequate word. I believe she was not what people call beautiful. She did not need to be; her charm was incontestable without it; too incontestable, I fear, for the peace of mind of more men than Alfred and George Gillespie.

She was standing by the newel-post, in a position startlingly like that she had maintained above; and while I shrank from the doubts thus called up, I could not but perceive in the straightforward look of her eyes, and the fierce clutch of her hands behind her, that some determination was absorbing all her energies; a determination little in accord, I fear, with the attitude of simple grief she made such an effort to maintain. Leighton appeared to see this also, for he set down the child he had been straining to his breast, and approaching his cousin, plied her with a few hurried questions.

But the coroner, who had shown some embarrassment at the appearance on the scene of so young and charming a lady, advanced at this juncture and prevented the answer which was slowly forming on her lips.

"If you are Miss Meredith, Mr. Gillespie's niece and assistant, you are justified in your grief. Mr. Gillespie has passed away under very extraordinary circumstances."

Her hands which had been behind her, came suddenly together in front, but she did not shift her eyes from the point where she had fixed them. Perhaps she dreaded to encounter the gaze of the three young men grouped behind the man addressing her.

"Have those circumstances been related to you?" resumed Dr. Frisbie with the encouragement in his tone which her loveliness and sorrow naturally called forth.

"No."

The answer came quickly, and with a sharp accentuation which showed her to be a woman of force, notwithstanding the condition in which we had first found her.

"Then this little one had said nothing," he continued with a glance at Claire who had nestled again at her cousin's feet.

"Claire?" she exclaimed in evident surprise. "Claire?" and her eyes followed his till they fell inquiringly upon the child whose presence up to this moment she had probably not noticed. "No, she has said nothing; at least nothing that I have heard." And her hand went out as if she would urge the child away. But she did not complete the gesture, and I doubt if anyone understood her movement unless it was myself.

The coroner seemed anxious to spare her feelings. "Dr. Bennett will communicate to you our conclusions in this matter," said he. "I simply want to ask you when you last saw Mr. Gillespie."

"Alive?" she asked, her eyes stealing towards the door of the little den.

"Yes, miss; you surely have not seen him dead."

"I was with him at supper," she returned. "We were all there"; and for the first time she let her gaze fall on each one of her cousins in succession. "My uncle seemed as well then as at any time since his illness. He ate a good meal and drank—"

"And drank," repeated the coroner with a stern look behind him at the young men who had all moved at this.

"His usual glass of wine at dessert. He drank it alone!" she suddenly emphasised, her tone rising in sudden excitement. "I can never forget that he drank it alone."

A sigh or a suspicion of a sigh answered her. It came from one of her cousins, but I never knew from which. At its sound she shrank as if heart-pierced, and put up her hands—those tell-tale hands—and covered her ears; then she as quickly dropped them, and regarded the young men before her slowly, separately, and with a heartrending significance.

"I would so gladly have joined him in this attempt at old-time sociability had I but known it would have been his last," she said, and dropped her head again with a sob.

At this look and simple action a burden rolled from my heart. But upon the coroner and the physician lingering near my side, both look and words fell with a weight which made this investigation, if investigation it could be called, halt a moment.

"I do not understand you," observed the former after a momentary interval surcharged with deep emotion. "Was Mr. Gillespie in the habit of sharing his wine with those who sat at his board, that you feel the pathos of that lonely glass so keenly?"

"Yes. I never knew the dinner to close before without some sort of toast from one of his sons. It is the coincidence that affects me. But I should not have mentioned it. No one could have known that this was destined to be our last meal together."

She was looking straight before her now. Though it seems more or less incredible, she was evidently unconscious of having raised the black banner of suspicion over the heads of her three cousins. But the blank silence which followed her words appeared to give her some idea of what she had done, for with a sudden start and a change in her appearance which startled us all, she threw out her arms with the cry:

"You are keeping something from me. How did my uncle die? Tell me! tell me at once!"

Leighton sprang for his child, caught her up and fled with her into a farther room. George tottered, then drew himself proudly erect. Alfred, who had been gnawing his finger-ends in restrained passion, alone stepped forward to her aid, though in a deprecatory way which robbed him of a large part of his natural grace. But she appeared insensible to them all. Her attention was fixed upon the doctor, whom she followed with an agonising gaze, which warned him to be brief if she was to hear his words at all.

"Your uncle is the victim of poison," said he. "But we have reason to think he took it some time later than at the evening meal. Prussic acid makes quick work."

The latter explanation fell unheeded. She had fallen at the word poison.

CHAPTER V

HOPE

This was the proper moment for me to leave, or rather it would have been had it not been for the communication in my pocket which remained to be delivered. To go without fulfilling my duty in this regard or at least without stating to the coroner that I held in charge a paper of so much importance, seemed an improper if not criminal proceeding, while to speak, and thus give up to public perusal an enclosure upon the right delivery of which the dying man laid such stress, struck me as an equal breach of trust only to be justified by my total inability to carry out the wish of the deceased as expressed to me in his last intelligible appeal.

That this inability was an assured fact I was not yet convinced. An idea had come to me in the last few minutes which, if properly acted upon, might open a way for me out of this dilemma. But before making use of it I felt it necessary to know more of this family and the ties which bound them. To gain this knowledge was, therefore, of not only great but immediate importance; and where could I hope to gain it so soon or so well as here.

I consequently lingered, and the young medical friend of George, having for some reason shown the same disregard as myself to the open hint thrown out by the coroner, we drew together near the front door, and fell immediately into conversation. As he seemed on fire to speak, I left it for him to make the opening remark.

"Fine girl!" he exclaimed. "Very fond of her uncle. Used to help him with his correspondence. I hate to see women faint. Though I have been in practice now two years I have never got used to it."

Anxious as I was to understand the very relationship he hinted at, it was so obnoxious to me to discuss Miss Meredith with this man whom I had first seen in a condition little calculated to prejudice me in his favour, that somewhat inconsistently, I own, I turned the conversation upon Mr. Gillespie.

"Mr. Gillespie was then a very busy man," I observed. "I judged so from the look of his den or study. Overwork often drives men to suicide."

The glance this called out from the now thoroughly sobered young doctor was a sharp one.

"Yes," he acquiesced; but it was an acquiescence which, from the tone in which it was uttered, had a most suspicious ring.

My position had now become an embarrassing one. I looked around for the coroner, and saw him talking earnestly with the old and enfeebled butler, who seemed ready to sink with distress. At the same instant, the rattling of two keys could be heard in their several locks. The dining-room was being closed against intrusion, and it was to the coroner the keys were brought.

Miss Meredith, who had been carried into an adjoining room, was slowly recovering. This was evident from the countenance and attitude of Alfred Gillespie, who stood half in and half out of the room, with his eyes fixed upon her face. This left the hall clear, and, as my companion chose to preserve silence, I presently could hear the story the old butler was endeavouring to relate.

"I was waiting on the table as usual, sir, and it was my hand which uncorked the bottle and set it down before Mr. Gillespie. The young gentlemen had nothing to do with that bottle; they did not even touch it, for none of them seemed inclined to drink. Mr. George said he had a headache, and Mr. Leighton, well, he makes a point of not touching port; while Mr. Alfred gave no excuse; simply waved it away when I passed it, so that the old gentleman drank alone. He didn't seem to feel quite happy, sir, and that was why Miss Meredith got so excited. She never could bear to see her uncle displeased with her cousins."

"And where is that bottle of port and the glass out of which Mr. Gillespie drank at the table?"

"O, sir, you must excuse me, sir, but—but—I drank what was left in that bottle. I often do when there is only a little left. Master didn't mind. He often said, if he was in the mood to remember me, 'You may finish that, Hewson,' and though he did not say it to-night, I made so bold as to remember the times he had. You see I have lived for twenty years in the family. I was a young man when Mr. Gillespie took me into his service first, and we had become used to each other's ways. As for the glass, that was washed, sir, long ago. He was well enough up to nine o'clock, you see, sir."

"Or until after he had taken the sherry?"

"Yes, sir."

"Which you also brought him?"

"No, sir; I took it out of the buffet, sir; but it was Mr. Leighton who carried it into the den. He rang for me from the dining-room, and when I came up he asked for his father's bottle of sherry, and I gave it to him. Then I went downstairs again."

"And that bottle has not been found?"

"I have not seen it, sir. Perhaps someone else has. It was not a full one. He had had a glass or two out of it before."

"You have not said where the glass came from, from which Mr. Gillespie drank the sherry?"

"From the buffet also. We always keep a supply in one of the lower cupboards, sir."

"Did you take it out?"

"I think so, sir."

"Did you take the first one you came to and hand it directly to Mr. Leighton?"

"I believe so."

"Was the room light or dark? Could you see plainly where to lay your hand, or did you have to feel about for a glass?"

"I don't remember it as being any too light. There was only one gas-jet turned on, and the room is a big one. But I saw the glasses plainly enough. I know just where to find them, you see, sir."

"Very good. Then you probably noticed whether the one you took out was clean."

"They are always clean. I wear my spectacles when I wash them." The old butler seemed quite indignant.

"Yes, yes; then you have to wear spectacles?"

"When I wipe the glasses? Yes, sir."

The coroner pushed the matter no further. I think he feared it would seem like an attempt to fix the guilt on Leighton. Besides, he had no time to do so, for at this moment Miss Meredith appeared on the threshold of the room into which she had been carried, and, pausing there, stood looking up and down the hall with an ardent and disquieted gaze which Alfred, who had started aside at her approach, tried in vain to draw upon himself.

"Claire? Where is Claire?" she asked. "I want to put her to bed."

"Here she is," answered Leighton, coming from the drawing-room with the child fast asleep on his shoulder. "Take her, Hope, and be careful not to wake her. Better lay her down as she is than have her frightened again."

Hope held out her arms. I was startled at her aspect. "Miss Meredith is not able as yet to carry the child upstairs," spoke up the doctor; but the child was already nestled against her breast.

"I can carry her," she assured him, drawing her head back as the father stooped to kiss the child.

"Are you sure?" asked Alfred.

"Quite." Her arms had closed spasmodically over the child.

"Let me go with you," he prayed. But catching the coroner's eye, he quickly added, "that is, if you feel the need of any assistance."

Apparently she did not, for next minute I saw her faltering figure proceeding up alone, while the scowl which had begun to form on George's forehead had smoothed out, and only Alfred showed discomfiture.

The next minute the coroner had concentrated the attention of us all by saying gravely to the three young men before him:

"You, as sons of Mr. Gillespie, will surely see the justice of my making an immediate attempt to find out how and when your father took the poison, which, to all appearance, has ended his invaluable life." Then, as no one replied, he added quietly:

"A bottle is missing; the bottle of sherry from which he drank a glass since supper. Will you grant me leave to search the house till I find it? So little time has passed, it must assuredly be somewhere within reach."

"I can tell you where it is," rejoined one of the brothers. "I wanted a drink. I had friends upstairs, and I came down and carried off the first bottle I saw. You will find it in my room above. We all drank our share, so there can have been no harm in it."

It was George who spoke, and I now saw why his lips had moved when this bottle was first mentioned.

The coroner showed relief, yet made a movement singularly like a signal towards the rear hall which I had supposed vacant since the servants had been sent out of it. That he was speaking in the meantime did not detract from the suggestiveness of the gesture.

"You and your friends drank of it?" he repeated. "Very good. That settles one doubt." And he waited, or appeared to wait, for some event connected, as I felt sure, with the step we all could now hear moving in that hall.

Suddenly these steps grew louder, and a young man, evidently as much of a stranger to the occupants of the house as to myself, approached from the servants' staircase with a bottle in his hand.

Quietly the coroner took it, quietly he held it up before the last speaker, without attempting to explain or to apologise in any way for the presence of the man of whom he had just made such dramatic use.

"Is this the bottle you mean?"

That young gentleman nodded.

The coroner held the bottle up to the light. Only a few drops remained in it. These he both smelled and tasted.

"You are right," said he, "the contents of this bottle seem pure." And he handed it back to the man, who immediately carried it out of sight.

Leighton looked as if he would like to demand who this fellow was, but he did not. Indeed it seemed hardly necessary. His confident manner, his alert eye which took us all in at a glance, satisfied us that the event we had all dreaded had transpired, and that a detective had entered the house.

Noticing, but not heeding, the effect which this unwelcome intruder had produced upon the proud trio he held under his eye, Dr. Frisbie proceeded with the questions naturally called forth by the acknowledgment made by George.

"You were on this floor, then, previous to your father's death, possibly previous to his taking the draught which has so unfortunately ended his life?"

"I was on this floor an hour or so ago; yes, sir."

"Did you see your father or anyone else at that time?"

"No. To tell you the truth, I was a little ashamed of my errand. It was early in the evening for the social glass, so I just took the bottle off the buffet and went back."

"And the glasses?"

"Oh, I always have enough of them in my room."

The coroner's hand went in characteristic action to his chin. Evidently he found his position difficult.

"No poison in this bottle," he declared. "None in the one your old butler drained, and, so far as we are able to judge, none in the phial of chloral found standing on the study mantelpiece! Yet your father died from taking prussic acid. Cannot one of you assist me in saying how this came about? It will save us unnecessary trouble and the house some scandal."

It was an appeal which the sons of Mr. Gillespie could little afford to ignore. Yet while each and all of them paled under the searching gaze which accompanied it, none of them spoke till the silence becoming unendurable, Leighton made an extraordinary effort and remarked:

"My father was a proud man. If he chose—I say, if he chose to end his troubles in this unfortunate way, he would plan to leave behind him no sign of an act calculated to bring such opprobrium upon his household. He would have acted under the hope that his death would be taken as the result of his late sickness. That is doubtless why you fail to find the phial from which the poison was poured."

"Hum! Yes! I see. Your father had troubles, then?"

The answer was unexpected.

"My father had three sons, none of whom gave him unalloyed comfort. Is not this true, George? Is not this true, Alfred?"

Startled by the sudden appeal which, coming as it did from a man of great personal pride, produced an effect thrilling to the spectators as well as to the men addressed, the brothers flushed deeply, but ventured upon no protest.

"You and father have always been on good enough terms," growled George, with an attempt at fairness which gained point from the dogged air with which it was given.

This brought a shadow over the face which a moment before had shone with something like lofty feeling.

"I cannot forget that we quarrelled an hour before he died," murmured Leighton, moving off with an air of great depression.

Meantime I had taken a resolution. Advancing from the remote end of the hall where I had been standing with their young medical friend, I spoke up firmly, calmly, but with decision:

"Gentlemen, I have been waiting to see what my duty was. I have reason to think, notwithstanding my position as a stranger among you, that the clue to your father's strange act is to be found in my hands. Will you allow me, before explaining myself further, to request your answer to a single question?"

The surprise which this evoked, was shared by the coroner, who probably thought he had exhausted my testimony at our first interview.

"It is a question which will strike you as strange and out of place at a time so serious. But I pray you to show your confidence in me by giving me a straightforward reply. Was Mr. Gillespie a man of dramatic instincts? Had he any special powers of mimicry, or, if I may speak plainly, had he what you might call marked facial expression?"

In the astonishment this called out I saw no dissent.

"Father was a man of talent," Alfred grudgingly allowed. "I have often heard Claire laugh at his stories, which she said were like little plays. But this is a peculiar if not inappropriate question to put to us at a time of such distress, Mr. Outhwaite."

"So I forewarned you," I rejoined, turning to the coroner. "Dr. Frisbie, I must throw myself upon your clemency. When I entered this house in response to an appeal from Mr. Gillespie's grandchild, I found that gentleman labouring under great mental as well as physical distress. He was anxious, more than anxious, to have some special wish carried out; and being tongue-tied, found great difficulty in indicating what this was. But after many efforts, he made me understand that I was to take from him a paper which he held in his clenched hand; and when I had done so, that I was to enclose it, folded as it was, in one of the envelopes lying on the table before us. Not seeing any reason then for non-compliance with his wishes, I accomplished this under his eye, and then asked him for the name and address of the person for whom this communication was intended; but by this time his faculties had failed to such an extent, he could not pronounce the name. He could only ejaculate: 'To no one else— only to—to—' Alas! he could not finish the sentence. But, gentlemen, while waiting here I have been enabled to complete in my own mind this final attempt at speech on the part of your father. Anxious to make no mistake (for the impression made by his dying adjuration not to deliver this letter into the wrong hands, was no ordinary one), I have not allowed myself to be moved by any hurried or inconsiderate impulse, to part with this communication even to those whose claims upon it might be considered paramount to those of a mere stranger like myself. But since seeing Miss Meredith, above all since hearing you address her by her name of Hope, I cannot help feeling justified in believing that this final communication from Mr. Gillespie's hand was meant for her. For when in my perplexity I pressed him to give me some sign by which I could make out whether it was intended for his doctor, his lawyer, or his household, he roused and his face showed an elevated look which I now feel compelled to regard as a dramatic attempt to express in action the name he could no longer utter. Gentlemen, I have described his action. What name among those you are accustomed to speak best fits it?"

"Hope," was the simultaneous reply.

"So I have presumed to think." And turning to Dr. Frisbie, I added: "I have been told that this young lady was in her uncle's confidence. Will you allow me to deliver this envelope to Miss Meredith, in accordance with the injunction I firmly believe myself to have received from Mr. Gillespie?"

There was a silence during which no movement was made. Then the coroner replied:

"Yes, if it is done in my presence."

I turned again to the young gentlemen.

"Commiserate my position and send for Miss Meredith," I prayed. "I feel bound to place this in her hands myself. If I make a mistake in thus interpreting the look given me by your father, it will at least be made under your eye and from unquestionable motives. With my limited knowledge of the family, I know of no one who has a better claim to this communication than she. Do you?"

None of them attempted a reply.

Dr. Bennett had already gone up for Miss Meredith.

CHAPTER VI

While waiting for this young lady, I surveyed the three Gillespies with a more critical attention than I had hitherto had the opportunity of giving them. As a result, George struck me as being the most candid, Leighton the most intellectual, and Alfred the most turbulent and ungovernable in his loves and animosities. All were under the same mental tension and in all I beheld evidence of deep humiliation and distrust, but this similarity of feeling did not draw them together even outwardly, but rather seemed to provoke a self-concentration which kept them widely apart. As I looked longer, Leighton impressed himself upon me as an interesting study—possibly because he was difficult to understand; Alfred as a good lover but dangerous hater; and George as the best of good fellows when his rights were not assailed or his kindly disposition imposed upon. None of them seemed to take any interest in me. To them I was simply a connecting link between their dead father and the letter I held in charge for Miss Meredith.

Meanwhile the coroner showed but one anxiety, and that was for the lady's speedy appearance and the consequent reading of the letter upon which all minds were fixed.

She came sooner than we expected. As her soft footfall descended the stairs a visible change took place in us all. Drooping figures started erect and furrowed brows grew smooth. Some of us even assumed that appearance of reserve which men unconsciously take on when their deeper feelings are stirred. Only Leighton acted in a perfectly natural manner; consequently it was in his direction her frightened glances flew when she realised that she had been summoned for some definite purpose.

"I don't know what more you can want of me to-night," she protested in a tone little short of a frightened gasp. "I am hardly fit to talk. But the doctor said I must come down. Why couldn't you have left me with Claire?"

"Because, dear Hope, this gentleman you see here, and who, as you know, was with my father when he died, says he has a letter, or some communication from your uncle, which he is sure was meant for your eye only. Do you think my father would be likely to leave you such a message? Have you any reason for expecting his last thoughts would be for you, rather than for his sons? Answer; we are quite prepared to hear you say Yes."

She had been trying to steady herself without laying hold of his arm. But she found this impossible. With an expression of deepest anguish she caught at his wrist, and then facing us, murmured in failing tones:

"He might. I have helped him lately a great deal with his letter-writing. Must I read it here?"

In this last question and her manner of uttering it there was an appeal which almost took the form of prayer. But it failed to produce any effect upon the coroner, favourably as he seemed disposed to regard her. With some bluntness, I had almost said harshness, he answered her with a peremptory:

"Yes, miss, here."

She was not prepared for this refusal, and her eyes, full of entreaty, flashed from one face to another till they settled again on the coroner.

"I cannot," she protested. "Spare me! I do not seem to have full use of my faculties. My head swims—I cannot see—let me take it to the light over there—I am a nervous girl."

She had gradually drawn herself away from Leighton. The envelope which had been given her was trembling in her hand, and her eyes, wandering from George to Alfred, seemed to pray for some encouragement they were powerless to give. "I ought to be allowed the right to read the last words of one so dearly loved without feeling myself under the eyes of—of strangers," she finally declared with a certain pitiful access of hauteur certainly not natural to one of her manifestly generous temperament.

Was the shaft meant for me? I did not think so, but, in recognition of the hint conveyed, I stepped back and had almost reached the door when I heard the coroner say:

"If the words you find there have reference solely to your own interests, Miss Meredith, you will be allowed to read them in privacy. But if they refer in any way to the interests of the man who wrote it, you will yourself desire to read his words aloud, as the manner and meaning of his death is a mystery which you as well as all the other members of his household must desire to see immediately cleared up."

"Open it!" she cried, thrusting it into the hands of the physician, who by this time had rejoined the group. "And may God—"

She did not finish. The sacred name seemed to act as a restraint upon the passion in whose cause it had been invoked. With her back to them all she waited for the doctor to read the lines to which she seemed to attach so apprehensive an interest.

It was impossible for me to leave at a moment so critical. Watching the doctor, I saw him draw out the paper I had so carefully enclosed in an envelope, and after looking at it, turn it over and over in such astonishment and perplexity that we all caught the alarm and crowded about him for explanation. Alas, it was a simple one! The paper concerning which I had endured so many qualms of conscience, and from the reading of which the young girl had shrunk with every appearance of intolerable dread, proved upon opening it to be an absolutely blank one.

There was not upon its smooth surface so much as the faintest trace of words.

CHAPTER VII

THE ELDERLY GENTLEMAN BY THE NEWEL-POST

"This is surprising. Do you understand this, Miss Meredith? There is nothing written here. The sheet is perfectly blank."

She turned, stared, and laughed convulsively.

"Blank, do you say? What a fuss about nothing! No words, no words at all? Let me see. I certainly expected you to find some final message in it."

What a change of manner! The moment before she had confronted us, a silent agonised woman; now her words rattled forth with such feverish volubility we scarcely knew her. The coroner, not noticing, or purposely blind to the relief she showed, handed her the slip without a word. The brothers had all drawn off, and for the first time began to whisper among themselves. As for myself, I did not know what to do or think. My position, if anything, had changed for the worse. I seemed to have played some trick. I wanted to beg her pardon and theirs, and seeing her finally let the paper fall to the floor with an incredulous shake of the head, I began to stammer out some words of explanation, which sounded weak enough under the tension of suppressed excitement called forth in every breast by this unexpected incident.

"I feel—I am persuaded—you will not give me credit either for good sense or for the sincerity of my desire to be of service to you," I made out to say. "I certainly thought from Mr. Gillespie's actions, above all from the expressions which accompanied them, that he had entrusted me with a communication of no little importance, and that this communication was meant for Miss Meredith."

To my chagrin, my plea went unheeded: she was too absorbed in hiding her own satisfaction at the turn affairs had taken, and her cousins in deciding to what extent their position had been improved by the discovery of a blank sheet of paper where all had expected to find words, and very important words, too. Consequently it fell to Dr. Bennett to answer me.

"No one can doubt your intentions, Mr. Outhwaite. Miss Meredith will be the first to acknowledge her indebtedness to you when she comes to herself. You have fulfilled your commission according to the dictates of your own conscience. That you have failed to effect all you hoped for is not your fault. As a lawyer you will rate the matter at its worth, and as a man of heart excuse the exaggerated effect it has to all appearance produced upon those about you."

It was a palpable dismissal, and I took it for such, or would have if Miss Meredith, whose attention the word lawyer had seemingly caught, had not honoured me with a look which held me rooted to the spot.

"Wait!" she cried, "I want to speak to that young man. Do not let him go yet." And advancing, she stood before me in an attitude at once womanly and confiding.

"Come back, Hope!" I heard uttered in the peremptory tones of him they called Leighton.

But though the spasm which passed over her face denoted what it cost her to disobey the voice of so near a relative, she stood her ground.

"I need a friend," she said to me. "Someone who will stand by me and support me in a task I may find myself too weak to accomplish unaided. I cannot have recourse to my cousins. They are too closely connected with the sorrows brought upon us all by this event. Besides, I find it easier to depend on a stranger,—one who does not care for me, as Dr. Bennett does; a lawyer, too; I may need a lawyer—sir, will you aid me with your counsels? I should find it hard to come upon another man of such evident sincerity as yourself."

"Hope! Hope!"

Entreaty had now become command; Leighton even took a step towards her. She faltered, but managed to murmur:

"You will not go till I have seen you again. You will not!"

"I will not," I rejoined, putting down the hat I had caught up.

The next minute she, as well as myself, perceived why she had been thus peremptorily called back.

The group around the newel-post had changed. A large, elderly man, with a world of experience in his time-worn but kindly visage, was standing in the place occupied by the coroner a moment before. He was bowing in the direction of Miss Meredith, and he held some half-dozen letters in his hand.

As her eyes fell on these letters he regarded her with an encouraging smile, and said:

"I am Detective Gryce, miss. I ask pardon for disturbing you, and I don't want you to lay too much stress upon my presence here or upon the few questions I have to put on behalf of the coroner who has just been called to the telephone. A few explanations are all I want, and some of these you are in a position to give me. You have been in the habit of using the typewriter for your uncle, I am told."

"Yes, sir."

"Did you use it for the writing of these five letters found upon his desk?"

"Yes, sir."

"To-night?"

"Yes, sir."

"At what hour?"

"Between dinner time and half-past eight."

This was the first time she had acknowledged having seen her uncle after dinner.

"So you were with him until half-past eight?"

"Yes, or thereabouts."

"And left him in the enjoyment of his usual health?"

"To all appearance, yes."

"Before or after your cousin Leighton came into the study?"

"Before."

"Why did you leave? Was Mr. Gillespie through with his work for the night?"

"I don't know; I don't think so, but I was tired, and he begged me to go upstairs."

"In his usual manner?"

"Yes."

"Not like a man anxious to have you go?"

"No."

"And when did the child come down?"

"Later."

"Not immediately?"

"No; a quarter of an hour or so later."

"Humph! The child was with him then a quarter of an hour before his death?"

"I suppose so; I do not know."

The detective waited a moment, then his hand closed over the letters.

"Miss, it is very important to know whether Mr. Gillespie anticipated death. This correspondence—you know it—a letter to Simpson & Beals, Attorneys, Dubuque, Iowa; another to Howard MacCartney, St. Augustine, Florida; this to the president of the Santa Fé Railroad; and this to Clarke, Beales & Co., Nassau Street, City. All business letters, I presume?"

"Entirely so, sir."

"And none of them, I judge, such as a man would write who expected to close all accounts with the world in less than an hour?"

"None."

How laconic she was for a girl scarcely out of her teens!

"From this correspondence, then, as you know it, he showed no intention of suicide?"

"On the contrary. In one of those letters, the one to Clarke, Beales & Co., I think, he made an appointment for to-morrow. My uncle was very exact in business matters. He would never have made this appointment if he had not hoped to keep it."

"Are you two in league?" the angry voice of George broke in. "Are you trying to make out that father died from violence?"

"In league?"

Did she say it or only look it? I felt my heart swell at her piteous, her agonised expression. Mr. Gryce, as he called himself, may have seen it, but he appeared to be looking at the slip of paper he now drew from his pocket, and which we all recognised as that which she had shortly before let drop.

"You see this," he said, "it looks like a piece of perfectly blank paper."

"And it is," she declared. "Why he should send it to me I do not know. It was given me in an envelope by the gentleman at the door, who says he got it from my uncle before he died. Everyone here knows that."

"Very good. Now let me ask from what sheet your uncle tore this scrap of paper? You recognise it as paper you have seen before?"

"O, yes, it is part of what is used in the typewriter. At least I suppose it to be. It looks like it."

"Sweetwater, bring me the typewriter!"

Sweetwater was the young man who had before shown himself in attendance on the coroner.

"O, what does this mean?" asked Hope, shrinking back.

An oath answered her. George had reached the end of his patience.

The placidity of the old man remained undisturbed.

Meanwhile the young detective called Sweetwater had returned with the typewriter in his arms. Setting it down on the library table, towards which they all immediately moved, he composedly strolled my way. We were now grouped as follows: the family and some others in the library, Sweetwater and myself at the front door.

Naturally, from the point I have just indicated, I could not look into the library; but my hearing being good and that of the young detective still better, we both managed to get the drift of what was being said, though we could not note the speakers.

I had seen a slip of paper protruding from the machine when it was carried past me, and it was to this piece of paper Mr. Gryce first called Miss Meredith's attention.

"There's an unfinished letter here, as you see. Did you have a hand in writing it?"

She did not answer very promptly, but when she did, it was with a "No" which was startlingly abrupt.

"Ah! then there's someone else in the house who uses the typewriter."

"Mr. Gillespie. He often used it when he was in a hurry and I not by."

"Mr. Gillespie? Do you think it was he who wrote these lines?"

"I do. There was no one else to do it."

Was my imagination too active, or had her voice a choked sound which spoke of some latent emotion she strove to conceal?

"Then," suavely responded the detective, "we need no other proof of Mr. Gillespie's condition up to the time he worked off this last line. I doubt if you ever made a better copy yourself, Miss Meredith. But why is it torn across in this manner? Half of the sheet is missing, and some portion at least of the letter is gone."

A sudden gasp which could have come from no other lips than hers was followed by certain short exclamations from the others indicative of interest if not surprise.

"Shall I take it out? Or will one of you read it as it lies here? I prefer one of you to read it."

We heard a few stammering sentences uttered by George or Alfred, then Leighton's voice broke in with the calm remark:

"It is about some shares lately purchased in Denver. If you think it necessary to hear what my father had to say concerning them, this is a facsimile of what he wrote a half-hour or so before he died:

New York, N. Y., Oct. 17, 1899.

James C. Taylor, Esq., 18 State St., Boston, Mass.

Dear Sir:—-

In regard to the financing of the $10,000,000, mentioned in our conversation on the 12th inst., it is of the utmost importance that I am placed as soon as possible in full possession of the facts regarding the propert

The rest is torn off, as you say. Do you consider this letter important?"

"Not at all, except as showing the sound condition of your father's mind immediately prior to his collapse at ten o'clock. It is not the letter itself which should engage your attention, but the fact that this portion of it which has been wrenched off cannot be found. I know," he went on, before a rejoinder could be made by anyone in the startled group about him, "that a strip seemingly of this same paper was received by Miss Meredith in an envelope a few minutes ago. Indeed, I have it here. But though it was evidently stripped from this same sheet—from the bottom part of it, as you can see from its one straight edge—it does not fit the portion left in the machine. Some two inches or so of the sheet is lacking. Now where are these two inches? Not in the room from which we brought the typewriter, nor yet on Mr. Gillespie's person, for we have looked."

Silence.

"No one seems to answer," breathed a voice in my ear.

Had this shrewd and seemingly able detective expected a reply? I had not. Silence had too often followed inquiry in this house.

"It is a loss open to explanation," mildly resumed the aged detective. "It is also one which the police deems important. We shall have to search for that connecting slip of paper unless, as I sincerely hope, someone here present can produce it."

"Search!" a commanding voice broke in—that of Leighton. "We know nothing about it."

"It is a pity," rejoined the old man, with a mildness unusual in one of his class. "Such a measure should not be necessary. Someone here ought to be able to direct us where to find this missing portion of a letter interrupted by so stern a fact as the writer's death."

Still no answer.

"Had there been a fire in the room—but there was no fire. Or had Mr. Gillespie left the room—"

"Speak out!" the stern tones again enjoined. "You think some of us took it?"

"I do not say so," was the conciliatory reply. "But this scrap must be found. Its remarkable disappearance shows that it has more or less bearing on the mystery of your father's death."

"Then we must entreat you to use your power and find it if you can." It was still Leighton who was speaking. "George, Alfred, let us accept the situation with good grace; we will gain nothing by antagonising the police."

Two muffled oaths answered him; their natures were more passionate than his, or possibly less under control. But they offered no objections, and the next minute the old detective appeared in the hall.

One look passed between him and the young man loitering at my side. Then the latter turned to me:

"This is to be my task," he whispered. "I don't know the house at all. I hear that you have been up."

From whom could he have heard this? From Dr. Bennett? It was possible. Such fellows worm themselves into the confidence of warier persons than this amiable old physician.

"I have passed through the halls," I admitted, none too encouragingly. "But I don't see how that can help you."

"It's a four-story building, I suppose. All the houses along here are."

"Yes, it's a four-story house."

He rubbed one hand awkwardly against the other; indeed, his whole manner was awkward; then he walked slowly down the hall. When he reached the library door he stopped and looked in with a shy and deprecating air. Suddenly he began to back away. Someone was coming out. It was Miss Meredith. When she was in full sight and he brought to a stand-still by the wall against which he had retreated, he spoke, but not to her, though his eyes were fixed upon her in a sort of blank stare she may have attributed to the power of her beauty, but which I felt was of a character to make her careful.

"Four stories!" he muttered. "Parlour floor, first bedroom floor, second bedroom floor, and the attic! Where shall I begin? Ha! I think I know," he smiled, and passed quickly down the hall.

She had given an involuntary pressure to her hands when he mentioned the word attic.

I thought of the position in which I had found her there; of the doubts expressed by the doctor as to how she could have received an intimation of her uncle's death before an alarm had been raised or her cousins fully aroused, and felt forced to acknowledge that the police were justified in their action, great as was the spell cast over me by her loveliness.

That, justified or not, they meant to do their work, I soon saw. With a steady eye the coroner held us all to our places, while the young detective disappeared above, followed only by Leighton, who had asked the privilege of accompanying him for fear of some alarm being given to his little child who was upstairs alone. From the way Miss Meredith's eyes followed them, I knew there was something to be feared from this quest which she alone had the power of measuring.

What was I to think of this young girl who chose to be reticent on a subject involving questions of life and death! I would not probe my doubts too closely. I steeled myself against her look, resolving to be the lawyer—her lawyer—if required, but nothing more, at least till these shadows were cleared up.

Her two cousins remained in the library, to which Mr. Gryce had returned after making the signal to his man Sweetwater. We were all under great restraint with the exception of the doctor, who was chatting confidentially with the coroner. What he said I could in a measure gather from the expression of Miss Meredith's face, who was nearer him than I. That it served to intensify rather than relieve the situation was apparent from the gravity with which the coroner listened. Later, some stray words reached me.

"Had the greatest dread of poison—" This I distinctly heard—"Never took any medicine without asking—" I could not catch the rest. "Tell him symptoms—all the poisons—like a child—he never poisoned himself." This last rung in my ears with persistent iteration. It rang so loud I thought everyone on that floor must have heard it. But I saw no change in Alfred's restless figure hovering on the threshold of the library door a few feet behind Miss Meredith; while George, conversing feverishly with Mr. Gryce, raised his voice rather than dropped it as these fatal words fell from the lips of one who certainly had the best of reasons for believing himself in the confidence of his patient.

Miss Meredith, who was listening to something besides this conversation, fateful as it was, was meanwhile schooling herself for Sweetwater's return. I could discern this by the change that passed over her face just when his steps began to be heard; and was conscious of quite a personal shock when I saw her hand fall involuntarily on her bosom as if the thing he sought was there and not in the rooms above.

Cursing myself for the infatuation which would not let my eyes leave her face, I turned with sudden impulse into the reception room opening on my right. But I speedily stepped back again. Miss Meredith, who seemed to have gained some confidence by my presence, had feebly uttered my name. It seemed that the child had been heard to cry above, and that the coroner had refused to let her go up.

I made my way to her side, and, despite Alfred's scowls, entered into conversation with her, urging her to be calm and wait patiently for the detective's return.

"The child has its father," I suggested.

But this did not seem to afford her much comfort. She wrung her hands in her anxiety, and showed no relief till her cousin, followed by the watchful detective, was again seen on the stairs.

Then she took my arm. She needed it, for life and death were in the gaze she fixed upon the latter. And he—well, I had never seen the man before that night; yet I felt as certain from the way his feet fell on the stairs he so slowly descended that he had been successful in his search, and that the piece of paper which rustled so gently in his hand was the one Mr. Gryce had declared to be of such importance, and which she—but what man can complete a thought suggestive of distrust, while the hand of its lovely object presses warmly on his arm, and the eyes whose glance he both fears and loves rest upon his in a confidence which in itself is a rebuke?

I gave up speculation and devoted myself to sustaining Miss Meredith in her present ordeal. As Sweetwater reached the last step she murmured these words:

"I tried; but fate has rebuked me. Now I see my duty."

Her eyes had not followed Leighton's figure as he joined his brothers in the library, but mine did, and it did not make my heart any lighter to see from the glance he tossed her on entering that he was prepared for some event serious enough to warrant all this emotion.

"You have found what you have sought!" she cried, intercepting the young detective in her anxiety to end the suspense it took all her strength to sustain.

His smile was dubious, but it was a smile. Meantime the paper he held had found its way into the coroner's hands.

"Call Gryce!" shouted out that functionary, with a doubtful look at the slip in his hand; "I shall need his experience in deciphering this."

The detective was at his side in an instant, and together they bent over the scrap. The suspense was great, and the moment well-nigh intolerable. Then we saw the detective's finger rest on a certain portion of the paper they were mutually consulting, and remain there. The coroner read the words thus indicated, and his face showed both strong and sudden feeling.

"Ah!" he ejaculated. "What do you make out of that?"

The detective uttered a few low words, and taking the piece which had been in the envelope he fitted it to the one held by the coroner. We could all see that they were part of the same sheet.

"I should like to see if it also fits the portion that was left in the typewriter," suggested the other, ignoring the anxious looks bent upon him from every side. Passing by us all, he laid the three pieces together on the library table with a glance at the young Gillespies which was not without its element of compassion.

"Let us see it. What's on it?" urged Alfred. "Why, this is worse than father's death."

"If Miss Meredith will tell me how this central portion came to be on the attic floor, I will presently oblige you," rejoined the coroner.

She who of all present showed no interest in the completed sheet answered instantly, and without any further attempt at subterfuge or denial:

"I carried it there. I had come upon my uncle lying dead in his study, and thinking, fearing, that he had been struck while at the typewriter, I flew to the latter, and, lifting up the carriage, consulted the letter attached to it for some indication of this, and saw—George, Leighton, Alfred," she vehemently cried, facing them with a look before which each proud and spirited head sank in turn, "I do not know upon which of your three souls the weight of this crime rests. But one of you, one, I say, lies under the ban of your father's denunciation. Read!" And her trembling finger crossed that of the detective and fell upon a line terminating the half-finished letter which they had already partially read.

This was the appearance of that letter as now presented:

New York, N. Y., Oct. 17, 1899.

James C. Taylor, Esq., 18 State St., Boston, Mass.,

Dear Sir:—

In regard to the financing of the $10,000,000, mentioned in our conversation on the 12th inst., it is of the utmost importance that I am placed as soon as possible in full possession of the important facts regarding the property covered by these bonds.

First, the actual cost per mile, and if such cost covers the necessary equipment for same both for freight and passenger service; also if these bonds are the first lien one of my sons he

"Those last words were written after he felt himself sinking under the poison," rang out in instinctive emphasis from her lips. "Contradict me, George! Contradict me, Leighton! or you, Alfred, if you can! It would give me new life. It would restore me—"

She was sinking, fainting, almost at the point of death herself, but not a voice was lifted, not a hand raised. This suggestion of crime had robbed them, one and all, of breath, almost of life.

CHAPTER VIII

Suddenly one voice rang out in passionate protest. "Hope! Hope! It was not I! It was not I!" And Alfred, leaving his brothers, stood before his young cousin, with self-forgetful gestures expressing a denial which was half-prayer.

George flushed, and his fist rose; Leighton drooped his head in shame—or was it sorrow; but the next minute he had that rebellious fist in his own clutch. Miss Meredith kept her eyes turned sedulously away from them all.

"I only want one of you to speak; the man who can exonerate his brothers by confessing his own guilt. Do not touch me!"

This to Alfred, whose hand had caught hold of her dress.

With an air of pride, the first I had seen in him, the youngest son of Mr. Gillespie withdrew from her side and took up his stand on the farther side of the hall.

"You are quick with your suspicions," he flashed out. "What sort of men do you think us, that you should allow an incoherent phrase like this at the end of a letter begun in health but finished in agony, prejudice you to the death against persons of your own blood? It would take more than that to make me think evil of you, Hope."

It was a natural reproach, and it told not only upon her, but upon us all. The words which had precipitated this situation might mean much and might mean little. Had the reputation of these young men been of a more stable character, or had no attempt been made to suppress this portion of the letter, suspicion would never have followed the discovery of this incongruous addition to the half-finished business letter found in the typewriter; "one of my sons he"—was that an accusation of crime? George and Leighton were on the point of asserting not, and Alfred had just begun to swagger with an air of injured pride, when Miss Meredith, recovering herself, laid her hand upon her bosom in repetition of her former action, and slowly drew forth a letter, the appearance of which evidently produced a new and still greater shock in the breasts of the three young men.

"I shall not try to vindicate myself," said she. "I have lived like a sister in this house, and you would have a right to reproach me if it were not for what I hold here. Alfred, you have complained that the few words left in the typewriter by your dying father were incoherent and unsatisfactory. Will you regard as equally meaningless this letter written four weeks ago? Sir,"—here she turned to the coroner,—"my uncle was ill a month ago. It was not a dangerous illness, but the remedies given—Oh! Dr. Bennett help me to say it—were remedies we all knew to be dangerous if taken in too great quantities. One night—I cannot go on—he had reason to think his glass was tampered with, and after that, he wrote this letter, and charged me with its delivery in case he—he—Ah! I need not say in case of what. You have seen his dear head lying low in the room over there. Only,—as this letter is addressed to my cousins conjointly, will you allow them to read it without witnesses if they will swear to respect it and restore it in an un-mutilated condition to your hands? It is the only favour I ask you to show them, and this I humbly entreat you to grant, if only in recognition of what I have suffered at having precipitated this horror when I only meant to—to—"

She was sinking—falling—nay, almost at the point of death herself. But she reached out the letter, and the coroner, giving it one glance, handed it over to Leighton as the one least shaken by the calamity which had just overwhelmed the house.

"God forbid that I should deny to sons the privilege of being the first to read the last letter addressed them by their father."

But he made no move towards drawing the curtain between himself and the room from which he was retreating, nor could he be said to have really taken his eye off any of them during the reading of this long letter.

"You see I had need of a friend," murmured Miss Meredith, swaying towards me.

I gave her a commiserating look. Was ever a girl more unfortunately situated? Two at least of the men against whom she had felt forced to utter this denunciation of crime, loved her (or so I believed), Alfred passionately, George with less show of feeling, but possibly with fully as much depth and fervour.

"You might have held the letter back," I whispered.

But she met me with a noble look.

"You mean if I have not drawn suspicion upon them by my first subterfuge. But with so much in their disfavour, how could I calculate upon another opportunity of seeing them all together. And they must read it together. So my uncle told me. But he never thought it would be with police-officers in the house."

Here the coroner advanced to question her, and I am happy to say that my presence gave her courage to bear up under the ordeal. This was what he elicited from her.

She did not know what was in the letter. It had been written by her uncle while still on his sick bed and after an experience which I will not relate here, as it will be found more fully stated in the letter itself. This letter I will reproduce for you at once, though it was weeks before I knew its whole contents:

GEORGE, LEIGHTON, AND ALFRED:

I may not have been a good father, but I have at least been a just one. Though each and all of you since coming to man's estate have given me great cause for complaint, I have never been harsh towards you, nor have I ever denied you anything from mere caprice or from an egotistic desire to save myself trouble. Yet to one of you my life is of so little value that he is willing to resort to crime to rid himself of me. Does this shock you, Leighton, George, Alfred? We are a Christian family, members of an honourable community, trained each and all in religious principles, you, by the best, the sweetest of mothers—does it move you to think that one of you could contemplate parricide and even attempt it? It moves me; and in two of you must awaken a horror, the anticipation of which affords me the sole comfort now remaining to my doomed and miserable life. For nothing will ever make me believe that this act was a concerted one or that the attempt which has just been made upon my life had its birth in more than one dark breast. One guilty soul there is among you, but only one; and lest to the remaining two the accusation I have just made may seem fanciful, unreal, the result of nightmare or the effect of fever, I will relate what happened in this room last night, just as I related it to Hope when she asked me this morning why I seemed so loath to see you before you went out to your several lounging places.

I was dozing. The lamp which since my illness has never been turned out in my room, threw great shadows on wall and ceiling. I seemed conscious of these shadows, though I was half asleep, but not so conscious that I was not aware of the light shining through the transom from the gas jet near the top of the stairs. This light has always been company for me, especially in wakeful nights or when I found myself troubled by dreams or any physical distress. It seemed to connect me with the rest of the house, and simple as it may seem to you, accounts for the cheerfulness with which I have declined the offers of my sons to sit with me during these last painful nights. I had no need of their company while this light shone; and as for pain—why, that is an evil which all men are called upon sooner or later to endure.

I was resting then, in this mild reflected light, when suddenly it went out. This woke me, for the orders are strict that this jet be left burning till the servants come downstairs in the morning. But I did not stir in my bed; I simply listened. Though aroused and somewhat disturbed by this palpable disregard of my wishes, I exerted all of my faculties to detect the step I now heard loitering about my door. But it was studiously cautious and made no distinct sound in my ear. I did not like this, and listened still more intently, whereupon I heard the door open and someone come in, softly, and with long pauses such as were not wont to accompany the entrance of any member of my household. I was deciding whether to raise an alarm or lie still and let myself be robbed of the money which I had just received from the bank, when I heard the whispered "Father" with which one and all of you approach me at night when you wish to ascertain if I am asleep or awake.

Why did I hear myself called and yet make no reply? What was in my heart, or what have I seen of late in your natures or conduct, that I should remain quiet under this appeal and lie there shut-eyed and watchful? I had no definite reason for doubting any of you. I knew you were in debt and that two of you at least were in crying need of money, but I hardly think I dreaded the rifling of my desk by the hands of one of my sons. Yet that approach so gentle and so measured! the drawn-in breath! the shadow that grew and grew upon the wall!—all these spoke of something quite different from the anxiety of a son keeping watch over a sick father's slumbers.

The desk was near the window towards which my eyes were turned in open watchfulness, and I hoped by lying still to catch sight of the intruder's figure at the moment of his passing between me and the faint illumination made on the curtains by the street lamp opposite. But the intruder did not advance in that direction. He passed instead to the little cupboard over the wash-stand, where, as you all know, my medicines are kept. This I was made aware of by the faint click made by one bottle striking another. "George has come home ill, or Leighton has one of his terrible headaches," was the soothing thought which then came to me, and I found it difficult not to speak out and ask who was sick and what bottle was wanted. But the something which from the first had acted in the way of restraint upon me, held me still, and I remained dumb while that sneaking hand continued to fumble among the phials and glasses. Suddenly a fear struck me, a fear so far removed from any which I had ever before known, that my whole attitude of thought towards my sons must have undergone an instantaneous change—a gulf opening where an instant before was confidence and love. The medicine was kept there from which my nightly dose was prepared; a medicine which you have all heard declared by my physician to be a deadly poison, which must be measured most carefully and given in only such doses as he had prescribed. Could it be that my son was feeling about for this? Had George bet once too often on that mare which will be his ruin, or Leighton found his religion an insufficient cloak for indiscretions which ever shunned the light of day; or Alfred—the child of my heart, he whom his dying mother placed as a last trust in my arms—confounded the ennui of inaction with that weariness of life which is the bane of rich men's sons? I know the despairs that come in youth, and I quaked where I lay; but it was not upon self-destruction that this man at the cupboard was bent. I felt my whole frame tremble and my heart sink in unutterable despair as he advanced, still quietly and with great pauses, up to the foot-board of my bed, then around to the side, protected, as you know, by a screen, till he crouched out of sight, but within reach of the small table where my glass stands with the spoon beside it, ready for my use if I grow restless and weary.

To have turned, to have intercepted the creeping figure in its work, and thus have known definitely and forever which one of you had thus furtively visited my medicine cabinet before proceeding to my bedside, might have been the natural course with some; but it was not my course. I was not content just to interrupt. I wanted to know the full extent of what I had to fear. A remark which Dr. Bennett had once let fall recurred to me, transfixing me to my bed. "If you were not a careful man," he had said in diagnosing my present illness, "I should say that you had taken something foreign into your system; something which has no business there; something which under other circumstances and in another man's case I should denominate poison." It had seemed nonsense to me at the time, and I laughed at what I considered a fatuous remark, uttered with unnecessary gravity; but now that there was really poison in the house, and one of my own blood stood hiding behind the screen within a foot of my medicine glass, I could not but choke down the cry which this thought caused to rise in my throat and listen for what might come. Alas! I was destined to behold with my eyes as well as hear with my ears the next move made by my unknown visitant. By the grace of God or through some coincidence equally providential, the gas at this momentous instant was relit in the hall, and I perceived, amid the old shadows thus called out upon the wall, a new one—that of a hand holding a bottle, which, projecting itself beyond the straight line cast by the screen, was now stealing slowly but surely in the direction of the table on which stood my glass of medicine. I did not gasp or cry. Thought, feeling, consciousness even of my own unfathomable misery seemed lost in the one instinct—to watch that hand. Would it falter? Should I see it tremble or hesitate in its short passage across the faintly illumined space upon which my eyes were fixed? Yes, some monition of conscience, some secret fear or filial remembrance made it pause for an instant; but even as my heart bounded in glad relief and human feelings began to re-awake in my frozen breast, it steadied and passed on, and though I could no longer see aught but a shadowy arm, I could hear one—two—three—a dozen drops falling into my drink—a sound which, faint as it was, made the guilty heart behind the screen quake; for the hand shook as it retreated, and I beheld distinctly outlined on the illumined space before me the end of the semi-detached label which marked the special bottle on which the word poison is printed in large letters.

No further doubt was possible. The medicine in my glass had been strengthened and by the hand of one of my sons.

Which one?

In the misery of the moment I felt as if I did not care. That any of you should seek my death was an overwhelming grief to me. But as thought and reason returned, the wild desire to know just what and whom I had to fear seized me in the midst of my horror, mixed with another sentiment harder to explain, and which I can best characterise as a feeling of dread lest I should betray my suspicions and so raise between my children and myself an insurmountable barrier.

Subduing my emotion and summoning to my aid all the powers of acting with which I have been by nature endowed, I moved restlessly under the clothes, calling out in a sort of sleepy alarm:

"Who's there? Is it you, George? If so, reach me my medicine."

But no George stepped forth.

"Leighton?" I cried petulantly. "Surely I hear one of you in the room." But my son Leighton did not reply.

I did not call for Alfred. I could not! He was the last son of his mother.

Did I wrong the others in not uttering his name also?

Meantime all was quiet behind the screen. Then I heard a quick movement, followed by the shutting of a door, and I realised that an escape had been effected from the room in a way I had not calculated on— that is, by means of the dressing-room opening out of the alcove in which my bed stands.

I had thought myself a weak man up to that hour; but when I heard that door close, I bounded to my feet and attempted to reach the hall before the man who had thus escaped me could find refuge in any of the adjoining rooms. But I must have fallen insensible almost immediately, for when I came to myself I found the foot-board of the bed within reach of my hand, and the clock on the point of striking two.

I dragged myself up and staggered back to bed. I had neither the courage nor the strength to push the matter further at that time. Indeed, I felt a sort of physical fear, probably the result of illness, which made it quite impossible for me to traverse the halls and creep from room to room seeking for guilt in eyes whose expression up to this unhallowed hour had betrayed nothing worse than a reckless disregard of my wishes.

Yet it was torment unspeakable to lie there in an uncertainty which threw a cloud over all my sons. For hours my thoughts ran the one gamut, George, Leighton, Alfred, clinging agonisedly to each beloved name in turn, only to drop into a dreadful uncertainty as I remembered the temptations besetting each one of you, and the readiness with which you all, from the oldest to the youngest, have ever succumbed to them. There was no determining point in the character of any of you which made me able to say in this solitary and awful communion with my own fears, "This one at least is innocent!" If I dwelt on George's generous good nature, I also recalled his wild extravagance and the debts he so recklessly heaps up at every turn he makes in this God-forsaken city; if some recollection of Leighton's strict ways in open matters of conscience came to soothe me, there instantly came with it the remembrance of the various tales which had reached my ears of certain secret attachments which drew him into circles where crime is more than a suggestion, and murder a possible attendant upon every feast. Then Alfred—youngest of all but the least youthful in his attitude towards the world and his fellow-men— what honourable ambition had he ever shown calculated to give me solace at this awful time, and make the association of his name with a damnable crime an impossibility and an outrage?

Meanwhile, my whole mental vision was clouded with the pictured remembrances of your faces as seen in childhood, in early youth, or at any other time, indeed, than the intolerable present. George's, when he brought home his first school medal; Leighton's, when he denied himself a new pair of skates that he might give the money to a crying street urchin; Alfred's, when the fever left him and his cheeks grew rosy again with renewed health. All these young and innocent faces crowded about me, awakening poignant suggestions of the change which a few short, short years had wrought in relations which once seemed warm and alive with promise. Then, a group of frank-eyed boys; now,—this awful question: which?

It was not till an hour had passed that I remembered that the phial had not been returned to the cabinet. In whose possession would it be found? Should I have a search made for it? I turned cold in bed at the debasing, the intolerable prospect of acting as detective in my own house. Then the poisoned glass! it still stood beside me; if I left it untouched it would show suspicion on my part, and suspicion might precipitate my doom. How could I avoid taking it without raising doubts as to my discovery of the trick which had been played so near me? In the feverish condition of my mind but one plan suggested itself. Throwing out my arm, I precipitated the glass to the floor, over which I heard it roll, with extraordinary sensations. Then I waited for daybreak, in much the same condition of mind in which a man awaits his last hour; for my heart yearned over my sons even while panting under the consciousness that one of them was a monster of ingratitude and innate depravity.

When Hewson and the girls came down, and I heard the stir of life in the house, I rang my bell and asked for Hope. She came in with beaming face and a smile full of happiness. She had risen from a beauty sleep and, possibly because my thoughts had been so dark, I had never seen her look so bright and lovely. But her cheeks paled as she approached my bedside and noticed my miserable appearance; and it was with sudden anxiety she cried:

"What a wretched night you must have had, uncle! You look poorly this morning. You should have sent for me before."

Again I summoned up all my powers of acting.

"I knocked over my medicine in the night. Perhaps that is why I look so wretched. I did not sleep after four. You can say so, if any of the boys ask after me at the breakfast table."

With a woman's solicitude she moved around to my side, where the screen stood.

"Why, what's this?" she exclaimed, stooping as her foot encountered some small object.

I expected her to lift the glass. Instead of that she lifted the bottle. It had been left there on the floor and not carried out of the room, as I had naturally supposed.

I endeavoured to look undisturbed and as if this bottle had been thrown over with the glass, but I failed pitiably. At the sight of her dear, womanly face and the affection beaming in every look, I broke down and raised my arms imploringly towards her.

"Come to my arms!" I prayed. "Let me feel one true head on my breast."

The next minute I was conscious of having said a word too much. Her look, which you all know and love, changed, and, while she submitted to my caresses and even warmly returned them, it was with an appearance of doubt which I almost cursed myself for having roused in that innocent breast.

"Why one true heart?" she repeated. "Are there not others in this house? George and Alfred love you devotedly; and little Claire—what child could show more fondness for a grandfather than she?"

Why had she not included Leighton?

I endeavoured to right myself with some mechanical phrase or other, but the attempt was not very successful, and she was leaving the room in great disturbance when I called her hurriedly back.

"I want you to smile as usual," I gravely enjoined. "George's extravagances and Alfred's caprices are no new story to you. I have been thinking about them, that is all, but I had rather they did not know it."

I could not mention Leighton's name, either.

Meantime she was standing there with the poison bottle in her hand. I could not bear to look at it, and motioned her to restore it to the cabinet. As she did so, I perceived her turn with half-open lips, as if about to ask some question. But she either lacked the courage or the will to do so, for she proceeded to the cabinet with the bottle, which she placed quietly on the shelf. But almost instantly she took it up again.

"Why, uncle," she cried, "there is not as much here as there ought to be! I am sure the bottle was half full last night."

And then I remembered it was she who prepared my medicine for me.

"And I left it on the shelf," she went on. "Uncle, how came it to be lying by the side of your bed? Did you try to strengthen the dose? You know you ought not to; Dr. Bennett said that three drops in half a glass of water were all you could take with safety."

I had not a word to say. My mind seemed a blank, and no excuse presented itself. The wish which I had openly cherished of seeing Hope married to one of my sons clogged my faculties. My protest confined itself to a slow shake of the head and a dubious smile she was far from understanding.

"I think I will stay with you," she gently suggested. "Nellie will bring my breakfast up with yours, and we can have a tête-à-tête meal at your bedside."

But this did not chime in with my plans.

"No," said I. "Nellie can stay with me if you wish, but I want you to go down. Your cousins will miss you if you are not there to pour the coffee for them. Alfred shows an astonishing punctuality of late, and George quite emulates his younger brother's precision and haste. Leighton was never late."

Her cheek grew the colour of a rose. Never before had I so much as suggested to her the secret wish you have one and all entertained ever since her beauty and affectionate nature brought sunshine into this cold dwelling.

I was glad to see this colour; at the same time I was made poignantly wretched by what it suggested. If Hope loved one of my sons, and he should be the one who had—I felt more than ever called upon to act warily. Here was someone besides myself to think of. Your mother is dead and in Paradise, but Hope is young and the crushing weight under which I staggered could not well be borne by her. For her sake if not for my own, I must locate the plague-spot that to my mind spread defilement over all my sons. I must know which of you to trust and which to fear; and that no mistake should follow my attempt at this, I made haste to insure that no warning should reach you through any change in Hope's manner. So I reiterated my old command.

"Let me see you smile," said I, "or I shall think you regard me as being in worse condition than I really am. Indeed, I am almost well, Hope. My disease has yielded to Dr. Bennett's treatment, and when I can rise above these sickly fancies, which are the effect, no doubt, of the powerful remedies I have taken, I shall be quite like my old self. After breakfast let me see you here again. I may have some letters requiring an immediate answer."

My natural tones reassured her. The force of my feelings had brought some colour into my cheeks, and I probably looked less ghastly. She turned away with a smile. Alas! her face renewed its brightness and shone with sweet expectancy as she approached the door.

Nellie brought me my breakfast and I forced myself to eat it. My mind was regaining its equilibrium and my will its power. Just as I was folding my napkin, Hewson came in. He had brought me an especial tid-bit, prepared in the chafing dish by Hope's own hands. But I could not eat it. The thought would rise that she had seen far enough into my mind to imagine I would dread eating anything she had not cooked for me herself. As Hewson was withdrawing, I asked if you were all well. His answer was an astonished Yes. At which I ventured to remark that I had heard someone up in the night. "That was Miss Meredith," he explained. "I heard her tell Mr. George at the breakfast table that she came down to your door about one in the morning to listen if you were quiet. She said she found the gas blown out in the hall, and that she lit it again. I had left the sky-light open; it don't do these windy nights, sir."

I was disturbed by this discovery. That she should have been at the door at a moment so fraught with danger and misery to myself was a thrilling thought; besides, might she not have been so happy or so unhappy as to have caught a glimpse of the man who crept out of my dressing-closet a moment later! Overcome by a possibility which might settle the whole question for me, I let Hewson go in silence; and when Hope came back, drew her gently but resolutely down on the bed at my side and said to her with a smile:

"I have just learned how my dear girl watches over her uncle's slumbers. You are too careful of me; I had rather have you sleep. George's room is on this floor; let him come and see how I am in the night, if you are so uneasy."

"George would never wake up without assistance," said she. "I could not trust you to his tender care, well meaning as he is."

"Leighton, then. He's a light sleeper. I have often heard you say that you have heard him pacing the floor of his room as late as three in the morning."

"But he sleeps better now. Alfred might stop on his way in; but Alfred does not stay out as late as he used to. He comes in quite regularly since you have been ill."

Were her eyes quite true? Yes, they were as true as the sky they mirror. I grasped her hand and ventured upon a vital question.

"Who was up at the same time you were last night? I am sure I heard a man's step in the hall, just about the time you relighted the gas."

"Did you know about the gas?" she asked. "I found it smelling dreadfully. But I didn't encounter anyone in the hall. I guess you imagined that, uncle."

"Perhaps!" was my muttered reply, as I wondered how I was to ask the next question. "When did you go upstairs?" I finally inquired.

"Oh, right away. I didn't wait a minute after I found you quiet. It was cold in the halls—Hewson had left the sky-light open, and my trip after a match chilled me."

"Was your cousin Leighton's door open?" I instantly inquired. "Or did you hear any door shut after you went up?"

She leaned over me and looked anxiously into my face.

"Why do you ask so many questions, uncle, and in so hard a voice? Would there have been any harm in my cousins being up, or in my running across one of them in the hall?"

"Not ordinarily. But last night—"

Here my weakness found vent. I must share my secret, if only as a safeguard; I could not breathe under the dreadful weight imposed upon me by this uncertainty. And she knew I had some dreadful tale to tell; this I was assured of by the white line creeping into view about her lips, and by the convulsive clasp with which she answered my clutch. Forgetting her youth, ignoring all the resolves I had made in the secret watches of the night, I drew her ear down to my mouth and gasped into it the few tell-tale sentences which revealed the dishonour of our house. I caught the thrill of anguish which went through her as I made plain the attempt which had been made upon my life, and never shall I forget her eyes as she slowly drew back at the completion of my tale, and surveyed me in the silent suspense which seemed to mirror forth my own deep heart-question: Which?

Sons, I could not answer the demand made by that look, nor can I answer it now. You all came in soon after, and each and all of you had something to say about the mischance of the night which had so visibly affected me. And I did not dare to read your eyes. Brought face to face with you, I seemed to shrink from, rather than seek for, the settling of this dreadful question. Perhaps because I regard you with equal affection. Perhaps because your mother's picture was visible over your heads, and it seemed like sacrilege to her memory to consider such a question under her loving and trusting eyes. At all events you left me with my mind still in doubt, to confront Hope again, and with her the wretched future which the night's experience had unfolded before us both. I found her filled with a confidence I could not easily share. She believed in the integrity of the man she held dearest, but she would not tell me which of you she thus loved. And I could only guess. But even this belief weakened a little as we talked together, and I soon saw by the arguments she used that peace and certainty would never be hers again as long as a doubt remained as to which of her cousins had conceived and perpetrated this criminal act. As for me, the future holds no comfort. I shall give each of you a thousand dollars to-night in celebration of my anniversary of marriage, and perhaps this will awaken the conscience of the one who loves my money better than my life. Then, though I shall not change my will, I shall publish abroad that I have had losses which only a fortunate speculation can make good, and see if by these means the cupidity which came near costing me my life may not serve to insure me a sufficiently prolonged existence for me to separate in my own mind the one black sheep from the white. But if these measures fail, if I am doomed to fall a victim to the unknown hand which I must henceforth see lifted over my life, if Hope's watchfulness and my own vigilance cannot prevent the repetition of an act which, if once determined upon, cannot fail of fulfilment in a house like this, then this letter read by you all in concert must prove the punishment of the guilty one. And since none of you will read these lines except under these circumstances of death and crime, I hereby charge that guilty one to speak, and as he hopes to escape my curse and the wrath of an outraged Deity, to avow his crime in her presence and in that of the two brothers he will thus exonerate.

Having done this, he may take or leave his portion of the estate. I shall be satisfied, and the God whose commandments he has doubly defied may forget to avenge a crime forgiven by its object.

To my two sons whose filial instincts have never been thus disturbed, I leave my blessing. May all happiness be theirs, whether this does or does not include the love of the dear girl whose future I have thus endeavoured to clear.

ARCHIBALD GILLESPIE.

I have inserted this letter here that you may understand the situation which ensued upon its perusal by the three brothers.

We, who had not read it, were simply startled to note the way in which these three young men drew back as from a common centre, as the last words fell from Leighton's well-nigh paralysed lips.

Then Alfred, in a rush of ferocious passion, bounded forward again, and striding up to George, shouted out in an awful voice, "You are the man!" and struck him without mercy to the floor.

CHAPTER IX

THE CLOCK THAT HAD RUN DOWN

In the commotion which followed, I noted two things. First, that at sight of this violence from one brother to the other, Leighton drew back without offering assistance to the one or rebuke to the other. Secondly, that Alfred's show of anger ceased as soon as it had thus expended itself, and that his next thought was for Hope.

But he was not allowed to approach her. The coroner now interfered with his authority, and all words were forbidden between these members of a disrupted household, till the police had finished an investigation, which had now become as serious as the crime which had called it forth.

The search was for the little phial which had held the acid, and when it was generally understood that the investigation would not cease till this was found, Miss Meredith, who had clung to me as her one stay in this overturning of every other natural support, asked me in agitated tones if I thought her cousins would be subjected to personal search. As no other course was open to the police after the direct accusation which had just been made by the infuriated Alfred, I answered in the affirmative; whereupon she attempted to flee the place, saying she could not endure to see them subjected to such humiliation.

But here Alfred, as if divining her thoughts, offered his person to Mr. Gryce with the remark:

"I have nothing to conceal. Look through my pockets, if you wish. You will find nothing to reward your pains. I am not the villain."

A growl of anger, bridled but concentrated, came from the other side of the room, and I caught a sudden glimpse of George, quivering under the restraining hands of Dr. Bennett and Sweetwater, in a mad attempt to reach his brother, whom he seemed to curse between his teeth.

"If you search him, you must do the same to me," were the words with which he seasoned this struggle. "You will find nothing more incriminating on me than on him; probably less, for my pockets are always open—while his—" A gnash of his teeth finished these almost inarticulate phrases. He was not as easily roused as his brother, but more tenacious in his passions, and less readily appeased.

"Peace, there! You shall both be satisfied," interposed a businesslike voice. In face of these open accusations, the coroner felt himself relieved from the embarrassment which had hitherto restrained him, and made no further effort to hide his suspicions.

Miss Meredith, who unconsciously to herself had drawn me as far as the drawing-room door in her efforts to escape the disquieting scene she had herself precipitated, paused as these words left the coroner's lips, and, yielding to the terrible fascination of the moment, caught my arm, and clinging thus with both hands, turned her eyes again upon the men under whose roof she had eaten, slept, and loved; ay, loved, as I knew by the tension of her body, communicated to me by the pressure of her hands.

Suddenly that pressure was removed. Her hands had flown to her eyes, shutting out the spectacle she could no longer confront. Nor was it easy for me to look on unmoved, or view with even an appearance of equanimity the scene before me.

I have not mentioned Leighton. He had not come forward with the other two, but he allowed his pockets to be searched without a protest when his turn came, though it was very evident that the proceeding caused him more suffering and a keener sensation of disgrace than it did the other two. Was this on account of the superior sensitiveness of his nature, or because he shrunk with a proud man's shame from the publicity entailed upon the anomalous articles which were drawn from his inner pockets? When some few minutes later my eyes fell on these objects lying piled on the library table, I marvelled over the character of a man who could gather and retain in one place a small prayer-book, a lock of woman's hair, the programme of some common music hall, and a photograph which after one glance I instinctively turned face downwards, lest it should fall under the eye of his cousin, whose delicacy could not fail to be hurt by it.

The phial had not been found on any of the young gentlemen.

When Miss Meredith became aware that the ordeal was over, she let her hands drop, and stepped hastily into the drawing-room. I did not follow her, but remained in the doorway watching the detectives as they moved from room to room in the search which was now being extended to all parts of the house. As I saw these men pass so quietly but with such an air of authority into rooms where a few hours before they would have hesitated to put foot even upon the genial owner's express invitation, I experienced such a realisation of the abyss into which this hitherto well-reputed family had fallen that I lost for a little while that sense of personal bitterness which the predictions evinced by Miss Meredith had so selfishly awakened.

But to continue the summary of events.

Seeing Leighton withdraw upstairs, followed by an officer in plain clothes, who had appeared on the scene as if by magic, I could not refrain from asking why he was allowed to separate himself from the others, and was much moved at being informed that he had gone up to sit by his child's bed, that child who of all in the house had found her wonted rest.

That he could calm himself down to such a task under the eye of one who could have little sympathy with his feelings, whether they were those of outraged innocence or self-accusing guilt, struck me as the most pathetic exhibition of self-control I had ever known; and more than once during the busy hour that followed, I was visited by fleeting visions of this silent man, sitting out the night under the watchful eye of one who moved if he so much as lowered his head to kiss the only cheek likely to smile upon him on the morrow as it had smiled upon him to-day.

That the search for the missing phial was likely to be a long-continued one soon became apparent to everyone. Two men who had carried the investigation into the room where the servants had been shut up since early evening, came back with the report that nothing had come to light in that quarter. At the same time two more returned from above with a similar report in regard to the sleeping-rooms of the three brothers. Sweetwater and Gryce, who had spent the last half-hour in the dining-room, appeared to have an equally unsatisfactory tale to tell, and I was wondering what move would now be made, when I intercepted a glance from the coroner cast in the direction of the drawing-room, and realised that the law was no respecter of persons and that she, she too, might be called upon to give proof of not having this tell-tale article upon her person.

The prospect of such an indignity offered to one I regarded with more than passing admiration unnerved me to such an extent that I was hardly myself when Dr. Frisbie advanced upon me with this remark:

"I regret the necessity, Mr. Outhwaite; but the emergencies of the case demand the same compliance on your part as on that of the other gentlemen found upon this scene of crime. It is needless to say that we have the utmost confidence in your integrity, but you were here when Mr. Gillespie died, and have been close to a certain member of this family many times since—and, in short, it is a form which you as a lawyer will recognise and—"

"No apologies," I prayed, recalling the one son of Mr. Gillespie who had not been on the scene of crime at the time of his father's death.

An intelligent glance from the coroner convinced me that he was thinking of him too. Indeed, he seemed to be more than willing to have me understand that he exacted this thorough search in order to fix the crime on Leighton. For if the phial was not to be found anywhere in the house, the necessary conclusion must be that it had been carried out of it by the one person known to have left it during the critical half-hour preceding Mr. Gillespie's death.

"I understand your thoughts," quoth the coroner, who seemed to read my face like an open book. "The phial may have been smashed on the sidewalk or thrown into some refuse barrel. But that would be the unwisest thing a guilty man could do. For its odour is unmistakable, and once it is found by the men I will set looking for it at daybreak—Well, what now?"

Sweetwater was whispering in his ear.

"The child? Do I remember that the father suggested she should be put to bed undressed? Oh, I cannot have you disturb the child. Used as I am to the subterfuges of criminals I find it impossible to believe that a father could make use of his child as a medium for his own safety."

"Or Miss Meredith?" the insidious whisperer went on.

"Or Miss Meredith. She may have the bottle on her own person, but she would never pass it over to the child. No, no! curb your extravagances and confine your attention to Mr. Outhwaite, who is kind enough to allow us to inspect his pockets—"

Here the curtain at the drawing-room door was disturbed and a pallid face looked forth.

"I pray you," came in entreaty from Hope's set lips, "spare this stranger, whose only crime has been to show kindness to a man he did not know, in an extremity he did not understand. Search me; search Claire; but do not subject this gentleman to an act so injurious. I swear that the phial is not on him! I swear—"

She hardly knew what she was saying. The heaped-up excitements of the last two hours were fast unsettling her reason.

She held out her hands imploringly. "I don't know why I care so much," she murmured in fresh expostulation, "but I feel as if I could not bear it."

From that moment I loved her, though I knew this interposition in my behalf sprang from her womanly instinct rather than from the spontaneous impulse of a freshly awakened heart. I must have shown how deeply I was moved, for the coroner looked distressed, though he gave no signs of modifying his intention, and I was beginning to empty my pockets before his eyes, when Sweetwater's expressive countenance showed a sudden change, and he rushed again to the rear. Here he stood a moment before the dining-room door, striking his forehead in wrathful indecision; then he disappeared within, only to shout aloud in another instant:

"Fool! fool! And I noticed when I first came in that the clock had stopped. See! see!"

We were at his side in an instant. He was standing by the mantelpiece, with the heavy French clock tilted up before our eyes. Under it, tucked away in the space allowed to the pendulum, we saw a small homoeopathic bottle. There was one drop of liquid at the bottom, which even before Mr. Gryce lifted the bottle to his nose we recognised by its smell to be prussic acid.

The phial which had held the deadly dose was found.

CHAPTER X

THE PENCIL

Under Sweetwater's careful guidance, the clock fell slowly back into place. It was one of those solid time-pieces which seem to form part of the shelf on which they stand. When it was again quite level, he pointed to its face. The hands stood at half-past nine, just ten minutes previous to the time of my entering the house.

"At what hour did Mr. Leighton Gillespie go out to-night?" he asked.

No one answered.

"Before half-past nine or after it?" urged the coroner, consulting the faces about him for the answer he probably had no expectation of receiving from anyone's lips.

"Leighton's all right," cried out a voice from the library. "I hate his puritanical ways, but there's no harm in him."

It sounded like Alfred, but the impression made by this interruption was not good.

"Will you allow me to state a fact," ventured Miss Meredith, coming impulsively forward. "If you hope to establish the guilt or innocence of anyone by the time marked by these hands, you will make a mistake. The clock has been out of order for some days. Yesterday it ran down. I heard my uncle say that it would have to go back to Tiffany's for repairs."

"Fetch in the butler or whoever has charge of this room," ordered Dr. Frisbie. "Let none of you attempt to speak while he is present. I wish to interrogate him myself and will have no interruptions."

We all drew back, and silence reigned in the spacious apartment which, lit up as for a dinner party, was yet in such a state of disorder that the orderly old butler groaned as his eyes fell upon the heaped-up rugs, the overturned chairs, and the great table stacked with fine china and cut-glass taken from the buffet and closets.

"Oh, what shall I do here?" he grumbled. "What would master—"

He did not finish; but we all understood him. The coroner pointed to the clock.

"When was this wound last?"

The old man stared at the time-piece, mumbled, and shook his head. Then his eyes fell on Miss Meredith.

"I don't remember," he protested. "It has not been running for days; has it, Miss? I have had to use my watch in order to be on time with the meals. Why do you ask, sir?"

He was not answered. This repeated closing up of every avenue of inquiry was beginning to tell upon the police.

"Mr. Gillespie looked very sober, very sober indeed, when he found he had to drink his wine alone," continued the butler, with a melancholy emphasis calculated to draw our attention back to the scene which had manifestly made such an impression upon him. "He lifted up his glass and held it out a long while before he drank it. I think he looked at each one of the young gentlemen in turn, but I didn't care to watch him too closely, for there was something solemn about him which made me feel queer, living so long as I have in the family and with every one of these young gentlemen babies in arms when I came here. He drank it finally, standing. But there was no harm in that glass, sirs, for I finished the bottle myself afterwards, and I am well, as you see. More's the pity!"

"Shut up!" shouted an angry voice from across the hall. "You are making a mess of the whole affair with your confounded drivel."

The coroner motioned the butler away.

The atmosphere of the house had now become oppressive even to me, and for the first time I experienced a desire to be quit of it, and would certainly have made some movement towards departure had it not been for my dread of leaving Miss Meredith alone with her own thoughts.

Meanwhile the coroner was issuing his orders.

"Dakin, request the gentlemen upstairs to come down again for a few minutes. Dr. Bennett, the body of your patient can now be moved."

"Ah, here we are again," he exclaimed, as Leighton was heard descending the stairs.

"Now, if the two other sons of the deceased will attend to my words for a moment I will state that under the existing circumstances I feel it my duty to call a jury and hold an inquest over Mr. Gillespie's remains. The phial smelling of prussic acid having been found in the dining-room, I shall only require restraint put upon the movements of the two sons of Mr. Gillespie who are known to have entered this room during the hour when this fatal dose was administered. The one called Alfred, having remained above, is for the present free from suspicion. I would be glad to show the same consideration to the others; but the facts demand a severity which I hope future developments will allow us to confine to the guilty party. Mr. Outhwaite, I must request you to hold yourself subject to my summons. Miss Meredith, I advise you to hold no communication with your cousins till this matter shows a clearer aspect."

He was moving off, when Alfred, who had been shifting uneasily under George's eye, stepped up to him and said:

"I don't want any discrimination made between my brothers and myself. I may be quite conscious of my own innocence, but I cannot accept any show of favours founded on a misconception. If George and Leighton are to be subjected to surveillance on account of entering the dining-room this evening, then I want to be put under surveillance too. For I was in that room as well as they, searching for a small gold pencil which I had dropped from my pocket at dinner-time."

This acknowledgment made under such circumstances and against such odds was calculated to enlist sympathy, and my heart warmed towards the man who in the heat of anger could strike a brother to the ground, but scorned at a less angry moment to take refuge in a misunderstanding which left that brother at a disadvantage.

But the imperturbability of the elderly detective, who at that moment found something to interest him in the chasing on a Chinese gong hanging from a bracket in the hall, warned me not to be too quick with my sympathies. Kindly as he beamed upon this favoured object of his attention, I saw that he took little stock in the generous attitude assumed by Mr. Gillespie's youngest son; and my attention being attracted to his movements, I was happily glancing his way when he suddenly approached Alfred with what looked like an empty tumbler in his hand.

"Is this the article you refer to?" he asked.

And then we saw that the tumbler was not empty,—that it held a small object standing upright in it, and that this object was a gold pencil.

"Yes, that is my pencil," Alfred acknowledged. "But—"

"Oh, I am accountable for putting it into the tumbler," the old man admitted. "The tumbler was a clean one, Mr. Gillespie. I assure you I examined it closely before making it a receptacle for this pencil. But the pencil itself—Let me ask you to put your nose to it, Mr. Gillespie."

It was a suggestion capable of but one interpretation. Alfred started back, his eyes staring, his features convulsed. Then he bent impulsively forward and put his nose to the object Mr. Gryce held out. With what result was evident from the sudden damp which broke out on his forehead.

CHAPTER XI

SOMETHING TO THINK ABOUT

"Fatality!" exclaimed Alfred. And, raising his head, he strode impetuously towards Miss Meredith. "You have enjoined a confession of guilt and forbidden us to assert our innocence," he cried. "But I shall assert mine now and always, whatever happens and whoever suffers. I should not be worthy of the happiness I aim at, if I did not declare my guiltlessness in the face of facts which seem to militate against me."

"I believe you—" she began, her hand trembling towards his. But the confiding impulse was stayed—by what thought? by what dread? and her hand fell and her lips closed before she had completed the sentence.

"I am innocent," he repeated, drawing himself up in proud assertion, nobly borne out by the clear regard of the eye which now turned alternately on George and Leighton, who were standing upon either side of him.

"What is the use of repeating a phrase you cannot back up with proof?" called out George, who was still gnawing his own special grievance. "I am as innocent as you are, but I scorn to take advantage of each and every opportunity to assert it."

Leighton neither spoke nor moved. The melancholy in which he was now completely lost repelled all attempt to break it. Nor did this expression of complete wretchedness alter during the hubbub that followed. When it did—but I must make clear the circumstances of this change. I was engaged in making my adieux to Miss Meredith, when Sweetwater, after a marked effort to meet my eye, motioned me to join him in the doorway of the den where Mr. Gillespie's body still lay. Not enjoying the summons, yet feeling it impossible to slight them, I ventured, for the last time, or so I hoped, down the hall.

The young detective was looking into the room which had already played so conspicuous a part in the events of the night, and as I drew up beside him, I perceived that his eyes were fixed not upon the out-stretched figure of its late occupant, but on the face and form of Leighton Gillespie, who was bending above it.

For all the humiliation I felt at thus sharing the professional surveillance entered into by this able young detective, I could not resist following his glance, which seemed to find something remarkable in the attitude or expression of the man before me.

The result was a similar interest on my part and a score of new surmises. The melancholy which up till now had been the predominating characteristic of this inscrutable face had yielded to what could not be called a smile and yet was strangely like one; and this smile or shadow of a smile, had in it just that tinge of sarcasm which made it the one look of all others least to be expected from a son who in common with his brothers laboured under a suspicion of having been the direct cause of his father's death.

With the memory of it fixed indelibly in my mind, I moved away, and in another moment was quit of the house in which I had spent four hours of extraordinary suspense and exciting adventure. As I passed down the stoop, I met a young man coming up. He was the first of the army of reporters destined to besiege that house before daybreak.

CHAPTER XII

GOSSIP

Next morning I routed up Sam Underhill at an early hour. Sam Underhill is my special friend; he is also my nearest neighbour, his apartment being directly under my own.

He is a lazy chap and I found him abed, and none too well pleased at being disturbed.

"What the dickens brings you here at this unearthly hour?" was the amiable greeting I received.

I waited till he had made himself comfortable again; then I boldly stated:

"You are a club-man, Sam, and consequently well up in the so-called gossip of the day. What can you tell me about the Gillespies?—the three young men I mean, sons of Archibald Gillespie."

"George, Alfred, and Leighton? What possible interest can you have in them? Rich fellows, spendthrifts, every one of them. What have they been up to that you should rout me up at this hour—"

For reply I opened out the morning paper which I had been careful to bring along.

"See here!" I cried: "'Archibald Gillespie, the well-known broker, died suddenly last night, from the effects of some drug mysteriously administered.'" I was reading rapidly, anxious to see what kind of a story the reporters had made of it. "'He had been ill for some weeks back, but seemed perfectly restored up to half-past nine o'clock last evening, when he fell and died without warning, in the small room known as his den. A bottle of chloral was found on the mantel but there is no proof that he took any of it. Indeed, his symptoms were such that the action of a much more violent drug is suspected. His little grandchild was a witness to his last moments.' George, Leighton, and Alfred are now more than rich fellows. They are rich men," I suggested, relieved that my name had not appeared in the headlines.

"They need to be," was the short reply. "One of them at least stood in great need of money."

"Which?" I asked, with an odd sensation of choking in my throat.

"George. He's about played out, as I take it. To my certain knowledge he has lost in unfortunate bets thirty thousand dollars since summer set in. He has a mania for betting and card-playing, and as his father had little patience with vices of this nature, their relations of late have been more than strained. But he's a mighty big-hearted fellow for all that, and a great favourite with the men who don't play with him. I heard he was going to be married. That and this sudden windfall may set him straight again. He's a handsome fellow; did you ever meet him?"

"Once," I acknowledged. Then with an effort of which I was more or less ashamed, I asked the name of the girl who was willing to take such a well-known spendthrift for a husband.

Sam did not seem to be as well posted on this point as on some others.

"I have heard her name," he admitted. "Some cousin, who lives in the same house with him. The old gentleman fancied her so much, he promised to give a big fortune to the son who married her. It seems that George is likely to be the lucky one. Strange, what odd things come up in families."

"There is another brother—Alfred, I think they call him."

"Oh, Alph! He's a deuced handsome chap, too, but not such a universal favourite as George. More moral though. I think his sole vice is an inordinate love of doing nothing. I have known him to lie out half the night on a club-divan, saying nothing, doing nothing, not even smoking. I have sometimes wondered if he ate opium on the sly. Life would be stupid as he spends it, if dreams did not take the place of the pleasant realities he scorns."

I must have shown my amazement. This was not the Alfred Gillespie I had met the night before.

"I have heard that everything was not quite smooth with him. I know I haven't seen him around lately, crushing pillows and making us all look vulgar in contrast to his calm and almost insulting impassibility. I wonder what he will do with the three or four millions which will fall to his share."

"Marry," I suggested, fillipping a fly from my coat-sleeve.

"He? Alph? I don't believe he could hold himself erect long enough to go through the ceremony. Besides, it would be such a bore. That's my idea of Alph."

It was not mine. Either he had greatly changed, or Sam Underhill's knowledge of him was of the most superficial character. As I wavered between these two conclusions I began to experience a vague sensation of dread. If love could effect such a transformation in so unlikely a subject as the man we were discussing, what might it not effect in an ardent nature like my own?

I hastened to change the subject.

"The third brother is already married, I believe."

"Leighton? Oh, he's a widower; has been a widower for years. He was unfortunate in the marriage he made. After the first year no one ever saw young Mrs. Gillespie in public. I don't think the old gentleman ever forgave him that match."

"What was the trouble? He seems to have a dear little girl. I saw her when I saw her uncle."

"Oh, the child. She's well enough, but the mother was—well, we will be charitable and say erratic. Common stock, I've heard. No mate at all for a man like him. Not that he's any too good either for all his hypocritical ways. I have no use for Leighton. I cannot abide so-called philanthropic men whose noses are always in the gutter. He's a sneak, is Leighton, and so inconsistent. One day you hear of him presiding at some charity meeting; the next night you find him behind the scenes at a variety theatre. And as for money—not one of Mr. Gillespie's sons spends so much. He has just drained the old man's purse, or so I've heard; and when asked to give an account of himself mentions his charities and many schemes of benevolence—as if the old man himself didn't spend thousands in just such lines."

"He doesn't look like a prig," I ventured.

"Oh, he looks well enough. But there's something wrong about the man. His own folks acknowledge it; something shameful, furtive; something which will not bear the light. None of those boys are chips of the old block. Let's see the paper. What are you holding it off for? Anything more about Mr. Gillespie's death? Do they call it suicide? That would be a sad ending to such a successful life."

"One question first. Was Mr. Gillespie a good man?"

"He was rich; yet had few if any calumniators."

I handed him the paper. There were some startling lines below those I had read out so glibly.

"They do not stop at suicide," I remarked; "murder is suggested. The drug was not administered by himself."

"Oh!" protested Sam, running his eye over the lines that were destined to startle all New York that morning. "This won't do! None of those boys are bad enough for that, not even Leighton."

"You dislike Leighton," I remarked.

He did not reply; he had just come upon my name in the article he was reading.

"Look here!" he cried, "you're a close one. How came you to be mixed up with the affair? I see your name here."

"Read!"

He complied with an eagerness which I suppose but faintly mirrored that of half the Tribune's readers that morning. What he read, I leave to your imagination, merely premising that no new facts had come to light since my departure from the house and the printing of the paper. When he had finished, he bestowed upon me a long and scrutinising look. "This knocks me out," said he, with more force than elegance. "I would never have believed it, never, of any of these men." Then with a sudden change quite characteristic, he ejaculated, "It was a rum chance for you, Arthur. How did you like it?"

I refused to discuss this side of the question. I was afraid of disclosing what had become the inner-most secret of my heart.

He did not notice my reticence—this, too, was like him—but remarked with visible reluctance:

"The weight of evidence seems to be against Alph. Poor Alph! So this is the result of those long, unbroken hours of silent dreaming! I shall never trust a lazy man again. When they do bestir themselves—"

"He has not been arrested yet," I interjected dryly. "Till the police show absolute belief in his guilt, I for one shall hold my tongue."

"Poor Alph!" was all the reply I received.

CHAPTER XIII

INDICATIONS

These concluding words of Sam Underhill show the trend of public opinion at this time. But I was not swayed by the general prejudice, nor, to all appearance, were the police. Though enough poison was found in Mr. Gillespie's remains to have caused the death of any ordinary man in fifteen minutes, no arrests were made, nor was Mr. Gillespie's favourite son subjected to any closer surveillance than the other members of this once highly respected family.

Meanwhile, the papers were filled with gossip about the case, which was now openly regarded as one of murder. In one column I read a semi-humorous, semi-serious account of how George Gillespie actually once won a bet in face of all odds and to the confounding of those who trusted in his invariable ill-luck; and in another how Leighton had worn out his father's patience by a most persistent association with the most degraded classes, an association which led him into all sorts of extravagances. As a sample of these, and to show how entirely his follies differed from those of his elder brother, he has been known to order breakfast at a restaurant and disappear in the wake of a Salvation Army procession before the meal could be served. They never knew at home when to expect him in, or at what moment he might leave the family circle. He was so restless, he rarely sat an evening out in any one place. Without any apparent reason, he would often leave in the midst of concert, sermon, or lecture, and has been known more than once to dash away from a theatrical performance as if his life depended upon his reaching the open air. And he never expected to be criticised or questioned. If he were, he found some apology to suit the occasion; but the apology was forced, and the person who called it forth rarely repeated the offence.

Only a small paragraph was devoted to Alfred. In it his temporary engagement to Miss Saxton of Baltimore was mentioned, and a somewhat cruel account given of the way he jilted this young lady on his return to the city. As this was coincident with the arrival of Hope at her uncle's house, I needed no further explanation of his fickleness.

All this gossip about people in whom I had come to take so deep an interest both worried and unsettled me; and I found myself looking forward with mingled dread and expectation to the public inquiry, which I had every reason to hope would separate some of these threads, in the network of which my own heart had become so unfortunately entangled.

It had been called for Thursday, and when that day came I was one of the first to appear upon the scene. Not a word of what passed escaped me; not a look nor a sign. Miss Meredith, who entered on the arm of Leighton, wore a veil thick enough to conceal her features. But I did not need to pierce that veil to imagine the expression of anxiety and distress she thus concealed from the crowd. George, who had resumed his usual manner, sat, conspicuous in height and good looks, among a group of witnesses, some of whom I knew and some not. Dr. Bennett sat at my side, and had so little to say that I did not attempt to disturb him, having respect for the grief with which he regarded the untimely end of his life-long friend and patient.

The first witness was myself.

As my testimony contained nothing which has not been already very fully related in these pages, I will pass over this portion of the scene, with the single remark that in the course of my whole examination, which was a lengthy and exhaustive one, I allowed no expression to escape me likely to prejudice the minds of those about me against any one of Mr. Gillespie's sons. For it was apparent, before I had been upon the stand ten minutes, that an effort was being made to fix the crime on Alfred; and what surety could I have that this result would not plunge a barbed arrow into the breast of her about whom my fancy had drawn its magic circle? As I sat down, I glanced her way, and it seemed to me there was meaning in the slight acknowledgment she made me with her ungloved hand. But what meaning?

The inquiry thus being opened, and curiosity roused as to the motive which led Mr. Gillespie to summon a stranger to his side at a moment so vital and under circumstances seemingly calling for the ministrations of those nearest and dearest to him, various experts and physicians were called to prove that his death had not been caused by disease, but by the action of prussic acid on a sufficiently healthy system. With the establishment of this fact the morning's inquiry closed.

As Miss Meredith was likely to be the first witness called at the afternoon session, I felt it my duty as her lawyer to approach her at this time with the following question, quite customary under the circumstances:

"Miss Meredith," said I, "you will probably soon be subjected to a searching inquiry by the coroner. May I ask if there is any special point or topic concerning which you would prefer to keep silence? If so, I can insist upon your privilege."

The look of mingled surprise and indignation with which she regarded me was a sufficient answer in itself. Yet she chose to say, and say coldly, after a moment of reflection:

"I have nothing to conceal. He can ask no question I shall not be perfectly willing to answer."

Abashed by the construction she had put upon my words, as well as greatly hurt by her manner, I bowed and drew off. Evidently she had felt her candour impugned and her innocence questioned, and, in her ignorance of legal proceedings, thought she had only to speak the truth to sustain herself in my eyes and in those of the crowd assembled to hear her.

This sort of self-confidence is common in witnesses, especially in such as are more conscious of their integrity than of the pitfalls underlying the simplest inquiry; and however much I might deplore her short-sightedness and wish that she had better understood both myself and her own position, it was plain that, in the light of what had just passed between us, all interference on my part would be regarded by her as an insult, and that I would be expected to keep silence under all circumstances, let the consequences be what they would.

It was an outlook far from agreeable either for the lawyer or lover, and the recess which now ensued was passed by me in a state of dread of which she in her inexperience had little idea.

Upon the reseating of the jury, her name, just as I had anticipated, was the first one called.

The emotions with which I saw her rise and throw aside her veil under the concentrated gaze of the unsympathetic crowd convened to hear her testimony, first revealed to me the absoluteness of her hold upon me; and when I heard the buzz of admiration which followed the disclosure of her features, I was conscious of colouring so deeply that I feared my secret would become the common property of the crowd. But the spell created by her beauty still held, and all regards remained fixed upon her countenance, now eloquent with feelings which for the moment were shared by all who looked upon her.

Her voice when she spoke deepened the effect of her presence. It was of that fine and resonant quality which awakens an echo in all sensitive hearts and carries conviction with it even to the most callous and prejudiced. It lost some of its power perhaps as the ear became accustomed to it; but to the very end of her testimony, I noted here and there persons who looked up every time she spoke, as if some inner chord responded to her tones—tones which, more than her face, conveyed the impression of a nature exceedingly deep and exquisitely sensitive.

She, meantime, failed to realise the effect which her appearance had produced. She had been questioned, and was striving earnestly and conscientiously to do justice to her oath, and relate as circumstantially as possible what she knew of her uncle's sudden death.

This is what I heard her say:

"I was my uncle's typewriter. I assisted him often with his correspondence and was accustomed to go in and out of his study as if it were my own room. On this night, I had written several letters for him, and being tired had gone upstairs for a little rest. But I was too anxious to be of assistance to him—his mail that evening was unusually large—to retire without one more effort to relieve him; so I went down again a little after ten. I had heard steps in the hall a few minutes before, and little Claire's voice somewhere about the house, but I did not encounter anyone in going down, perhaps because I went by the way of the rear stairs, as I often do when I am in a hurry. Little, little did I imagine what was before me. When I reached my uncle's door,—but you know what a terrible sight met me. There lay my kind— my good—"

We all waited, our hearts in our mouths, but in a moment more she choked down her emotion and was ready to go on.

"He was dead. I knew it at first glance, yet I raised no cry. I could not. I seemed in an instant to have become marble. I saw him lying at my feet and did not weep a tear. I did not even touch him. I merely staggered to the table at the side of which he had fallen, and mechanically, but with a stoppage of my heart's action which made the instant one of untold horror to me, lifted the carriage of the typewriter which he had evidently been using when struck with death, and looked to see what his last words had been. I had reason for believing that they would convey some warning to me or at least an explanation of his sudden death. And they did, or so I interpreted the isolated phrase I came upon at the end of the unfinished letter I found there. God knows I may have been mistaken as to what those five words meant, but I was so impressed with the belief that they were added there for my personal enlightenment that I reeled under the responsibility thus forced upon me, and, hardly conscious of what I was doing, tore off, with almost criminal haste, the portion containing these words, and fled with them out of the sight and reach of everyone in the house. It was a mad thing to do, and I speedily regretted the insane impulse which had actuated me, for I was very soon discovered in the remote spot to which I had fled, and the piece of paper was found, and—and—"

How could she be expected to go on?

"Have we that piece of paper here?" asked the coroner.

It was produced, identified, and passed down to the jury.

It was my opinion at the time, and is still, that she told her story thus fully in order to elude the questions which any apparent reticence on her part would assuredly have evoked. But, having reached this point, it seemed impossible for her to go farther. She drooped, not under the eyes of the crowd, but under the fixed gaze of her three cousins. Had she hoped for some signs of sympathy from them which she failed to receive, or, at least a partial recognition, on their part, of the suffering she was undergoing in the cause of truth and justice? If so, no such recognition came. George's fine face showed anger and anger only; Leighton's, a cold impassibility which might have passed for the stolidity of an utterly unfeeling man if his hands had not betrayed his inner restlessness and torment; while Alfred's flashing eye and set lips made plain the fact that his emotions clung to his own position rather than to hers—as was natural, perhaps, with that slip of paper going the rounds of the jury, and calling up from that respectable body startled, uneasy, or menacing looks, according to the nature of the man examining it.

You remember that slip; a business communication broken into by these totally irrelevant words, "one of my sons He". Is it any wonder that these twelve commonplace men keenly felt their position in face of what looked like a direct accusation from the father's hand?

Yet as these five words, simple in themselves and gaining meaning only from the effort which this young girl had made to suppress them, were capable of being construed in a hundred different ways, the faces which at first blush mirrored but one thought gradually assumed a non-committal aspect, which would have been more encouraging to the men thus compromised, if the facts still to be brought out in explanation of Miss Meredith's conduct towards them had not been of so damaging a character.

Hope, who surmised, if she did not know, the contents of the letter she now heard rustling in the coroner's hand, awaited his next question with evident perturbation. Alfred, who may have hoped that this letter would not appear so early in the examination, forgot himself for a moment and cast a look at his brothers, which they took pains to ignore, perhaps because of the effort it cost them to preserve their own countenances in face of the impending ordeal.

I was witness both to this appeal and its rebuff, but to all appearance Dr. Frisbie saw neither. He was deciding with what form of words to introduce his new subject.

"Miss Meredith," he said at last, "you will now take this letter in your own hand. Have you ever seen it before?"

"Yes, sir, it was a letter which was entrusted to me by my uncle, and which I was told to preserve in secrecy so long as he retained his health and life."

"It is addressed, as all may see: To my three sons, George, Leighton, and Alfred Gillespie. Miss Meredith, did you understand by these words that the enclosed was intended equally for your three cousins?"

"Yes, sir. My uncle Archibald told me so. He expressly said, in giving it into my charge, that in the event of his sudden or unexplainable death, his three sons were to read this letter together."

"It has been opened, I see. Is that a sign it has been so delivered and read?"

"Yes, sir. When on the night I made that inconsiderate attempt to suppress the slip of paper on which my uncle had transcribed the five words you have just shown to the jury, one of my cousins reproached me with having drawn erroneous and unwarrantable conclusions from what was there written. I justified myself by handing over this letter. Though I was never shown its contents, I was well aware of the circumstances under which it was written and—and I was certain it would prove my best excuse for what would otherwise have seemed monstrous in one—who—"

She was too disturbed to proceed.

The coroner looked at her kindly, but it was no part of his duty to allow any sympathy he might feel for the witness to interfere with his endeavour to reach the truth. He therefore urged her to relate the circumstances to which she alluded; in other words, to explain how this letter addressed collectively to her three cousins came to be written.

She grew still more distressed.

"Does not the letter explain itself?" she remonstrated. "Spare me, I pray. My uncle's sons have been brothers to me. Do not make me repeat what passed between my uncle and myself on that unhappy morning when he first unburdened himself of his intolerable grief."

"I fear that I cannot spare you," replied the coroner; "but I will grant you a short respite while this letter, or such portions of it as bear upon Mr. Gillespie's death, is being read to the jury. Gentlemen, it is written in Mr. Gillespie's own hand, and it is dated just a month prior to his unhappy demise. Miss Meredith, you may sit."

She fell rather than sank into the chair offered her, and for a moment I felt myself the prey of a boundless indignation as I witnessed the callousness shown towards her by the three men who up to this time had presumably regarded her with more or less affection. To me her position called for their especial sympathy. The heroism she evinced was the heroism of a loving woman who sacrifices herself, and what is dearest to her, to her idea of justice and law. And while such action may be easy for a man, it is hard beyond expression for a woman, who, as we know, is much more apt to listen to the voice of her heart than to any abstract appeal of right and justice. Yet these same relatives of hers sat still and scarcely looked her way, though she glanced repeatedly and with heartrending appeal in their direction.

I am quite ready to admit that I was too prejudiced a witness to be just to these men. Had I not myself been under the influence of a sudden and violent passion, I would have seen that Alfred needed sympathy as well as she; for Alfred was the man most menaced by the contents of the letter now on the point of being read; and he knew this as certainly as she did.

As this letter is better known to you than it was to me up to this hour, I leave you to judge of its effect upon the jury and the excited crowd of spectators thronging the room at every point. Heads which had wagged in doubt now drooped in heaviest depression; and while all eyes seemed to shrink from an attempt to read the three white faces on the witnesses' bench, the attention of all was concentrated there, and it was with quite a sense of shock that Dr. Frisbie's voice was heard rising again in renewed examination of the young lady whose precipitate action had brought to public notice this touching letter of a heartbroken father.

His first question was a leading one. Had Mr. Gillespie followed up his former confidences by any further allusions to the attempt which had been made upon his life?

Her answer was a direct negative. Though she had detected in her uncle signs of great unhappiness, he had held no further conversation with her on this topic, and life had gone on as usual in the great house.

"But he talked of poisons, and refused to take any more of the medicine which came so near killing him?"

"Uncle Archibald took no more of this medicine, certainly. That is, I saw no more of it in the house. But he never talked of poisons, that is, publicly or in my presence."

"Not at the table?"

"Not after that night, sir."

"He had before?"

"Only incidentally. He had laughed at some of Dr. Bennett's remarks, and once I heard him mention the danger of taking an overdose of the remedy that was doing him so much good. It was while jesting with me upon my refusal to allow anyone else to portion it out for him."

"That was your duty, then?"

"Assuredly."

"Were you in the habit of preparing his glass when alone or in the presence of his sons?"

"As it happened, sir. I had but one dread; that of miscounting the drops."

"And he took no more of this medicine after that especial night?"

"No, sir. He asked Dr. Bennett for a narcotic of less dangerous properties, and was given chloral."

"Did you hear any remarks made on this change?"

"None."

"What became of the phial which held the remainder of this medicine marked 'Poison'?"

"I emptied it out at my uncle's request."

"You were your uncle's nurse, then, typewriter, and friend?"

"He trusted me, sir, in all these capacities."

"Did he trust you with his business concerns?"

"Not at all. I merely wrote letters to his dictation."

"Did you know, or have you ever heard, the value of his estate?"

"I have never even asked myself whether he counted his fortune by thousands or millions."

The dignity, the simplicity, with which this was said made it an impressive termination to a very painful examination. As I noted the effect it produced, I was in hopes that she would be allowed to retire for the day. But the coroner had other views. With a hesitancy that more or less prepared us for what was to come, he addressed her again, saying quietly:

"I have spared you a public reading of certain portions of your uncle's letter, referring to yourself and the wishes he openly cherished in your behalf. In return, will you inform me if you are engaged to marry any one of these young men?"

The thrill, the start given to the witnesses' bench by this pointed question, communicated itself to officer and spectator. In George's fiery flush and Alfred's sudden paleness, emotions could be seen at work of sufficient significance to draw every eye; though few present, I dare say, ascribed these emotions to their rightful sources. To myself, divided as I was in feeling between the anxiety I could not but feel as her lawyer to see her parry a question too personal not to be humiliating, and the interest with which, as her lover, I awaited a response which would solve my own doubts and make clear my own position, there was something in the attitude of both these men strongly suggestive of a like uncertainty. Were her feelings, then, as much of a mystery to them as they were to me? Did George fear to hear her say she was engaged to Alfred, and Alfred dread to hear her admit that she was irrevocably pledged to George? If so, what a situation had been evolved by this question publicly put by a city functionary! No wonder the young girl dropped her eyes before venturing a reply.

But the spirit of self-protection, always greater in woman than in man where heart secrets are involved, gave her strength to meet this crisis with a baffling serenity. Raising her patient eyes, she replied with a sweet composure which acted like a tonic upon the agitated hearts about her:

"There is no such engagement. I have lived in their house like a sister. Their father was my mother's brother."

Another man than Coroner Frisbie would have let her go, but this honest, if kindly, official was strangely tenacious when he had a point to gain. Flushing himself, for her look was directed quite steadily upon him, he gravely repeated:

"Do you mean to say that no words of love ever passed between you and any of these gentlemen?"

This was too much. Expecting to see her recoil, possibly break down, I eagerly looked her way for the permission to interfere, which she might now be ready to give me. But with a proud lift of her head she showed herself equal to the emergency, and her answer, given simply and with no attempt at subterfuge, restored her at once to the dignified position we all dreaded to see her lose.

"I mean to say nothing but the truth. Mr. George Gillespie has more than once honoured me by making me an offer of his hand. But I did not consider myself in a position to accept it."

Dr. Frisbie showed her no quarter.

"And your cousin Alfred?"

"Alfred?" Her eyes no longer met those of the coroner or anyone else in that cruel crowd. "He," she stammered proudly, "has never interfered with whatever claims his brother may have been supposed to have upon my favour."

It was a statement to awaken turmoil in more than one of the uneasy hearts behind her. George bounded to his feet, though he quickly subsided again into his seat, ashamed of this betrayal, or fearful of the effect it might have upon his brother. Alfred, on the contrary, sat still, but the bitterness visible in his smile spoke volumes, and, seeing it, the whole crowd recognised what had long been apparent to myself, that these two brothers were rivals in the love they bore this woman, and that it was through her desire to shield the one she favoured, that she made the first false move which had drawn the attention of the police to the doubtful position held by Mr. Gillespie's sons.

That her choice had fallen upon the man who had not interfered with his brother's rights seemed only too probable, and I expected the coroner to force this acknowledgment from her lips, but he grew considerate all at once and inquired instead if Mr. Gillespie had been made aware of his elder son's wishes. She replied to this by saying:

"They were no secret in the house"; and, with a look, begged him to spare her.

But this man was inexorable.

"And did he approve of the match?"

"He did."

"Yet you failed to engage yourself?"

This she deemed already answered.

"If the younger brother had pressed his suit for your hand, do you think that under the circumstances your uncle would have sanctioned such rivalry?"

This, perhaps, she could not answer. At all events she was as silent as before.

"Miss Meredith," proceeded her tormentor, utterly oblivious or entirely careless of the suffering he caused her, "do you know whether your uncle and his youngest son ever had any words on this subject?"

Her hands involuntarily flew out in piteous entreaty.

"Ask this question of the only person who can answer it," she cried. "I only know that I have been treated with great respect in the house of my uncle."

With that, the proceedings closed for the day.

CHAPTER XIV

A SUDDEN TURN

Dr. Frisbie's point had been made. As we separated to our several destinations for the night, it was with the universally expressed conviction that this young girl, for all her beauty and attractive qualities, had been an apple of discord in her uncle's house, and that in this fact, rather than in an impatient desire to enjoy the wealth of a man who was never close with his sons, the unnatural crime we were considering had originated.

The evidence elicited from the first witness called to the stand on the following morning tended to substantiate this conclusion.

Nellie Stryker, an old inmate of the Gillespie house, answered the coroner's questions with great reluctance. She had been maid to Mrs. Gillespie, nurse to all the children, and a trusted servant in the household ever since the latter grew beyond her care. Of the attempts made upon her master's life, the last of which had been only too successful, she knew little and that only by hearsay, but she was not quite so ignorant concerning a certain conversation which had been held one morning in Mr. Gillespie's room between that gentleman and his youngest son. She was sitting at her needle in the adjoining dressing-closet, and, whether her presence there was unsuspected by her master or simply ignored, they both talked quite freely and she heard every word.

Urged to repeat this conversation, the good old soul showed a shamefaced reluctance which bore out her reputation for honesty and discretion. But she was not allowed to escape the examination set for her. After repeated questions and a show of extreme patience on the part of the coroner, she admitted that the topic discussed was the state of Mr. Alfred's affections. This young gentleman, as was publicly known, had lately engaged himself to a Southern lady of great pride and high social distinction; and his present disagreement with his father arose out of his wish to break this engagement. His father had no patience with such fickleness, and their words ran high. Finally, Alfred threatened to follow his own wishes in the matter, whether it gave satisfaction all round or no; declaring that he had been a fool to tie himself to a girl he cared nothing about, but that he would be a still greater one if he let the mistake of a moment mar his happiness for life. But the old gentleman's sense of honour was very keen, and he continued to urge the claims of the Southern lady, till his son impetuously blurted out:

"I thought you wanted one of us to marry Hope?"

This caused a break in the conversation.

"Do you care for Hope?" the old gentleman asked. "I thought it was well understood in this house that George, not you, was to be given the first opportunity of winning her."

The oath with which Alfred answered was shocking to Nellie's ears, and affected her so deeply that she heard nothing more till these words caught her attention:

"George has everything he wants; unlimited indulgence in each and every fancy, the liking of all the men, and the love of all the women. I am not so fortunate; I am neither a favourite with my mates nor the petted darling of their sisters; I like my ease, but I could give that up for Hope. She is the only woman I have ever seen capable of influencing me. I have been quite a different man since she came into the house. If that is love, it is a very strong love; such love as makes a man out of a nobody. Father, let me have this darling girl for my wife. George does not care for her,—not as I do. He would be a better fellow if he did."

Mr. Gillespie seemed quite upset. He loved this son as the apple of his eye, and would very possibly have been glad to see the matter so adjusted, but it did not tally with his idea of what people had a right to expect from his sons, and he told Alfred so in rather strong language.

"Can you remember that language?" asked the coroner.

She tried to make him believe, and herself too, no doubt, that her memory would not serve her to this extent; but her honesty eventually triumphed over her devotion to the family interests, and she finally admitted that the old gentleman had said:

"While I live I will not put up with rivalry of any kind between my sons. George is fond of Hope, and I long ago gave him my permission to woo and marry her. That you are the child of my heart shall not make me blind to the rights of one I loved before you ever saw the light. Were I to permit such shilly-shallying, George would have a right to reproach me with his wasted life. No; the influence which you call so great must be exerted in his behalf rather than yours. He needs it, Alfred, as much, if not more than you do. As to your present engagement, you may break it or you may keep it, but do not expect me to uphold you in any love-making with your brother's choice till Hope has openly signified her absolute refusal of his attentions. This she is not likely to do; George has too many conspicuous attractions."

"She has refused him once."

"Not because her fancy was caught by his younger brother, but because she wished to see some reformation in his habits. In this she was perfectly right. George will have to change his mode of life very materially before he can be regarded as worthy of such a wife."

"The same might be said of me; but I am no George. I am anxious to make such a change. Yet you give me no encouragement in my efforts, and even deny me the opportunity of winning her affections."

"You were not the first to enter the field. Your older brother has the prior right, and, as I view the matter, the only right, to approach Hope in the attitude of a lover."

The oaths which this excited turned the poor old listener cold. Alfred could not see the justice of his brother's course, and stormed away about fairness being shown to the young girl herself, who possibly looked upon the matter in another light than he did.

"Then you have been making love to her on the sly!" vociferated Mr. Gillespie, totally forgetting himself.

But this the young man denied. If he understood her better than others did, it was because he loved her better. He was positive that she did not care for his brother, and all but certain she did care for himself. At all events he flattered himself to this extent. This called forth a few more bitter words from his father, and Alfred went out, banging the door behind him.

"And did you see any change in the manner of Mr. Gillespie towards his sons after this misunderstanding with Alfred?"

The witness appeared to weigh her words; but, when she answered, it was evident her care arose from a desire to present the subject fairly.

"I thought Mr. Gillespie talked less and looked about him more. And the young gentlemen seemed conscious of this change in him, for they were very careful not to show their feelings too plainly in his presence."

"Yet there was a manifested distrust between them?"

"I fear so."

"Amounting to animosity?"

"That I cannot say. I never heard them exchange hard words; only neither of them would leave the field open to the other. If Mr. George stayed home, Mr. Alfred found some excuse for doing so also; and if Mr. Alfred showed a disposition to linger in the parlour, Mr. George brought in his friends and made a social evening of it."

"And is this all you can tell us?"

"On this topic? Yes."

"You never saw Miss Meredith speaking apart to either of these two men?"

"No, sir; on the contrary, she appeared to avoid all private conversation with any of them."

"Nor ever heard either of these men swear he would have Miss Meredith for his wife, no matter who stood in the way, or what means were taken to stop him?"

"Oh, I once heard Mr. Alfred make use of some violent expressions as I was passing his door, but I can not be sure he spoke the precise words you mention. He falls into fits of anger at times and then is liable to forget himself. But his ill-temper does not last, sir. It is quite unusual for him to show unkindness for any length of time."

After the close of this examination, so painful to the witnesses and so humiliating to the three persons whose most cherished feelings were thus exposed to the public eye, the three sons of Mr. Gillespie were called up, one after the other, and questioned.

Leighton made the best impression. Not being involved in the delicate question which had just come up, he had no blushes to conceal nor any secret animosities to hold in check. George, on the contrary, seemed to have reached a state of exasperation which made it difficult for him to preserve any semblance of self-possession. He stammered when he talked, and looked much more like having it out with his brother in a hand-to-hand fight than submitting to an examination tending to incriminate one or both of them on a charge of murder. Alfred showed less bitterness, possibly because he felt securer in his position towards the woman whose beauty had occasioned this rivalry. Of the facts brought out by their accumulated testimony I need say little. They added nothing to the general knowledge, and the inquiry adjourned with promise of still more serious work for the morrow.

Hitherto the evidence had been of a nature to show, first, that a crime had been committed, and, secondly, that the relations between Alfred and his father had been such as to occasion a desire on the former's part to be free from the watchful eye of one who stood between him and any attempt he might make to win the affections of the woman upon whom he had set his heart. On this morning the testimony took a turn, and an endeavour was made to show a positive connection between Alfred Gillespie and the drug which had ended his father's life,—or so it appeared at the time. The visit he paid to the dining-room during the fatal hour preceding his father's death was brought out, and the acknowledgment reached that he went there in search of his missing pencil.

Then the detectives were called to the stand and requested to relate the circumstances connected with the finding of a certain cork and phial, the one under the edge of the dining-room rug, and the other under the clock on the mantel-shelf. These aforementioned articles were then produced, and after positive declaration had been made that they had not been allowed to come in contact since falling into the hands of the police, they were severally handed down to the jury, who immediately proceeded to satisfy themselves that the scent of bitter almonds was nearly as marked in one as the other. This point having been reached and universal expectation raised, Sweetwater handed up another article to the coroner, saying:

"In this box, which is as nearly air-tight as I could procure offhand, I caused to be placed, as soon as possible after finding it, the pencil which we came upon in our search of the dining-room floor. Like the phial and the cork, it was kept isolated in a perfectly clean glass till this box could be procured, and, with this fact in mind, may I ask you to open the box and hand the pencil round among the jury?"

Instantly a great stir took place in the whole body of spectators. Necks were stretched, heads were craned, and a general sigh swept from end to end of the room as the coroner wrenched the cover from the box, lifted out the pencil, raised it to his nose, and then passed it down to the jury. Only one person in sight failed to follow these significant movements with looks of curious interest; and that was the unhappy man who thus saw the finger of suspicion, which had been simply wavering in his direction, settle into immobility and point inexorably towards him. A white face and a sinking heart were shown by Alfred Gillespie at that moment; and in the features of Hope, disclosed for one instant under the stress of her mortal anxiety, I saw his anxiety reflected as in a mirror.

The jury whispered together with nods and significant looks as this small pencil passed from hand to hand—I had almost said from nose to nose. Then silence was restored, and the coroner, with a sudden change of manner startling to observe in one whose bearing and tone reflected his feelings almost too openly, called an expert in poisons to the stand.

His testimony established three facts: that the smell of prussic acid is unmistakable; that this poison, though volatile in its character, preserves its own individual odour for a long time if not subjected to too much air; and, lastly, that if the pencil smelt of the bottle, the pocket in which they both had lain would also give out the same odour of bitter almonds.

When the expert was seated, Detective Sweetwater was called back. And then for the first time I noticed a large package encumbering the coroner's desk. As this package was being unrolled, I stole a look at the witness, who, from his assured air, evidently had the thread of Alfred's future destiny in his hand, and was astonished to see how attractive a very plain man can sometimes become.

Perhaps I have not spoken of this young detective's plainness. It was so marked and of such an unrelieved type that, after once seeing the man, you could never again think of him without recalling his lank frame and inharmonious features.

Yet as he stood there, calm amidst the tremor of this throng, his eye sparkled with such intelligence that I trembled for the man whose cause he was expected to damage with his testimony. Seeing that my feelings were shared by those about me, I glanced back at the coroner's table to see what the unrolling of that package had revealed, and saw, hanging from the coroner's hands, three vests, which he proceeded to display, one by one, before the witness.

"What are these?" he asked, with a stern look down the room, calculated to suppress any too open demonstration of interest.

"Vests; the property of the three gentlemen members of the present Gillespie household; in other words, those severally worn by Messrs. George, Leighton, and Alfred Gillespie on the evening of their father's death."

"How do you know these particular vests to be the ones then worn?"

"From their material and cut, of which I took especial note at the time."

"No other way?"

"Yes, sir. Foreseeing the difficulties which might arise if it ever became necessary to distinguish the vests then worn from the half dozen others which we should doubtless find in their well-supplied wardrobes, I took the precaution of secretly running my finger over a freshly inked pen before taking hold of their vests in the search I had been commanded to make of their persons. If the marks of my finger can be seen on the white linings of the vests now in your hand, you may be sure they are the ones subjected to my search on that night, as I communicated my intention to no one and have since been exceedingly careful not to take anyone into my confidence concerning this little trick."

The coroner turned the vests. On the back of each a black spot was plainly visible to the remotest observer in the room. A murmur of mingled admiration and suspense responded to this discovery, and the coroner turned again to Sweetwater.

"May I ask," said he, "if you are in a position to tell us to which of these young gentlemen these several vests belong?"

"The Messrs. Gillespie can be trusted to identify their own property," was the answer. "But I doubt if you will consider this a necessary formality. There is no scent of bitter almonds lingering about any of these pockets. There was none on that night. This I made it my especial business to ascertain." And he glanced at Alfred as much as to say, "Thank me for doing you what justice I can."

Such surprise followed this unexpected acknowledgment from one whose manner had given promise of a very different result, that it was hard to tell where the effect was greatest. Hope's veil was shifted again, and the three brothers looked up simultaneously and with an equal show of relief.

But their countenances fell again as they noted the witness still on the stand—waiting.

My countenance fell too, or rather my heart began to throb apprehensively as I now perceived the face and form of Mr. Gryce slowly appearing round the corner of a certain jut in the wall where he had held himself partially concealed during most of the day's proceedings. If this sagacious but sickly old detective thought it worth his while to come forward, I thought it worth mine to note upon whom or on what his glance first fell. But I had forgotten his habit, known to most men who have had anything to do with this celebrated detective. He had looks for nothing save the umbrella he rolled round and round between his palms; though his face—if this indicated anything—was turned towards the seat where the three Gillespies sat, rather than towards the witness with whose testimony past, present, and to come he was probably fully acquainted.

Meantime the coroner was speaking.

"When you failed to find the tell-tale scent of bitter almonds tainting the pockets of any of the clothes worn by these young gentlemen at the time you searched them, what did you do?"

"As soon as opportunity offered, that is, as soon as I found myself unobserved, I searched the wardrobes of these young gentlemen for other vests and pockets."

"Ah, and did you come upon any article of clothing giving signs of having at any time come in contact with this pencil or this bottle?"

"I found that," he returned, indicating a fourth garment, which the coroner now deftly drew forth from the paper where it had hitherto lain concealed.

This garment was a vest like the others, and, like them, of a plain and inconspicuous pattern. As it was lifted into sight, a groan was heard which seemed to spring from the united breasts of the three young men behind him. Then one bounded to his feet.

"That is my vest," he shouted. "What damned villain says there is anything the matter with it?"

It was George. The two other brothers had shrunk back out of sight.

CHAPTER XV

THE MISSING POCKET

The excitement was intense. To see suspicion thus suddenly, and, I must say, deftly, shifted from the man hitherto regarded guilty to one whom nobody had seemed inclined to doubt, was to experience an emotion of no ordinary nature. I was so affected by it that I quite forgot myself, and stared first at the vest thus recognised by its owner, then at the witness, who was calmly awaiting an opportunity to speak, with deep bewilderment only cut short by the coroner's abrupt words:

"Where did you find this vest I now hold up before you?"

"In the closet of the dressing-room adjoining the apartment where Mr. George Gillespie is said to sleep."

"Does this dressing-room communicate with the hall or with any other room than the said Mr. Gillespie's sleeping apartment?"

"No."

"Is it a large room or a small one; a mere closet or a place big enough for a man to turn about in with ease and do such a thing, say, as change his vest without being seen too plainly by persons in the adjoining room?"

"It is a six-by-ten room, sir. If anyone chose to do what you suggest in the especial corner where the wardrobe stands, he certainly would run little chance of being seen by anyone sitting near the fireplace of the sleeping apartment."

"Why do you speak of the fireplace?"

"Because the evidences are strong that this was where Mr. Gillespie's three friends were sitting when he came up from below, with the half-empty bottle of sherry in his hands."

"What evidences do you allude to?"

"The fact that we found four chairs standing there about a table strewn with cards. I did not see the gentlemen in their seats."

"But you did see this vest hanging on one of the nails in the wardrobe?"

"Yes, sir."

"A near nail or a remote one?"

"The remotest in the closet."

"Very good. Now, what is the matter with this vest?"

"It lacks a pocket."

Ah! So that was it!

The coroner turned the vest in his hand.

"What pocket?"

"The lower right-hand one, the one where a gentleman usually carries a pen, knife, or pencil."

"What has happened to it? How could a pocket be lost from a vest?"

"It has been cut out."

"Cut out!"

"Yes, sir; we found an open knife lying on the dresser, and if you will look again at the vest you will see that the missing pocket was slit from it with a very hasty jerk."

"I avow—" shouted the voice of the owner from the seats behind.

But the infuriated man who thus attempted to speak was quickly silenced.

"You will be allowed to explain later," remonstrated the coroner. "At present we are listening to Mr. Sweetwater. Witness, what course did you pursue after coming upon this vest?"

"I endeavoured to ascertain if its owner had gone into his dressing-room after coming up from the room below."

Here we heard sobs; but they were only a child's, and the inquiry went on.

"Did you succeed?"

"I request you to call up Mr. James Baxter as a more direct witness."

His request being complied with, Mr. James Baxter came forward, and expectancy rose to fever-point. He was one of the three gentlemen whose voices I had heard over the cards that were being played in George Gillespie's room during the hour his father had succumbed to poison. I recognised him at once from his burly figure and weak voice; having noticed this eccentricity at our first meeting. He was not sober then, but he was very sober now, and the effect he produced was, on the whole, favourable.

Glancing at George as if in apology, and receiving a tiger's glare in return, he waited with a certain sang froid for the inevitable question. It came quickly and with a peremptoriness which showed that the coroner now felt himself on safe ground.

"Where were you sitting when George Gillespie left you to go downstairs for wine?"

"At the card-table near the fire, with my face towards the dressing-room at the other end of the room."

"Had wine been passed then, or any spirituous liquors?"

"No."

"You were all in a perfectly sober condition therefore?"

"Tolerably so. Two of us had had dinner at Delmonico's, but I had been dining at home and was dry. That is why Mr. Gillespie went down for the wine."

"What did you do while he was downstairs?"

"Bet on the Jack about to be turned up."

"How much money passed?"

"Oh, ten dollars or so."

"And when your host returned, what did you do?"

"I guess we drank."

"Did he drink too?"

"I did not notice. He put the bottle down and went into his dressing-room. When he came back he stood a minute by the fire, then he sat down. He may have drank then. I didn't observe."

"What did he do at the fire? Was he warming himself? It was not a cold night."

"I don't know what he did. I saw a sudden burst of flame, but that was all. I was busy dealing the cards."

"You saw a flame shoot up. Was there wood or coal in the grate?"

"Deuce take me if I remember. I wasn't thinking of the fire. I only knew we were roasting hot and more than once made some movement towards shifting the table further off, but we got too interested in the cards to bother about it."

"It must have been a lively game. Were you too interested in shuffling and dealing to notice why Mr. Gillespie went to his dressing-room?"

"Yes, I never thought anything about it."

"You didn't watch him, then?"

"No."

"Cannot say whether or not he went towards his wardrobe?"

"No."

"Or, perhaps, whether the door between you was closed or not?"

"He didn't close the door; I should have noticed that."

"How long was he in that room?"

"I can't say. Long enough for me to drink my wine and shuffle the cards. Before I had dealt them he had set down."

"One question more. Can you truthfully assert he did not cross his dressing-room before your eyes, change his vest in the corner where the wardrobe stands, and come back in the same coat, but with a different vest on?"

"No. I cannot even say what kind of clothes he wore that night. I am no dude, and all vests, so long as they are not striped or plaid, are alike to me."

This remark, which was facetious only from the humorous contrast between the small and highpitched voice and the large and stalwart figure of the speaker, caused a smile to appear on several faces. But this expression was soon replaced by one more befitting the occasion, as a change in witnesses once more occurred and Hewson appeared upon the stand. This old servant of the family was loath to look at the vest held out before him, and seemed desirous of denying that he had noticed what his young master had worn at dinner that night. But his precision and habitual attention to details were too well known for him to succeed in any evasion, and he was forced to declare that the vest with the thumb mark on the lining was not the one Mr. George had worn at dinner.

This was a fatal admission and George's case was looking very black, when a sudden cry mingled with a burst of childish sobs was heard in the room, and little Claire, breaking away from the restraining hands that sought to hold her back, rushed out in face of coroner and jury, and stretching out her arms to her father, cried:

"Uncle George didn't cut the pocket out of his vest. I did. I—I wanted a little bag for my beads, and Hetty wouldn't make me one; so I stole into uncle's room and snipped out the little pocket. It was before grandpa died, and I'm so—so sorry."

She fell into her father's arms and was crushed, nay, strained against that father's breast. Never had a child's naughtiness brought a more perfect joy; while from floor to ceiling of the great room, cries and shouts of relief went up from the surcharged hearts of the spectators which for once the coroner failed to rebuke.

Possibly he was as much touched as anyone. There was so much natural impulse, so much spontaneity in the child's words and actions, that no one could doubt her candour or the fact that this outburst had been prompted by her own contrition.

Even Mr. Gryce accepted the explanation without demur, though he must have realised that it demolished at a blow the case he had so carefully reared against the oldest son of Mr. Gillespie. He was even seen to smile benignantly and with a kind of soothing tenderness on the knob of his umbrella before he rested his chin upon it in quiet contemplation.

Hope, who had made an impetuous movement as the child flew by her, let her eye fall for a moment on the curly head almost nestled out of sight in the paternal embrace. Then with a glance at George, scarcely long enough to note the relief this childish hand had brought him, she let her eye travel slowly on to Alfred, who, biting his lips to keep down the flush which these rapidly succeeding events had called up, did not catch her look, precious as it doubtless would have been to him.

Then and not till then did her gaze seek mine.

Alas! this recognition of my interest, so eagerly anticipated and so patiently waited for, was inspired by no deeper sentiment than a desire to gather my present idea of the situation and what was now to be expected from the baffled officials.

If my answering look conveyed undue confidence in the outcome, I had certainly sufficient excuse for it in the attitude of those about me. The explanation which George was able to give of the causes which had led to his changing his vest on the evening in question were received with respect, if not with favour, and as it was natural enough to gain credence, enthusiasm in his regard rose to such a pitch that it presently became evident that it would be next to impossible to push the case farther before this jury.

Indeed, the reaction was so strong that after some futile attempts to reopen the inquiry on fresh lines, the coroner finally gave in and called for the jury's verdict.

It was, as might be expected:

"Death from the effects of prussic acid, administered by some hand unknown."

Meantime, the will of Mr. Gillespie had been admitted to probate; but as he had never made any secret of his intentions, and the share and share alike of his sons had been left without a disturbing codicil, little help was afforded by its terms in settling the harassing problem which more than ever occupied the minds of the community and presented itself as an almost unanswerable puzzle to the police.

Even Mr. Gryce, whose sagacity no one could doubt, showed how unpromising the affair looked to him by the line of care which now made its appearance on his forehead; a forehead which had remained singularly unclouded till now, notwithstanding his sixty or more years of experience with such knotty problems.

This I had occasion to note in an interview I held with him some few days after the rendering of the abovementioned verdict.

He had sought me with the intention of satisfying himself that the ground had been thoroughly gone over, and no possible clue had been ignored. But he gained nothing new from me, not even my secret, and went away at last, looking older and more careworn than my first view of his benevolent and naturally composed countenance had led me to expect.

But while moved by this to consider the seriousness with which these men regarded their duty, I was much more deeply impressed by the corresponding marks of secret disturbance which I presently discovered in my own countenance. For, in my case, the trouble indicated did not depend upon the settlement of an exciting case, but was the result of a lasting impression made upon me by a woman who gave little sign of sharing a passion likely to prove the one absorbing experience of my life. Do what I would, I could not forget her or the position she held among these three men. Was she still the object of George's attentions or—worse still—of Alfred's passionate hopes? Did she respond to the latter's devotion, or was she still restrained by doubts of an innocence not yet entirely proved?

I longed to know. I longed to see for myself how she bore all these uncertainties.

But no excuse offered itself for a second intrusion upon her privacy, even if I had been sure I should find her still living with her cousins; and in this unrest and state of anxious waiting, the days went by, till suddenly I heard it casually mentioned at the Club that Miss Meredith was with a distant connection of the Gillespies in Fifty-seventh Street.

This was like fire to tow. Without waiting to question my own motives or to ask whether it would be for my happiness or misery to see her again, I called at the Penrhyn mansion and inquired for Miss Meredith.

To my great relief and consequent delight she consented to receive me, and I presently found myself seated in a choice little reception-room awaiting her coming. Only then did I begin to realise my own temerity. With what words should I accost her? How open conversation without suggesting griefs I was burning to make her forget? I had no time to decide. She was at the door and in the room before my mind could frame the simplest greeting; and, once brought face to face with her, I forgot everything but herself and the irresistible charm which her presence exerted over me.

She had been weeping, and I could not but see that the sight of my face recalled scenes suggestive of the deepest suffering. In my dismay I found my tongue and attempted some conventional expressions of good-will. These she no sooner heard than she cut me short by an irrepressible exclamation.

"Pray,—" she entreated. "You have been with me during a time of too much misery for such formalities as these to pass between us." Then, before I could protest, "What is wanted of me now? I know you desire explanations of some kind; everybody does who approaches me; even my best friends. Yet I unburdened myself of everything I knew that first night."

I may have looked hurt. I certainly felt so; but she did not notice this result of her abrupt attack; she was too full of the feverish anxiety roused by the subject she had herself introduced.

"But you are a just man and a good one," she went on. "I do not need to be told so; I see it in your face. You will be honest with me, and will at least acquaint me with the motive underlying any questions you may put. Others deceive me, and lead me into confidences they afterwards turn against me or against those I have reason to be true to, though I was the first to betray them."

Her cheek, so pale at her entrance, was burning red now, and she spoke quickly, almost disconnectedly. I saw that she needed rallying, and smiled.

"Now it is you who are pressing the subject you abhor. I have not asked you anything; I shall not. I have not come here to satisfy either my curiosity or the demands of the law. I am here to inquire after your health and to renew my offer of service. May I be excused for my interest in yourself? It is involuntary on my part and so sincere that your uncle, were he living, could not object to it."

Soothed by my voice as much as by my words, she sat down and endeavoured to open conversation. But there was a constraint in her manner which convinced me that she was labouring under a too vivid remembrance of the scene where we had last met.

"What a position is mine!" burst at last from her lips. "I have three natural protectors, yet I do not know of an arm on which I can place my hand with implicit confidence. This is my reason for being in this house; and why I hail with eagerness, too great eagerness, perhaps, the prospect of a friend."

It was an appeal for which I found myself poorly prepared, especially as it was made with such simplicity and in such evident disregard of the feelings which made my presence there of such import to myself. It recalled to me her position; and remembering that she was a comparative stranger in town, and that since her coming she had been all in all to her uncle in capacities which had kept her much at home and out of the society where she might have made friends and found support in this dreadful emergency, I composed myself, and, leaning forward, took her hand in mine with a respect she could not but feel, since it permeated my whole being.

"I am a stranger to you," was my plea, "notwithstanding the vivid experiences which have brought us together. You know little of me beyond my name and the fact that my one wish, since first seeing you, has been to serve you and save you from every possible annoyance. This must be obvious to you, or you would not have accepted me so unhesitatingly for your lawyer. Will you add to this title—a title which you have yourself given me, the more personal one you have just mentioned? Will you let me be the friend you need? You can find no truer one."

She broke into a confused stammering, amid which I heard: "I will. You give me confidence." Then she sat still, her hand trembling in mine and her eyes shining with a new light. It was an innocent one, that of a child who has stumbled on a protector in the dark; but to me it was the very glow of heaven, the first ray of promise by means of which I could discern, even in fancy, the fairy-land of my dreams. Was it any wonder it intoxicated me? Forgetting that I had not been to her all that she had been to me for the last few weeks; forgetting everything but that she was an unhappy woman whom I passionately loved, I gazed in her face as a man gazes at a woman but once in a lifetime.

She did not lower her eyes; would that she had! but met my looks with a half smile whose open and indulgent kindness should have warned me to recover my ground while it was safe. But a sudden madness had seized me, and seeing simply that it was a smile, I found it impossible to realise in the frenzy of the moment that the feelings I had hitherto ascribed to her were true. She had liked, not loved her cousins. They had been good to her, and in return she had given them a cousinly regard which in one instance, perhaps, approached the warmth of love. But it was a love far from necessary to her life— or so I dared dream; while my passion for her was a part of my being, so close a part that I felt forced to speak and claim her as my own in this hour of her greatest trouble and perplexity. Before I knew it; before she had time to restrain me by word or look, I was pouring out my soul before her. Not in the respectful, measured way I had foreseen when looking forward to this hour, but wildly, hotly, as a man speaks when the treasure of his life is to be won by one strong effort.

It was sudden; it was perhaps unwarranted; but my sincerity moved her. That was perhaps why she listened so patiently, and it was to this recognition of my candid regard I attribute the look of wistfulness which crept over her features when I ceased.

"Oh!" she murmured, "why cannot I accept the love of this good man?" And, rising up, she walked away from me to the other end of the room.

Breathlessly I watched her; breathlessly I noted her walk, the droop of her head, the agitated working of her hands. Would my good angel stand by me and turn her trembling heart my way, or must I prepare myself to see her pause, turn, and come back to me with denial in her looks? The suspense of that moment I shall never forget. It has never been repeated in my experience. Never since have I suffered so much in any one moment.

Suddenly it was all over. She turned and I read my doom in her sorrowing face.

"You are good," she cried, "and it would be an infinite rest to be lifted out of the agony I am in and be cared for by someone I could perfectly trust. But I cannot accept a devotion which fails to awaken in me aught but simple gratitude and friendliness. Unfortunately for me, and perhaps unfortunately for him whom I cannot trust myself to name, I have given my whole heart—" She choked back the words with a certain wildness. Then she faced me with mournful dignity and avowed calmly, and with a certain finality which caused my hopes to sink back into the depths from which they had so inconsiderately sprung, "I have fixed my heart where perhaps I should not. Pity me, but do not blame."

I blame, I! who had committed the same folly, was suffering from the same mistake!

"He may be the one true heart amongst them. Sometimes I think he is; sometimes I think his faults are blemishes upon a nature noble enough for any love and worship; then doubt comes, horrible, corroding doubt, and I see in him a fiend, a monster, a being too dreadful to contemplate, much less dream of and adore. Oh, if I did but know—"

"You shall know!" I burst forth, forgetting my own misery in hers. "I have been selfish in urging my personal wishes upon you when I should have been occupied with yours. Henceforth I shall think only of you. To see you happy, to see you at peace, shall be my joy and prove my consolation. I cannot rejoice at the task, if task it can be called, but from this day on my energies shall be devoted to the settling of that doubt which, while it exists, robs you of all peace of mind. If Alfred is the guiltless man we are fain to believe him, you shall know it. I feel that it is possible to prove him so, and my feelings have often been very reliable guides in difficult undertakings."

She was startled; she was more than startled; she was alarmed. "I don't understand you," she cried. "What can you do? If the one guilty heart among my cousins refuses to respond to the appeal made to it by my uncle, how can you hope to move so callous a soul to a sense of its duty?"

"I cannot. With the hand of the law raised in threat against him, he would be throwing away his life to proclaim his guilt to anyone now. It would be folly on our part to expect it. But there are other means by which this question may be settled. We do not gather figs of thorns or grapes of thistles. Consider, then, in which of these three breasts the thorns are found thickest; and, if uncertainty yet remains, to which of your cousins your uncle's death offered the greatest release."

"Have I not already asked myself these questions? Have I not repeated them over and over in my own mind till their ceaseless repetition has well-nigh maddened me? I think I know George, yet I dare not say he has a heart incapable of crime. I think I know Alfred and I think I know Leighton; but what certainty can this imaginary knowledge give me of the integrity of men who hide their best impulses under wild ways or cloud them with plausible hypocrisies? There is not an open soul among the three; and unless one of them consents to confess his crime, we can never feel sure of the two true men who are guiltless. That is, I never can. I should be haunted by doubts just as I am to-day, and to be doubt-haunted is misery, the depth of which you cannot judge unless you know my history."

"And that I cannot ask for—" I began.

"Yet why should I keep it from you? You have earned my confidence. You are, and are likely to remain, my only friend; then why should I hold back facts well known to those who come in daily contact with me? I am unfortunate in having a father who is no father to me. From earliest childhood till I left him to come to New York, I had never received from either parent a caress which was more than a formality. My father's lack of sympathy rose from the mortal disappointment he suffered when, of his two children, it was the girl and not the boy who survived the illness which prostrated both. My mother—but I will not talk of her; she has been dead a dozen years—only you will believe me when I say that all tokens of affection were lacking to my childhood and that the first word expressive of warmth and protection came to me from the cousin who met me at the train the day I entered upon my new life in my dear uncle's home. Do you wonder this unexpected tenderness blinded me a little to faults which I had no reason then to think would ever develop into anything worse?"

I rose to leave; my self-control was not strong enough for me to bear up against these repeated attacks. As I did so, I said:

"Miss Meredith, you have heard my promise. May I be prospered in my undertaking, for success in it means not only satisfaction to myself but great relief to you. Why do you tremble?"

"I fear—I dread your interference. Sometimes I wish never to know the truth. You will call me inconsistent, unreasonable. Indeed, I know I am; but what can you expect from a girl upon whom the blessing of God has never rested?"

This was a new phase in her nature, the more distressing to me, that, knowing little of women, I did not understand her. She saw the effect of her outburst, and melted immediately.

"This is a bad return for your generosity," she cried. "Ascribe it to my weakness and the dread I feel lest he—"

"The guilty man," I interposed, "is not a subject for sympathy. But he whom you love is not the guilty man," I bravely assured her. "Take my word and my hope for that. A man who could win your regard has no such black spot in his breast."

And, bowing over her hand, I escaped before she could propound any of the many questions my declared purpose was likely to call up.

BOOK II

THE MAN

CHAPTER XVII

THE MONOGRAM

I had made my promise to Miss Meredith with an apparent hopefulness which may have deceived her, but did not deceive myself. When the glow of my first enthusiasm passed, I sat down in the solitude of my own room to reconsider the events of the day, but one thing was clear to me, and that was the unpromising nature of the task I had set myself to perform. What excuse had I for the self-confidence I had shown? What means were at my command which were not also at the command of the police? She herself had asked this same question, and I had parried it. But I could not parry the demands of my own intelligence. They must be met and answered. But how? In vain I pondered ways and means; laid innumerable plans and relentlessly discarded them; projected interviews which I knew were fruitless, and worked myself through labyrinths of reasoning which ended in nothing and left me no farther advanced at the end than I was in the beginning.

Wearied at last in mind and body, I retired, and during my sleep had an inspiration upon which I proceeded to act early the next morning. Revisiting Sam Underhill's apartment, I told him my difficulty and opened up my scheme. Sam Underhill, with all his faults and numberless eccentricities, was a good fellow at bottom, and just the man to respect my confidence. He was, besides, the only person within the range of my acquaintances who could assist me in the plan I had formed; a plan which demanded the active cooperation of someone not so well known to the police as myself. Hampered as I was by my well-known connection with the Gillespie poisoning case, I could not personally make a move towards the ravelment of its mystery without subjecting myself to the curiosity of the people among whom my investigations might carry me, even if I escaped drawing upon myself the attention of the District Attorney's office and the suspicion of the men whose business I was in a measure attempting to usurp. But he was a free agent; he could come and go without arousing distrust or awakening professional jealousy. At all events he, and he alone, could put me into communication with the private detective whom I had decided to employ. As I had always been accustomed to visit Sam's rooms, my presence there at any hour of the day or night would raise no comment. I had only his laziness to fear, a laziness which with him was as marked a characteristic as it was with Alfred Gillespie, whom he so carelessly criticised.

Seated with him over an impromptu chafing-dish breakfast, I first tested his good nature by a sally or two, and finding it well up to the mark, took him, as I have already said, sufficiently into my confidence to rouse his interest; then I put the blunt question:

"Which of the three Gillespie boys do you, upon mature reflection, consider the most capable of the crime attributed to this family?"

His manner changed at once.

"Oh, come now!" he cried, "don't calculate upon putting me in that box. Like the rest of the world I prefer to await developments before committing myself on so delicate a matter. Why, Outhwaite, prejudice is as bad as the hangman! If I had settled positively in my own mind which of the three had emptied that phial of poison into the old gentleman's evening glass, I would not impart my convictions. These fellows have enough to carry without my throwing the least weight into so trembling a balance."

I girded myself for the struggle.

"Wait," said I; "have I fully made clear to you Miss Meredith's position?"

"Yes, I comprehend that well enough."

"Very well, then. Which is most important; to assist this unhappy woman to escape from her anomalous position, or to prevent prejudice from being formed in my mind, when you know how impossible it would be for me to misuse it to my advantage?"

"I am not so sure of that," he retorted. "I don't know of a fellow more likely to be carried away by his convictions than yourself. If you were not a lawyer you would be doing all sorts of quixotic things; but, being hemmed in by professional conventionalities, you show some restraint, though not enough to warrant me in trusting you with my opinion on this matter—since it is only an opinion."

Naturally, I became eager to know what lay behind this break. Opinions are not formed without some show of reason, and the lightest reason might suffice to put me on the track I sought. He saw my resolution in my face, and made an effort to resist.

"I am as sorry as you are for Miss Meredith," he drawled, helping me to fresh coffee. "If I had seen her the day she gave her testimony I might be sorrier still; but I did not have that pleasure, and so am willing to leave the matter with those whose duty it is to see that justice is meted out to the guilty."

"Do you think their efforts are likely to be successful?"

"Oh, the question will be solved some day."

"Do you think so?"

At this repetition of the phrase, which I had made forcible by my intonation, he raised his eyebrows and, emptying his cup before answering, gave me an opportunity to add:

"With nothing to go upon but an accusation which, while involving all three of Mr. Gillespie's sons, specifies none, how can any official action be taken beyond that very ordinary one of submitting the whole household to a continual surveillance? Unless fresh evidence comes in, or conscience drives the guilty to confession, weeks, months, nay, years will go by, and the hand which hesitates to move now will hesitate still; justice needing something more definite to go upon than a suspicion equally divided amongst three men."

"You are right there, but what can you do to better the situation? It appears to me that you will have to wait too."

"Which contradicts your former assertion."

"Very possibly; man is full of contradictions at so early an hour as this, and with only one cup of coffee between him and the possible nightmare of the night before."

"Drink another cup, then, while I tell you what my hopes are. Guided by impressions which more than once in my life have proved infallible, I mean to run my man down till he succumbs to the pressure I will bring upon him, and confesses. This, I believe, can be done if all my force is concentrated on one man. At all events it is the only way I see of attaining the desired end. Now, will you assist me to choose the one out of these three most open to attack?"

"I don't like it; it is against all my principles, but if you must know the exact state of my feelings on this matter, come to these rooms to-night at nine sharp and I will allow you to hear from the lips of a certain acquaintance of mine a story which may serve to give you some enlightenment. He's not a man you will want to meet, so I must ask you to content yourself with an easy chair in my den. He will be received in this room, and the door yonder can be left conveniently open. Do you object to this arrangement? It smacks of conspiracy and other things not altogether agreeable; but it's the best I can do for you at this time, and poor Yox won't care; it's your feelings I am mainly considering."

"I will be here," I doggedly replied. I was resolved to let nothing, not even my prejudices as a gentleman, interfere with the successful pursuit of this undertaking. "Will his story contain any reference to Miss Meredith?"

"Not the least in the world. Why?"

"Because I always find it difficult to sit still when I hear ladies spoken of in any way short of the deepest respect; and you say he is not a gentleman."

"He won't transgress to that degree. If he does, trust to my bringing him to order. Sorry I must place an embargo on the cigars you will find on the table. Smoking on your part would give away your presence; for the man whose story you are coming to hear is one of those fellows who smell a rat round the corner. In other words, he's a private detective with whom I was once thrown in a peculiar way. What now?"

"Perhaps he's the very fellow I want. I have use for a private detective."

"So—I—suppose."

This sentence, so long in coming, was uttered in a peculiar way, and at the moment we were rising from table. Though I said nothing, I experienced an access of courage. Unpromising as Sam's manner had been, he was really in sympathy with me, and willing to lend me a helping hand.

That day the law suffered, or, rather, I should say, such clients as were misguided enough to come to my office. The uncertain nature of the disclosure I awaited, and the doubt as to which of the three brothers it would chiefly affect, kept me restless up to the hour set apart for my return to Sam Underhill's room. Not till nine o'clock arrived and I found myself in the small apartment called his den, did I recover my poise and show anything like a steady countenance in the long mirror stretched above the mantel. This has always been a characteristic of mine. Great agitation up to the moment of action, and then an unnatural calmness. In this case it was an event I awaited; but the characteristic remained unchanged.

Sam Underhill, on the contrary, never appeared more at his ease. I could hear him singing between the whiffs of his cigar, and, as I followed the mellow strains of one of the finest tenors I have ever known, I recalled the fact that I myself had not sung a note since the experience which had made such heavy inroads into my life. Was I growing misanthropic? Sam had not been without his dark days. I remembered quite well all the talk that went about at the time of his mad passion for Dorothy Loring,— that bewitching madcap who afterwards found her match in Steve Wilson,—and I could not reconcile that disappointment with his present gaiety.

But these reflections cannot be of any interest to my readers; enough that they occupied me at the time and killed my impatience, till a sudden stoppage in the strain I objected to warned me that the expected visitor had arrived. I squared myself for the ordeal, held my breath, and prepared to listen.

The greetings were commonplace. Sam is a proud chap and does not put himself out much for anybody. To this man he scarcely showed common courtesy. Perhaps he was afraid of awakening distrust by any betrayal of interest in the coming interview; perhaps he recognised that a barely civil greeting was all the man expected or desired.

"Halloo, Yox!"

"Good evening, Mr. Underhill."

"Did I ask you to call on me to-night?"

"You certainly did, Mr. Underhill, and set the hour."

"Well, well, I suppose you are correct. Sit down. My memory is not much longer than this cigar, which you may observe is almost smoked up. Have one, Yox; you won't get a better in your shop; and now, what have you come to tell me?"

"Not much. Dennison bought seven shares last Tuesday and Little invested in as many more yesterday. Both men show confidence, and to-morrow's report will be all you can wish."

"Good! How much do I owe you? Will that do?"

I heard a rustle, then a short laugh preceding the remark, "You might halve it and still please me. Oh, I'll take it. Not too much grist comes to my mill."

Here there was a silence. Underhill was evidently lighting a fresh cigar. When they spoke again it was to drift into generalities, to which I listened with an impatience in marked contrast to the complacency of Sam, who seemed just too tired to live; that is, if I could judge from his tone and the total absence of interest he expressed in anything said either by himself or his somewhat vulgar guest. But suddenly there was a change, not in Underhill, whose voice was even more languishing than before, but in myself; for I heard Sam remark between two prolonged whiffs:

"What is that story you were trying to tell me the other night about the row in lower — Street? I thought it promised to be interesting at the time, but the other fellows were in such a hurry I couldn't stay to hear it out. Tell it again, Yox, just as you did then; perhaps it will wake me up."

The answer came more quickly than I expected.

"Oh, that? Well, I don't mind. It was a curious adventure and brought me too near the police for me to forget it in a hurry. I wish I knew who that fellow was. Did I show you the match-box I found in one of the pockets of the coat he gave me? The monogram—"

"Never mind the monogram. We'll talk about that afterwards," broke in Sam in the sleepiest tones imaginable. "I don't care so much about the man as the way he acted. This struck me as being strange for a gentleman. But begin, Yox; you relate adventures well. I have heard you talk more than once."

Yox, who was not above flattery, hemmed, hawed, and launched out in the following tale. I transcribe his words as nearly as I can remember them. At first he did not interest me much.

"You see, I had business at old Mother Merry's. Do you know the place? It's not likely, so I will describe it; you need to know something about it in order to understand my story.

"It's an old fish-market, or, rather, that was its use once; now it's a sort of lodging-house, standing half on the dock and half on piles, somewhere down near — Street. I like the place. That is, it has a mysterious air which we fellows don't object to. Seen from the docks and in daylight, it has the appearance of four squat walls without windows. But if you take the trouble to crawl around on the river side, you will find two glazed loopholes overlooking the water, one on the lower story and one under the roof. There is also, I am told, a sky-light or two up above, but I can't swear to that. By night, the one bright glimmer you see on getting near it shines through the door. This stands open in the summer, or, rather, the upper half of it does, for it is made in two parts, like the old Dutch ones you see in the pictures; but in winter time an agreeable light shines through the four small holes arranged along the top half. A calico curtain blows in and out of this door on such nights as we have been having lately; for Mother Merry likes a fire, and the little stove she sits at, netting, heats the one big room below to smotheration, and the men won't stand it. If this curtain blows high you can, if you're nervy enough, get a peep at the inside, stewing with a horrible smell of fish, and bright with kerosene lamps and the busy little stove. You won't see much furniture, for Mother Merry don't spend her money on anything she can do without; but there is a table or two and some chairs, and in one of the corners a door which sometimes stands half open, but more often is to be seen tight shut. Behind this door whatever mischief the house hides takes place. You can tell this from the old woman's eye, which is always on it; and, if you know her well, it is quite enough to watch her twitching underlip to satisfy yourself as to whether the mischief is big or little; prosperous in its character, or of a kind likely to damage her reputation and empty her well-stuffed pockets. She is no fool, this old Mother Merry; and though she has not much of what we men call nerve, and trembles like a leaf at the approach of a policeman, she has more control than you would think over the tough crowd of boatmen who knock their heads together in that little room. I have even been told that she is feared quite beyond all reason by the few stray females who find a refuge in the scanty garret rooms, which have given to this shanty the highfalutin name of lodging-house. What harm goes on under her twinkling red eye, I do not know. I have been in the place altogether three times, but have never yet found out what that door conceals. The men play at some sort of game around a large table, on which black bottles and thick glasses take up as much room as the cards; but I do not think it is gambling only which makes it next to impossible for a fellow to get in there at night. There is something else—but I won't stop over that. It is a hell of a place, as you can judge, and unless one's business led him there, scarcely a spot where a man would brag of being found.

"One night—the night I am telling you about—I got in, but got in late. There was some sort of password necessary, and I had a hard time getting hold of it, and a harder time yet making old Mother Merry hear it when I had got hold of it. Yet she isn't deaf and doesn't pretend to be. This trouble over, and the door passed, I encountered another check. A man was there; a slouchy, disreputable wretch, and it was he, instead of Mother Merry, who was watching that mysterious door, which for once stood far enough ajar for one room to share the smells, sights, and uproar of the other. I did not like this man. I did not like the way he stood, or looked, or held his tongue. There was something peculiar and unnatural in his whole manner, and I glanced at Mother Merry to see what she thought of him.

"Evidently nothing bad; for she moved about quite comfortable-like, and did not so much as look at the door I had never before seen her let out of her sight a moment.

"'Who can he be?' I naturally asked myself, a little put out by my doubts; for my business would soon take me into the inner room, and I did not like to imagine myself under his eye.

"'Drink!' I suddenly shouted, to see if I could make any impression on him.

"But I might as well have shouted at a hitching-post. Mother Merry brought me whiskey, but the man did not budge. I began to think of putting off my affair to a more convenient season, when I was taken with a sudden curiosity to see just what he was staring at.

"Approaching gently, I looked over his shoulder. A portion of the inside room was all I could see, but in that portion sat a man with a red face and a cruel jaw. It was this face which held the attention of the boatman before me; and while I was wondering what he found in it to hold him stock-still for so long, I heard a sigh escape from under the coarse jacket I dreaded touching with my own, and, much amazed at this show of feeling in a den of such boiled-down filth and wickedness, I moved back to where Mother Merry stood, and whispered in her ear:

"'Who's that man? Do you know him? Has he any business here?'

"Her gaunt shoulders lifted in a shrug—she is far from jolly, cheerful as her name is—then she drew near the man and I saw her touch him. At that, or some low words she uttered, he roused and cast a quick look about him, then he pointed towards a door on the other side of the room.

"She answered by a nod, and he moved off with a poor try at a slouchy gait. When I saw this I knew he was no sailor.

"As the door closed behind him, a sound of women screaming and scolding came from the docks, then a child's cry cut into the night, after which there was quiet in that quarter and in the house, too. For Mother Merry, with a scared look, jumped towards the room where the men were sitting, and, pushing her way in, held up her hand so as to draw all eyes.

"'The warning,' she cried. 'It's the cops! See if you can get out by the window.'

"One of the men arose and went to the window, looked out, and came crawling back, putting out a light as he did so.

"'They're on the water,' he whispered; and, whether I am a fool or not, that whisper sent the creeps up my back.

"'Both front and back?' she cried. 'That means business; you'll have to squeeze into the hole, boys.'

"Another light went out.

"Meanwhile I had crept to the door.

"''Ware there! that fellow's trying to sneak,' shouted a voice.

"I drew back. Old Merry came to my aid.

"'Don't be a fool,' she whispered. 'Stay here or they'll think you're in with them!'

"The growl of some half-dozen of them brought the warning home. I laughed and got in line with the boys, grumbling aloud as I did so:

"'Then they'll make a mistake. If you are wanted by the cops, I am, too. But how about that other fellow?' I whispered, getting close to Mother Merry in the hubbub.

"She didn't hear me; she was telling how something was to be done. Then another light went out. The place now was in nearly total darkness.

"'Hush!' came from the doorway where the curtain blew in and out.

"'Hush and quick,' came in hoarse echo from Mother Merry's quivering lips.

"Suddenly the room was empty. Of the half-dozen drunken figures I had seen moving about me the minute before, not one was in sight. I heard a creak, then a scuffle, and then a bang, and the room stood empty. Only a few bottles and a pack or two of cards were left on the dirty top of the old pine table, as proof that a tough crowd had been there raising Cain. The old woman cleared the table and shoved the lot into a cupboard; then she sat down. Never have I seen a woman so steady and at the same time so frightened.

"'There is room for one more,' she quickly said, pointing to where the men had disappeared. 'It's over the water, and the floor is full of holes, but the police haven't got on to it yet. Will you go down?'

"'I wasn't with the crowd,' I told her.

"'That won't help you. You're in the house—Ah!'

"It was almost a cry she gave; the door to the upper rooms had opened and the sailor who had struck me as such a peculiar chap stood in the room before us. 'I forgot,' she wailed out. 'What am I to do with him?'

"The sailor, who was no sailor, stared straight before him, as well he might, for he had left a lighted room and found a dark one. Yet in that stare there was a look of pain easily to be seen by the light thrown out by the red-hot stove. He didn't mind Mother Merry's cry. He had something else on his mind. He looked like a man suddenly wakened up, and I had a strange idea that his dreams, if he had had them, held him just then in a closer grip than the facts he had come among.

"'Is it so late?' he sighed; and I started, for the voice was the voice of a gentleman.

"The words, and the way he said them, seemed to bring fresh trouble to Mother Merry.

"'Oh, the ill-luck!' she wailed. 'The cops are at the door. The place has been threatened for a month, and to-night they are closing round. Will you face them, or shall I open the trap again—Oh, don't!' she groaned, as he gave a sudden reel backward; 'it makes me feel wicked. I ought to have warned you.'

"'It would have made no difference,' he said. 'I should still have gone up. Help me, if you can, and remember what you have sworn. To-morrow I will send money. O God! O God! to leave now—'

"'You cannot leave. Hark, that is the second signal! In another moment they will be here. Do you want to fall into their hands?'

"'I had rather die. Quick! Some place! Money is no object. Let that fellow I see over there help me. He looks as if he wasn't afraid of the police. Let him change togs with me.'

"'I am a private detective,' I whispered, going very close to him in the dark. 'My name is Yox, and you will find papers to support the name and business in my coat pocket. They may hold you for a day, but no longer,' and I handed over my coat.

"'I am sorry that I cannot confide my name to you with the same ease I do this coat,' he replied, as he threw me the garment which had so disfigured him. 'But my name is the secret I would defend with my life. Say that you are Benjamin Jones.'

"'First fork over the cash which you say is no object to you!' I cried.

"'You must trust me for that,' he answered. 'If I get off without discovery you will receive a hundred dollars at your address within the week. I have left all I had above.'

"'Chaff!' I muttered.

"'He will pay,' Mother Merry assured me.

"'Then here's my cap,' I grumbled, not any too well pleased.

"He took it, and though it was a common one enough, he looked like another man in it.

"'Support me in my character!' he ordered, just as that blowing curtain was caught and held back by a hand from without and the face of a policeman looked in.

"'Hey, there! lamps up!' was the order. We got a light flashed over us from the doorway.

"The man at my side advanced to meet it, and I saw him talking with the officer who had pushed his head through the upper half of the door. Then everything about and before me became mixed in the rush the police made from every side, and I failed to see anything again for some minutes. When a minute's quiet came about again, and I had the chance to use my eyes, I did not find the man to whom I had lent my coat and my name. He had been allowed to slip away.

"But I had no such luck. The place being turned over, and only a few women found, they turned on me. But I was game, and was soon able to show them I was one of their own sort. At which there naturally came the question as to who the other fellow was. But I did not help them out on this, and it ended in my being taken to Jefferson Market with the rest.

"We all got off next day and without much trouble. I have always thought that fellow paid the fines; at all events, one week from that day I found an envelope addressed to me, lying on my desk at the office. It contained bills to the amount agreed upon.

"Now, Mr. Underhill, who was this man? I have been asking myself that question ever since I pocketed his money. The fellow who can pay out hundreds like that is a man to know."

I waited for the answer, which was slow in coming. But then Underhill was always slow. When he did speak it was lazily enough.

"Didn't you say you had some clue to his identity; a match-box or something of that kind, which you found in one of the pockets of the coat he gave you?"

"Yes, I have that."

"And that there were initials on it which you had not been able to decipher?"

"Oh, yes, initials; but what can a fellow make out of initials?"

"Not much, of course. Have you that match-box with you?"

"I just have. I sport it everywhere. I think so much of it I have even talked of having my name changed to fit the letters of this monogram."

"Let me see it, will you?"

The fellow drew it out.

A minute passed, then Underhill drawled out:

"It's not as easy to make out as I expected. Will you let me compare it with a collection I have in a book here? I may have its mate."

"Sure, sir."

Underhill came my way. The sudden heat into which I was thrown by this unexpected move acted as a double warning. I must beware of self-betrayal, and I must take care not to give away my presence to the sharp-eyed, sharp-eared man whose perspicacity I had reason to dread. I therefore rose as quietly as possible and met Underhill's entering figure with a silent inquiry, nicely adjusted to the interest I was supposed to feel in the matter. He was no less careful, but there was a sparkle in his eye as he handed over to my inspection the match-box he had just taken from Yox, which contradicted his air of unconsciousness, and led me to inspect with great interest the monogram he displayed to my notice. It was by no means a simple one, as you will see by the sub-joined copy.

As I studied it, Underhill wrote on a sheet of paper lying open on the table:

"I have seen that match-box a dozen times." Then, separating the letters of the monogram, he wrote them out in a string, thus:

L L D G

"Leighton Gillespie?" I inquired in a kind of soundless whisper.

"Leighton Le Droit Gillespie," he wrote.

It was the name with which my own mind was full; the name with which it had been full ever since the inquest.

THE PHIAL

The moment was not propitious for a fuller understanding between us. Sam lowered the light and sauntered back into the outer room, remarking lazily to Yox:

"If I were you I wouldn't sport this thing around too openly. If judiciously kept out of sight it may bring you in another hundred some day."

"How's that? You know those initials?"

"Know Louis Le Duc Gracieux? Well, rather. But as long as you have not the honour, keep quiet, lie low, and await events. That is, if you care about the money. What have you done with the blouse?"

"Put it away in cotton."

"Oh, I see. Well, put the match-box with it."

"I will."

"Have another cigar?"

"Thank you. I don't often have such a snap. Well, what is it, sir?"

"Oh, nothing."

"I thought you looked as if you wanted something from me."

"I? Not the least in the world."

Silence, then a lazy movement on the part of Sam which disturbed something on the table at which they were sitting. The small noise had the effect of eliciting another word from Sam.

"I thought your story had more to it when I heard it last. Didn't you say something about a small parcel which this mysterious man took out of his pocket before handing over his blouse?"

"Perhaps; but that wasn't anything. I wonder you remember it."

Long silence on the part of Sam.

"I never forget anything," he observed at last. "Was it a big parcel or a little?"

"It was a small one."

"How small?"

"Oh, a thing a man could hold in his fist. Why do you ask about it?"

"Whim. I am trying to wake myself up. What was the shape of this parcel?"

"Bless me if I've given two thoughts to it."

"You'll get that blessing, Yox; for you've given more than two thoughts to it."

"I?"

"Yes, or why should you have described it as minutely as you did the other night?"

"Did I?"

"Undoubtedly; I can even recall your words. You said the fellow was pretty well shaken up for a man of his size and appearance, and after handing you the blouse he caught it back and took something out of one of the pockets. It looked like one of those phials the homoeopaths use. You see, you were inclined to be more dramatic on that occasion than on this. Indeed, I have been a little disappointed in you to-night."

"Oh, well! a fellow cannot always cut a figure. I'll try to remember the bottle next time I tell the story."

Sam did not answer; I heard him yawn instead. But I did not yawn; that word "phial," had effectually roused me.

"As you say, it is a small matter," Underhill finally drawled. "So is the straw that turns the current. He was a philosopher who said, 'The little rift within the lute,' etc., etc." Then suddenly, and with a wide-awake air which evidently startled his companion: "Do you suppose, Yox, that Mother Merry runs an opium-joint in those upper rooms?"

The answer he received evidently startled him.

"She may. I hadn't thought of it before, but I remember, now, that when those women were brought down there was amongst them one who certainly was under the influence of something worse than liquor. Faugh! I see her yet. But it wasn't opium he had in that bottle; that is, not the opium which is used for smoking. The firelight shone full upon it as he passed it from one pocket to another, and I saw distinctly the sparkle of some dark liquid."

Sam Underhill, who seemed to have fallen back into his old condition of sleepy interest, mumbled something about his having been able to see a good deal, considering the darkness of the place. To which his now possibly suspicious visitor replied:

"I would have seen more if I had known so much was to be got out of it. Can you give me a point or two as to how I'm to get that extra hundred?"

Whereupon Sam retorted, "Not to-night," in a way to close the conversation.

As soon as the man had left I rushed in upon Sam without ceremony. He was still sitting at the table smoking, and received me with a look of mingled amusement and anxiety.

"How did the comedy strike you?" he asked.

I attempted a shrug which failed before his imperturbable nonchalance.

"How did it strike you?" he persisted.

"As cleverly carried out, but not so cleverly that the fellow will not suspect it to be a comedy."

"Oh, well! So long as he does not associate the right name with those four initials we are safe. And he won't; I know Yox well enough for that."

"Then you know him for a fool. Louis Gracieux! Who is Louis Gracieux? Besides, the phial—why, the whole town is talking about a phial—"

"I know, but not about a match-box that is worth another hundred dollars to the man holding it. Yox isn't a member of the regular police; he's in business for himself, which means he's in it for what he can make. Now, he knows—or, rather, I flatter myself that I have made him see—that there is more to be got out of this matter by circumspection and a close tongue than by bragging of his good luck and giving every ass about him a chance to chew upon those letters. Oh, he'll keep quiet now, for a week or two at least. After that I cannot promise."

"Do you think his version of this affair reliable?"

"Absolutely. He would have exaggerated more if he had been forcing an invention upon us."

I sat down and, regarding Underhill across the table, remarked somewhat pointedly:

"Now that the name has been mentioned between us, we can talk more openly. What date have you been able to give to Yox's adventure? You surely have not failed to get from him the day he went down to Mother Merry's?"

Sam rose—he who detested rising—and, going to a little side table where a pile of newspapers lay, he pulled off the top one and laid it open before me, taking care, however, to stretch his arm across the upper margin in a way to cover up effectually the date.

"Read," said he, pointing to a paragraph.

I followed his finger and read out a brief account of the descent which had been made on Mother Merry's, and a description of the proceedings which had ended in the release of the women involved.

"Now take a look at the date," he went on, lifting his arm.

I did so; it was a memorable one,—the evening of Mr. Gillespie's death.

"The affair at Mother Merry's took place on the preceding night," commented Sam. There was no languishing note in his voice now.

I sat silent; when I did speak it was plainly and decidedly.

"I see what you mean. You think he went to that place to get the acid."

Sam puffed away at his cigar.

"It has been a mystery to everyone where that acid came from," I continued; "a mystery which has evidently baffled the police. If a druggist in the whole range of this great city had lately sold a phial of this poison to anyone answering the description given of these brothers, we would have heard from him before now. Equally so if a doctor had prescribed it."

"A second Daniel come to judgment," quoth Sam, sententiously.

"And now we, through chance or special providence, perhaps, have stumbled upon a clue as to how this deadly drug may have entered the Gillespie family."

"I regret to agree with you, but that is the way it looks. But, Outhwaite, you must remember—and as a lawyer you will—that a long and tangled road lies between mere supposition and the establishment of a fact like this. This phial, so carefully transferred from a pocket where a seemingly more valuable article lay hid, has not been identified as holding poison, only as holding a liquid. Much less has it been proven to be the bottle found under the clock in the Gillespie dining-room."

"All very true."

"Yet this fellow's story of—well, let us say, Louis Gracieux' appearance and conduct in this more than doubtful place, warrants us in thinking the worst of his errand."

I felt the force of this suggestion.

"Quite true." I assented. Then, in some agitation, for my thoughts were divided between the relief which a knowledge of this night's occurrences might bring to Hope and the terrible results to the man himself, I went on to say:

"His little girl—you never saw his little girl, Sam. Well, she's a fairy-like creature, and the last time I saw her she had her arms about his neck."

"Don't talk about children," he hastily objected. "You'll make a muff of me," and then I remembered he had a great weakness for children. "I had rather you'd talk about Miss Meredith. Nothing but the interest I take in the peculiar position held by this young lady gives me the requisite courage to stir in this matter. I have known those boys too long and too well; that is, I have drunk too many bottles with George and sat out too many nights in full view of Alfred's handsome figure, stretched out in the mysterious apathy I have alluded to. With Leighton I have fewer associations; but I have seen enough of him to know perfectly well the match-box which Yox handed out."

"Do you suppose there was anything in those pockets besides the match-box; anything, I mean, calculated to give away the wearer of that foul blouse?"

"No. If there had been; if, in other words, he had found anything there which suggested a member of the Gillespie family, he would never have aired the matter in the presence of their friends. He would have gone at once to the police, or endeavoured to make such capital out of it as such a find would suggest."

"Then you really think he does not know that the tools he is playing with have mighty sharp edges?"

"I am confident he does not."

"That is a relief; yet he cannot remain in such ignorance long if I call him to my assistance."

"That depends."

"How, depends?"

"Upon what you want him to do."

For this I had no answer. My plans were as vague as the wandering smoke-wreaths curling upward at that instant from my neglected cigar.

"You have never liked Leighton," I remarked, in the hope of adjusting my thoughts before entering upon the more serious portion of this conversation. "Neither have I, since surprising a very strange expression on his face the night of his father's death."

"Yet three-quarters of the people who knew him would tell you that he is a good man, a very good man, the best of the three, by far."

"Notwithstanding his low associates?" I ventured.

"Notwithstanding everything. People are so deceived by a few words uttered in prayer-meeting, that their judgment is apt to be blunted to the real character of a man like Leighton Gillespie."

"He must be an odd one," I observed. "The lights and shades of such a nature are past finding out. In appearance and manner he is a gentleman, yet if Yox's story is true he finds no difficulty in visiting the worst of places under circumstances and in a garb which bespeaks a personal interest in them. The nature of that interest we have dared to infer from the part played in his visit by the mysterious phial. But how account for such instincts, such murderous impulses in a man brought up as he has been? The motive must have been a serious one to drive a man of his connections into crime. Can you name it? Was it the need of money, a craving for perfect liberty to pursue his own strange courses unchecked, or just the malice of a revengeful spirit cherishing some rankling grudge, which only the death of its object could satisfy?"

"Do not ask me. I'm not going to supply facts and reasons, too, in this matter. What! going?"

"Yes, I never don my thinking-cap to any purpose save in privacy and under the influences emanating from my own room and its familiar surroundings."

"Very good—you shall seek such inspiration as is to be found there in just another moment. But first let me give you a little further insight into the character of the man we are discussing. This is something I saw myself: One day last fall I was going down West Broadway when I came upon Leighton Gillespie standing near an elegant turnout, talking with an ill-shod and bedraggled woman. As philanthropy is his fad and occurrences of this kind a common affair with him, I was passing by with no further display of interest than an inward sneer, when I noted his expression and stopped short, if not from sympathy, at least in some curiosity as to the woman who could draw it forth. Outhwaite, she was a wild-eyed, panting creature, with chestnut-coloured hair and nervously working lips; not beautiful, not even interesting—to me. But he—well! I have seen few faces look as his did then, and when she started to run—as she presently did, he caught at the muddy shawl she wore and pulled her back as if his very life depended upon restraining her at his side.

"I even saw him take that shawl in his hand—such a shawl! I would not have touched it for a champagne supper, and there have been times when he has shown himself more squeamish on some subjects than I. But he was not squeamish now—far from it, for he not only held that shawl, but fumbled with it, almost clung to it, talking all the while with voluble persistency. At last he asked her some questions which brought out a passionate refusal. But if discouraged, he did not show it; on the contrary, he continued his plea with increasing earnestness, and finally pointed to his carriage. She gave it one look and shrank back with a gesture of fear; then she grew steadier and her head fell forward on her breast. He went on pleading with her; and then I saw a strange sight. With an air such as only a swell like himself is capable of assuming, he signalled to his driver to draw up at the curbstone before him. Then, as he might hand in one of the four hundred, he handed her in and took his seat beside her. Not a look to the right nor left,—he was simply the perfect gentleman; and, obnoxious as he had always been to me up to that hour, I could not but respect his manner if not himself. It was admirable, and so was that of the man who sat upon the box. Though the latter must have cringed when that disreputable foot struck the step and what might be called a bundle of rags entered among his pearl satin cushions, he did not turn a hair or lose a jot of that serene absorption in his own affairs which characterises all the Gillespie coachmen. I watched him expressly to see. A valuable fellow that, for a master of the eccentric tastes of Leighton Gillespie!"

"You interest me," said I. "Did you watch them drive off?"

"Yes, and stood there staring till they were half down the block, for she had not accepted the situation with the same ease as himself, and I felt that something would happen. And there did. Before the polished panels were lost to my sight, the door burst open and I saw her wild figure jump out and plunge away in the direction of the river. This time he made no attempt to follow her; the carriage rolled on and he with it. Nor did he do what I would have done,—let the door stand open till the air of that carriage had been purged of its late unwholesome occupant. Altogether, it was an odd experience. What do you make out of it, Outhwaite?"

"He's a fellow who will bear studying. Is he always so respectful to the paupers he befriends?"

Sam shrugged his shoulders.

"I have related my sole experience with Leighton Gillespie in his rôle of philanthropist. My other memories of him suggest simply the millionaire's son."

CHAPTER XIX

I MAKE MY FIRST MOVE

To attempt to fathom such a nature as this leads to little but mental confusion. Before I had spent a half-hour in trying to untangle the knotty problem offered by Leighton Gillespie's opposing characteristics, I decided to follow the example of my friend Underhill, and keep to facts.

These in themselves were startling enough to occupy my mind and convince me absolutely of Leighton's guilt. But this was not convincing Miss Meredith. Probabilities, possibilities even, which might satisfy me, would count for but little with her. With her nice sense of justice, she would demand a positive and unbroken chain of evidence before she would allow herself to acknowledge the guilt of the man whose innocence I presumed to challenge, and this clear and unbroken chain I did not have. How, then, could I strengthen the evidence just obtained? Not by showing motive. There seemed to be no motive. To be sure, Leighton was in debt,—so were they all,—and he was known to have quarrelled bitterly with his father more than once. But these were not new facts, nor were they sufficiently condemnatory to settle, even in her mind, the torturing question embodied in that one word already alluded to: which?

Something of an absolutely criminating character must be found against this man; some proof so direct and unanswerable that even her scrupulous conscience would be satisfied; something like positive evidence, say, that he had visited Mother Merry for the purpose of obtaining in secret the poison he dared not buy openly, or that the glass of sherry he poured out for his father had held poison as well as wine.

As all attempts to establish this latter fact had proved abortive; as the police had not only failed to prove that such a mixture had been made, but to settle the exact medium by means of which Mr. Gillespie received the poison, I turned my attention to the easier task and decided to concentrate my energies upon establishing the fact that the bottle carried from Mother Merry's by the would-be sailor contained prussic acid, and that this would-be sailor was positively the man we supposed him to be,—Leighton Gillespie.

With these facts indubitably established, even Miss Meredith must feel that the man who could be guilty of obtaining a deadly drug through such under-handed agency, and at such a risk to his reputation, must have had a purpose in so doing which could only be explained by the tragedy which took place in his home so soon afterwards.

This point reached in my meditations, I next asked myself how the necessary inquiries could be started without risk to their success. I could not go openly to Mother Merry, or, rather, it would be undesirable for me to do so. If, as I sometimes suspected, I was myself under surveillance, I could make no such move without attracting the attention of the detectives to a matter which I hoped to keep a sacred secret between Hope and myself. Remember that I was not working to bring the guilty to justice, but to free a pure heart from a soul-torturing doubt.

But if I could not go there myself, whom was I to send? What man of my acquaintance was judicious enough to be entrusted with such a message? Yox? I did not like the man. I looked upon him as a very shady individual and shrank with strong distaste from further contact with him. Underhill? I laughed at the suggestion. Who, then? Not a single name rose in my mind till, by an association of ideas not entirely illogical, I remembered the habits of certain members of the Salvation Army, and how easy it would be for one of them to enter such a vile haunt as Mother Merry's and interview the depraved beings to be found there without attracting the notice of the police or rousing the least suspicion as to their intentions. But could I reach such a man, and, if I could, would I find him willing to undertake such an errand without understanding its full purport and just what use was to be made of the knowledge thus obtained? This seemed very doubtful, and I was seriously deliberating over my next move, when my mind flew straight from the topic engaging it to that memorable moment in my experience when, amid the alarm and hurry following the suspicions expressed by the physician called in at Mr. Gillespie's death, the glass fell from Hewson's hand and broke into a hundred pieces on the dining-room hearth. The tinkle made by the shattered glass, the gasp which escaped the old man's lips, all came back to me, and with it the startling conviction—strange that it had not struck me before!—that this old and tried servant of a disrupted household knew who had tampered with that glass, and by this sudden breaking of the same had sought to shield him. Now, if I should find out that this man regarded Leighton with an especial fondness—But such thoughts were for further contemplation. With a resolution born, perhaps, of the lateness of the hour, I forced my mind back into its former channel and resolutely asked myself how a connection was to be established between Mother Merry and myself. The small confidence I have always had in third parties, especially when a matter of delicate inquiry was to be pushed, made it imperative for me to see her myself. Yet how—Ah! an idea. What if I took the bull by the horns and openly requested the assistance of the police in my adventure? That would disarm suspicion and render me independent of special surveillance.

The idea was a happy one, and, relieved by the prospect it offered, I resigned myself to sleep.

Next day I went boldly to police headquarters and asked for assistance in making some inquiries in a dangerous quarter of the town. I said that the case then before me necessitated some evidence which could only be gathered from a certain old woman whose name and place of living I had yet to learn by judicious questioning in that quarter of the city where she had been last seen. Would they give me a man to make my projected tour safe? They would. Could I have him now? I could.

Satisfied with the result of my first move, and more than satisfied with the unintelligent appearance of the man they picked out to escort me, I made for Mother Merry's, but not in a direct course or with any appearance of knowing where I was going. I tried several lodging-houses and chatted across several bars, and, noting the indifference with which my thick-headed companion followed me, I really began to cherish hopes of coming through my task without any unpleasant consequences to myself. Sometimes he tried to help me; but as I had given no names and confined myself to a somewhat vague description of the person I wanted, this help was naturally futile, and I found myself approaching my goal without any seeming advance having been made. Should I proceed at once to the docks or should I play the fox's game a little longer? As I weighed these alternatives my eyes fell on a Salvation Army sign, and the idea I had scouted the day before returned to me with renewed force.

Pointing to the windows across which it was displayed, I said that here were people who might possibly tell me where to find the woman I sought, and, leaving the officer outside,—he seemed quite content to stay in the fresh air,—I went in and respectfully approached the sweet-faced woman I saw before me.

"I am come for assistance," I began. "I am in search of a woman—" Here the words died in my throat. Opposite me and quite near enough for me to catch what they were saying, I saw two men. One was a Salvation Army Captain and the other was Leighton Gillespie.

CHAPTER XX

THE LITTLE HOUSE IN NEW JERSEY

The surprise was great, but I doubt if I betrayed the fact to the unsuspicious eye of the patient lass who attended me.

"I wish to see one of your captains," I explained. "I will gladly await his convenience."

"Captain Smith will be at liberty soon," she answered, going back to her work.

I was thus left to study the face of the man whom at that very moment I was bent upon connecting with a great crime.

I had not seen him since that touching scene at the inquest; and I found him looking both older and sadder. Perhaps his health was broken; perhaps there were other and deeper reasons for the great change I saw in him.

I had instinctively withdrawn a few steps when the lass left me and stood in as inconspicuous a position as possible, with my face turned from the light. But I had not retreated far enough to lose a word of the conversation going on so near me.

They were discussing an approaching meeting; Leighton with deep interest, the Captain with an embarrassment not often seen in one of his calling. Listening, I heard these words.

"It will be a full one, won't it?"

This from Leighton.

"It usually is on a day like this," was the hesitating reply.

"Do women come?"

"More women than men."

"I should like to speak at the meeting."

The Captain, with an uncomfortable flush, fumbled with the ribbon on his cap, and said nothing. Leighton repeated his request.

The Captain summoned up courage.

"I am sorry, sir," he remarked, in an apologetic tone. "You have given the Army much help, and we have listened to many good words from you, but I have received orders not to let you speak again; that is, from the platform."

A painful silence ensued. Then Leighton remarked, with a forced composure and something more than his usual melancholy:

"Because of the unhappy prominence given me by the circumstances attending my father's death?"

"That, and something else. I may as well be frank, sir. We have heard of the little house, leased under your name, in New Jersey."

"Ah!"

A chord had been touched which vibrated keenly in this mysterious breast. I saw his hand go to his throat and fall again quickly. Meantime the Captain went on:

"We are not frightened by sin and we hold out our hands to sinners; but we have no use for a man who prays in New York and has his pleasure on the other side of the North River. It shows hypocrisy, sir, and hypocrisy is the enemy of religion."

A smile, whose dark depths betrayed anything but hypocrisy at that moment, crossed Leighton's pale lips as he remarked without anger (which I could not but consider strange in a man so openly attacked):

"That little house is empty now. Has the thought struck you that my heart might be so too?"

The Captain, who evidently did not like his task, seemed to experience some difficulty in answering; but when he had settled upon his reply, spoke both clearly and with resolution:

"The house of which you speak may lack its occupant just now, but everything goes to show she is always expected. Or why are the lamps invariably lighted there at nightfall, the rooms kept warm, and the larder replenished? Some birds in flitting come round again to their forsaken nest. Your bird may; meanwhile the nest remains ready."

"Enough!" The tone was sharp now, the words cutting. "You do not understand me nor my interest in the poor and forsaken. As for my place among you, let it be filled by whom you will. I have my own griefs, and they are not light, and I have anxieties such as visit few men. A ban is upon me and upon all who bear the name of Gillespie. This is known to you and possibly to every man and woman soon to assemble here. Perhaps you do well not to submit me to their curiosity. But there is something you can do for me—something which you will do for me, I am sure; something which would place me under lasting obligation to you without doing you or anyone else the least harm in the world. A woman may come in here; a woman, wild-eyed, unkempt, but with a look—I am sure you will know her. There is an unearthly loveliness in her wan features. She has—But what use is there in my attempting to describe her? If she answers to the name of Mille-fleurs—some persons call her Millie—she is the woman I seek. Will you give her this?" (He had torn the edge off a newspaper lying near and was rapidly writing on it a few words.) "It will do no harm to the cause for which you are working, and it may save a most unhappy woman. Of myself I make no count, yet it might save me, too."

He handed over to the Captain the slip carelessly folded. It was received with reluctance. Mr. Gillespie, noting this, observed with some agitation:

"You are here to do God's work. Sometimes you are called upon to do it blindly and without full enlightenment." And having emphasised this with a bow of remarkable dignity he went out, little realising that the possible clue to his own future fate lay in the hands of one he at that moment passed without a look.

"These are the crosses we are called upon to bear," spoke up the Salvation Army Captain as the door closed upon the man they had once held in deepest reverence. "Now, what am I to do with this?" he added, turning over in his hands the half-rolled-up slip which had just been given into his charge.

Involuntarily my hand went out to it. It was a perfectly unconscious action on my part, and I blushed vividly when I realised what I had done. I had no authority here. I was not even known to the good man and woman before me.

The Captain, who may or may not have noted my anxiety, paid no heed either to my unfortunate self-committal or to the apologetic question with which I endeavoured to retrieve myself.

Turning to the lass beside him, he handed her the slip, with the look which a man gives to a woman on whose good sense and judgment he has come to rely.

"Take it, Sally," he said. "You will know the girl if she comes in, and, what's more, you'll know how to manage the matter so as to give satisfaction to all the parties concerned. And now, sir?—" he inquired, turning towards me.

But at this instant a diversion was created by the arrival of Detective Sweetwater, a man for whose presence I was certainly little prepared.

"The gentleman who has just gone out passed you something," he cried, approaching the lass without ceremony, though not without respect. Me he did not appear to see.

"The gentleman left a note with us for one of the poor women who sometimes straggle in here," was her quiet response. "He is interested in poor girls; tries to reclaim them."

"I am sorry," protested the detective "but I must have a glance at what he wrote. It may be of immediate importance to the police. Here is my authority," he added in lower tones, opening his coat for a moment. "You know under what suspicion the Gillespie family lies. He is a Gillespie; let me see those lines—or, stay, read them out yourself—that may be better."

The young woman hesitated, consulted the Captain with a look, then glanced down at the slip trembling in her hand. It was half unrolled, and some of its words must have met her eye.

"Why do you think this has anything to do with the serious matter you mention?" she ventured to ask.

The detective approached his mouth to her ear, but my hearing did not fail me even under these unfavourable circumstances.

"Everything has connection with it," I heard him say. "Everything they do and think. I wouldn't trust one of them round the corner. I should make the greatest mistake of my life if I allowed any secret communication written by a Gillespie to pass under my nose without an attempt to see what it was. This one may be of an innocent nature; probably is. The gentleman who left it with you passes for a philanthropist, and as such might very readily hold communication with the worst characters in town without any other motive than the one you yourselves can best appreciate. But I must be sure of this. I have been detailed to watch his movements, and his movements have brought him here. You will therefore oblige me, Miss, if you can make it clear that the cause of justice—by which I mean the cause which I here personally represent—will not suffer injury by the free transmission of this slip to the person for whom it is meant."

"I will read you what he has written here," replied the girl. "He left it open or almost open to anyone's perusal." And I heard her read out, in low but penetrating tones, the following words:

When I last saw you, you were suffering. This is an unbearable thought to me, yet I cannot go to you for reasons which you can readily appreciate. Come to me, then. The house is always open and the servants have received orders to admit anyone who asks for me.

This was certainly warm language from a mere philanthropist to a city waif whose misery had attracted his notice. But no remarks passed, and Sweetwater did not seek to hinder even by a look the careful refolding of the slip and the putting of it away in the young lass's desk. Indeed, he seemed to approve of this, for the next moment I heard him say:

"That's right; take good care of the slip. If the young woman comes in, give it to her. I suppose you know her?"

"Not at all; he simply described her to us; or attempted to. She may not come in at all."

"Then keep a grip on those lines. What kind of a person did he say she was?"

"Oh, I don't know. He said she was wild-looking, but beautiful, and that she answered to some such name as Millie."

"It's likely to be a fake, the whole mess. Good-day, Captain; good-day, Miss." And Detective Sweetwater stepped away.

I had thought him keen, yet he had paid no more attention to me than if I had been a stick. Was the corner in which I sat darker than I thought, or had he been so full of his own affairs that he failed to recognise me? I had kept my face turned away, but he assuredly must have known my figure.

When he was gone the two laid their heads together for a moment, then began to bustle towards me. In the meantime I had planned a coup d'etat. I had considered if, by a little acting on my part, I could put them in the wrong, I might succeed in getting from them some positive facts to work upon. Accordingly, I was in a state of suppressed feeling when the Captain found himself face to face with me.

"I heard you," said I, flinging down the book I had taken up. "I have ears like a hare and I couldn't help it. I know Mr. Gillespie, and it made my blood boil to hear him addressed with suspicion. How anyone who has ever heard him speak to the poor and unfortunate could associate him with the atrocious death of his father, I cannot imagine. So good to poor girls! So bountiful in his charities! I thought you were Christians here."

The Captain may have been a Christian, but he was also a man, and, being a man, looked nettled.

"It was a mistake for us to discuss Army affairs within reach of two such sharp ears," said he. "Mr. Gillespie has done some good work, and far be it from me to add myself to those who have associated his name with the crime which has just made the family notorious. I simply fail to stand by him because he uses us as a cloak for his personal indulgences. He is infatuated with a woman whom he has never presumed to present to his family. This won't do for us. The other matter belongs to the police."

I allowed myself to cool down a trifle.

"I beg your pardon; you know your own business, of course. But it's a little hard for me to believe that such a refined man as Mr. Gillespie could find any other than a charitable interest in any woman likely to come straying in here. Did you ever see his home, his child, his friends?"

The Captain shrugged his shoulders and curtly replied:

"I can imagine." Then in a tone calculated to end the interview so far as this topic was concerned: "We count nothing as strange in this place, sir. We come too near the unregenerate heart. Human nature's the same, sir, in rich and in poor. And now, sir, your business? It's most time for our noon meeting, so I must ask you to be concise."

I had almost forgotten I had any business there, but I pulled myself up under his eye and told him I was on the search for a woman, too.

"But she's an old one," I made haste to assure him; "a lodging-house keeper who is in the possession of evidence of great importance to a client of mine. Her name, as told me, is Mother Merry; do you know any such person?"

He did not, but informed me that there were several queer old places down by the wharves where I might hear of her. This was enough. I had now an excuse for penetrating the district towards which I had been pointing from the first.

Thanking him, and asking his pardon for my few brusque words, I went out, and, giving my policeman a wink, turned in the direction of the river.

CHAPTER XXI

MILLE-FLEURS

The complications which had surrounded Leighton Gillespie were, through his own imprudence, in the way of being cleared up, though hardly to his advantage. This was not all. Either from indifference or ignorance—I hardly thought it was indifference—he had not only called attention to his own secret passion, but laid such a trap for the object of it that she could hardly fail to fall ultimately into the hands of the police.

Under these circumstances was it my duty to proceed with the task I had imposed upon myself? Was my help needed when Mr. Gryce's right-hand man was at work? It would not seem so. But—as I was happy enough to remember before my hesitation resolved itself into action—the one clue connecting him to this murder was to be found in my hands, not theirs. I alone knew where to look for the woman who had procured him the phial of poison. This in itself created an obligation I dared not slight. I must continue my quest, if I desired to fulfil my promise to Hope Meredith.

The day was Friday and the fish-stalls were doing a lively business. By the time I had threaded my way through innumerable sheds, I had got enough of this commodity into my nostrils to satisfy my appetite for a week. I was glad when I stepped out upon the wharf.

"Is it along there you want to go?" asked the officer under whose protection I moved.

I looked, and saw fluttering before me the calico curtain which had blown in and out of Yox's story.

"Yes, if it's where an old woman named Merry is to be found."

"I'll ask."

He approached a brother officer whose presence I had not noticed, spoke to him, and came back.

"That's the place," said he. "Do you want me to go in with you?"

"Not if it's safe."

"Oh, it's safe enough at this hour. You haven't any too much cash on you, I judge? Besides, I'll hang about the door, and if you don't come out in ten minutes I'll just inquire the reason why. You see, the place's on our books and we don't want to keep too open an eye on it."

I was glad to be allowed to go in alone. I had not dared to hope for this and felt correspondingly relieved.

An unexpectedly quiet interior met my eye. The bare walls, the busy stove, the woman whose gaunt frame and lowering eye I had heard described by Yox, were before me, but nothing of a sinister, or even suspicious, appearance. I had surprised Mother Merry's quarters at a happy hour; that is, happy for her and possibly so for me.

But perhaps I convey a wrong impression in speaking of the walls as bare. They were not so; for, stretched from side to side of the steam-reeking, stifling room, were lines on which coarse garments were hanging up to dry; and on the wall directly before me I saw a pair of rough seaman's breeches, pinned up in a ghostly and grotesque fashion over the little stove which even on this mild afternoon was doing its best to keep out undesirable visitors.

The old woman, who was bending over a table on which a few broken victuals lay, was, without doubt, Mother Merry herself; and, recognizing her as such, I assumed the half-audacious, half-deprecatory manner I thought best calculated to impress her. With a broad smile, I thrust my hand into my pocket. Then as I perceived her hard eye melt and the coarse lines about her mouth twist into something which was as near encouragement as one could expect from a being always on her guard against strangers, I whispered with a careful look about me:

"Anyone here? My errand won't stand peering eyes or listening ears."

She gave me a penetrating glance.

"What do you want?" she grumbled.

I took out a dollar and laid it on the table. Her hand was over it in an instant.

"A morsel of drug," I whispered. "Three drops of something that'll do up a man in five minutes. The man is myself," I added, as her eye darkened.

She continued to regard me intently for a minute; then cast a quick glance down at the hand which covered the coin.

"Sorry," she muttered, with a reluctant lift of that member; "but I'm not in the way of getting any such stuff. Who sent you to me?"

I hesitated, then made my great venture.

"The man you helped out of here the night the police came down on you. He had better luck than I. You didn't refuse it to him."

"You lie!" she cried.

Startled by these uncompromising words, I fell back. Had I made a great mistake?

"He never got any such stuff from me," she went on shrilly. "That wasn't what he came for, or else he made more of a fool of me than I knew."

"What did he come for?"

Her look of inquiry turned into one of suspicion.

"Did you come here to ask that? If so, you'd better go. I'm not one of the blabbing sort."

I drew out another dollar.

"Perhaps he got it upstairs," I insinuated.

"Oh!" she cried, spreading out her long fingers so as to cover both pieces. "That may be; those girls have strange ways with them."

"May I have a peep at them? May I have a peep at her?"

The emphasis I placed on the last word called out from Mother Merry a long stare, which I bore as best I could.

"She hasn't a drop left of what you were talking about," said Mother Merry at last. "If she gave it to him it's all gone."

"Perhaps she can get more where she got that," I made bold to suggest.

The old hag gave a grunt and looked gloatingly at the coins sparkling between her bony fingers.

"How many of these have you saved up?" she asked.

"Ten."

"And with ten dollars in your pocket you come here for poison?"

Her amazement was quite real. Ten dollars in my pocket and wanting poison! It took her some minutes to grasp the fact; then she said:

"And how many of these are for me?"

"Five."

She pawed at the coins till they were well under her palm.

"I'll call her down; will that do?"

"Yes."

"She may not be just right."

"No matter."

"She may be all right herself and not think you so."

"I'll risk that, too."

"Then stand near the stove so she won't see you when she first comes in. She wouldn't stay a minute if she did."

Obeying the old hag, I watched her sidle to the door already familiar to me in Yox's narrative; the door upstairs, I mean. As she disappeared behind it I glanced at the table near which she had been standing. The two silver dollars were gone.

"I'll never see them again," was my inward decision.

And I never did.

The presence of the wet clothing hanging so near me was anything but agreeable. Moving around to the other side of the stove, I at least avoided some of the fumes which in that stifling atmosphere were almost insufferable; but I was more exposed to view, something which the old woman noticed when she reëntered.

"You have moved," she suspiciously snarled. "Come back and let the clothes hide you. Perhaps I can make the girl sing if she don't see you. She seems to be in one of her queer moods. Would you like to hear her sing?"

As the old woman evidently expected an enthusiastic assent I gave it with as much force as I could muster up on such short notice.

"Hush! she is coming. You mustn't mind her laugh."

It was well she gave me this warning, for the sudden wild shout of hilarious mirth which I now heard from the region of the staircase was so startling, that without these words of caution I might have betrayed myself. As it was, I kept my post in silence, watching for the girl who I had every reason to believe had given the bottle of prussic acid to Leighton Gillespie. Would she prove to be the wild, unkempt woman whose beautiful look he had endeavoured to describe to the Salvation Army Captain? I hoped not; why, I hardly knew.

Suddenly there broke upon my eyes a sight I have never forgotten. A woman came in—a woman, not a girl—and while her look was not beautiful—far from it—she had that about her which no man could see for the first time without emotion. Her features were ordinary when taken by themselves, but seen together possessed an individuality whose subtle attraction had been marred, but not entirely destroyed, by the countless privations she had evidently undergone. And her hair, wild and uncared-for though it was, was wonderful; so was the air of vivacity and rich, exuberant life which characterised her. Though her cheek was pale and her arms thin, she fairly beamed with that indefinable but spontaneous gladness which springs from the mere fact of being alive, a gladness which at that moment did not suggest drugs or any unwholesome source. I was astounded at the effect she produced upon me, and watched her eagerly. No common unfortunate, this. Yet it would have been hard to find among the city's worst a woman more bedraggled or more poorly nourished.

"Sing!" cried old Mother Merry, with an authority against which I instinctively rebelled, though I had seen the object of it for only a couple of minutes. "You feel like it, and I feel like hearing you. SING!"

The woman's throat throbbed. She stopped just where she was and threw out her arms. Then she smiled and then—she sang.

I have heard Guilbert, I have heard Loftus, but neither of them ever made my temples throb, my heart swell, or my breath falter as this woman did. That she chose the saddest of all sad songs—she who a moment before seemed hardly able to contain her laughter—could not quite account for this effect; nor the fact that these flights of tragic melody rose from out a misery which no laughter could cover up. It was genius, great and wonderful genius, misdirected and lost, but still heaven-given and worthy of an artist's recognition. As she sang on I yielded her mine, for my heart swelled almost to bursting, and when she had finished and stood poised, rapt, ecstatic, enthralled with her own melody and beautiful with her own feeling, I found my cheeks wet with tears. I had never wept at anyone's singing before.

"Dance!" came in fresh command from the miserable hag behind me.

I had forgotten Mother Merry.

But the raised face I was contemplating drooped forward at these words, and the arms, which had moved all through the singing, fell inert.

"I have no strength," she wailed. Yet in another instant she was swaying, turning, rising, and falling in mazes of movement so full of grace and charm that I scarcely missed the music which should have accompanied them. It was more than a dance: it was a drama; instinctively I followed her feelings and knew as by a species of revelation what each motion was meant to convey. I watched her as I would some charmed being; for the marks of care had vanished from her features, and the lips, which had been drawn and white, burned redly, and the hair, which had hung in dishevelled locks, now blew out in live curls, athrill with passion and breathing forth rapture and love. Suddenly she paused. Mother Merry had pointed me out with the words:

"The gentleman is looking at you."

Instantly her beauty shrivelled and vanished. Her hands went up to her face; and she crouched like a lost thing against the floor.

"No, no!" she wailed, and would have fled, but Mother Merry forced her back.

"The gentleman wants something. He wants a drop of what you gave the other one that night. You remember, the night the boys slid away and left us to the police."

Instinctively her right hand went to her bosom and her eyes looked wildly into mine. Suddenly she saw the moisture on my cheeks.

"Oh! he's been crying, Mother Merry, been crying. Perhaps now I can cry, too. I should like to; it's better than singing." And she broke into sobs so violent that I stood aghast in mingled pity and amazement.

Just then the policeman looked in.

"How now?" he cried. "What's up?"

My impulse was to shield her from this fellow's curiosity. Motioning him away, I whispered in her ear:

"You haven't said whether you would give me what I have come for."

"What is that?"

"A drop of what kills trouble; kills it at once, instantly, and forever. I am wretched, heartbroken." (God knows I spoke the truth.)

She stared, and what remained of light in her face went out.

"I have none—now," she hoarsely assured me.

"Then get it where you got that."

"I cannot. I got that when it was easier to smile, and dancing was not followed by dreadful pain. Now—" She tried to laugh as she had a few moments before, but her jocund mood had passed. One would never imagine from her present aspect that she had just floated through the room an embodiment of joyousness and grace.

"You gave it all to him, all?" I questioned.

The emphasis did not strike her, or rather it assumed a different place in her mind than on my lips. "To him?" she repeated, shrinking back with evident distrust.

"Yes," I pursued, following her and speaking in her ear; "the sailor lad who took it away from here that night. Poison—prussic acid—a phial you could hide in your hand."

She broke into laughter, not the expression of joy, but that of defiance if not derision. She was but a common woman now.

"Sailor lad!" she repeated, and laughed again.

I felt that the moment had come for speaking the significant word. Looking around and seeing that Mother Merry was not too near, I whispered:

"A sailor lad with a gentleman's name. You know the name; so do I—Leighton Gillespie."

She had not expected me to go so far. Smothering a frightened cry, she struck her hands together over her head and dashed towards the door by which she had come in. Mother Merry stood before it laughing. Then she turned to escape by the street; but there she was confronted by the heavy form of the policeman, who had thrust himself across the threshold. Crouching, she folded her arms over her breast and made a plunge for the door communicating with the den beyond. It opened under her pressure and she fell gasping and bruised upon the threshold. I hastened to her aid, but she was up before I could reach her.

"I don't know the man you talk of; I don't know you. I am a free woman! a—free—woman!—" she shrieked, bounding to the trap and opening it. As she uttered the last words she swung herself down. I tried to stop her, but she was as agile as a cat. As I leaned over the hole I saw her disappearing among a confusion of oozy piles; and shuddering with the chill of the mephitic air that came pouring up, I drew back.

"That's the end of her for to-day," muttered the harsh voice of Mother Merry behind me. "When she's like that you might as well make for other quarters. But you've had your money's worth. You've heard her sing; you've seen her dance. It's not every man can boast of that. She's shy of men; at least she'll never sing for them."

Perhaps I looked surprised; perhaps I only looked dejected. Misinterpreting the expression, whichever it was, old Mother Merry sidled up closer, and, as I made for the door, whispered with a leer:

"If you really want what you say, come back in a week; and if I can get it you shall have it."

I gave her another coin.

"What do you call that girl?" I asked, with my hand on the latch.

The money made her loquacious.

"Millie," she answered. "That is not how she speaks it, but it's how we all call her."

It was, then, as I had thought. I had seen and listened to Mille-fleurs, the woman to whom Leighton Gillespie had addressed those appealing lines.

CHAPTER XXII

A DISAGREEABLE HOUR WITH A DISAGREEABLE MAN

This interview made an astonishing impression upon me. Never had I supposed myself capable of being stirred to such sympathy by a being so degraded as this wonderful Mille-fleurs.

Was it the contrast between her genius and the conditions under which that genius had shown itself? Possibly. Or was it that a recognition of the latent sweetness underlying her wild nature had caused a feeling of rebellion against the degradation into which a creature of such amazing possibilities had fallen?

Whatever it was, I was conscious of a haunting sense of regret such as had followed few experiences in my life, and began to look upon the man who could make use of such a ruin of womanhood for the obtaining of a deadly drug, with something deeper and more active than mere distrust.

Leighton Gillespie was a man of the world. He knew this wretched creature's weak points and what would procure him the poison he dared not buy from any druggist or chemist. Anyone who saw this woman could read her story. Gay as she was, buoyant as her spirit rose in certain moments of ecstatic passion, she had corresponding moods of morbid depression, possibly of actual suffering, which only morphine could relieve. He knew this and used his knowledge without let or scruple. Was he a monster of selfishness, or only another instance of a good man gone to the bad for the love of a worthless woman? The latter theory seemed the more probable, since all good instincts could not be lacking in a man who had been confessedly helpful in many ways towards rescuing the needy and aiding the unhappy.

Undone by a woman! Was that the situation? It is a common one, God knows. Yet I found it hard to allot her the place suggested by this theory. She did not look like one capable of inclining a man to murder. Yet might I not be playing the fool in cherishing so generous an estimate of her? Might I not be as yet too much under the spell of her peculiar grace to rightly judge the nature underlying it? What did I know of him or of her, that I should burden him with all the blame; and in what did my own wild, uncalculating passion for a woman who not only did not love me, but of whose real character I knew little save as it shone for me through her captivating face, differ from the feeling which might easily be awakened in a still more ardent breast by a creature of so much grace and fire?

Certainly the words I had overheard Leighton Gillespie use in his colloquy with the Salvation Army Captain showed the existence of feelings far beyond those usually associated with a commonplace passion; so did the lines he had left behind him for this waif. But if it was love which moved him, it was a love which did not shrink from involving its object in crime. This she had herself recognised, else why had she shown such terror at the mention of his name and made such a hazardous attempt at escape when threatened by the prospect of further association with him?

The progress which I had made in the case I had undertaken against this man may seem to have reached a point justifying me in communicating the result to Hope. But though I had succeeded in supplying one of the missing links heretofore mentioned as necessary to that end, I nevertheless hesitated to approach her till the whole chain was complete. Her very desire to believe her youngest cousin innocent would make her slow in accepting conclusions too much in the line of her own wishes. She might even now be moved by secret hopes in this direction, might cherish convictions and calm herself with soothing anticipations of restored confidence in Alfred, but she would require the most positive evidence that the potion, however and by whomever obtained, had been actually and knowingly administered by Leighton. To the establishment of this last link in the chain, I must therefore address myself; an almost hopeless task, from which I shrank with very natural misgivings.

Two paths of inquiry, and two only, offered any promise of success. One of these struck me as practicable; the other not. But the practicable one was not within my reach, while the other was little more than a dream. I allude in the first instance to the knowledge supposed to lie hidden within the breast of the old butler; while the dream—well, the dream was this: For some time I had suspected the existence of a secret and as yet unknown witness of this crime, a witness for whose appearance on the scene I had daily looked, and from whom I did not yet despair of gleaning valuable testimony. What basis had I for this dream? I will endeavour to explain.

In presenting to your notice a diagram of the parlour floor of the Gillespie house, I was careful to show the window to be found at the left of Mr. Gillespie's desk. But I drew no attention to this window, nor did I think it worth my while to say that I found the shade of this window rolled up when I first followed Claire into the room. Later, I drew this shade down, but not before noticing that a window stood open in the extension running back of the Gillespie yard from the adjoining house on Fifty- — Street, and that in the room thus disclosed a man was to be seen moving uneasily about.

Now, if this man had been in that room for any length of time, the chances were that his glances had fallen more than once on the brilliantly lighted interior of Mr. Gillespie's den, lying as it did directly under his eye. If so, how much or how little had he seen of what went on there? That is what I now proposed to find out.

That this person, who was a total stranger to me, had given no sign of being in the possession of facts withheld from the police, did not deter me from hoping that I should yet learn something from him. Many men, among them myself, have an invincible dislike to the publicity inseparable from the position of witness, and if this unknown man imagined, as he naturally might, that the police were ignorant of the opportunity which had been given him of looking into Mr. Gillespie's house at a moment so critical, the chances were that he would keep silent in regard to it. That his appearance at the window had been simultaneous with my sight of him, and thus too late for him to have seen more than I did of what went on in Mr. Gillespie's den, was a possibility which would occur to any man. Also, that he might have been there and in full sight of the window from the first, yet had distractions of his own which kept him from making use of his opportunities.

Nevertheless, the probabilities were favourable to the hope I had conceived; and, deciding that in my present uncertainty any action was better than none, I made up my mind to ascertain who this young man was, and whether any means offered for my making his acquaintance.

Sam Underhill was the only man I knew capable of bringing this about. I therefore went below in search of him, and was fortunate enough to come upon him just as he was returning to his room for some theatre tickets he had forgotten to put into his pocket. I attacked him before he could back out.

"What is the name of those people who live in the first house west from Fifth Avenue on Fifty- — Street?" I asked. "Don't you remember the house I mean? That very narrow brown-stone front, with a vase of artificial flowers in one of the parlour windows."

"— me if I know," he protested, in a high state of impatience, as he snatched up the tickets he was looking for. Then, seeing that I was in no condition to be fooled with, he admitted that the name was Rosenthal, and carelessly added, "What do you want to know for? Oh, I see, you are still on the scent; still harping on that Gillespie poisoning case. Well, the Rosenthals may live near the people just mentioned, but there's nothing in that for you or anyone else interested in this crime."

"Why?"

"Because they move in a totally different set from the Gillespies. They have absolutely no connection with them."

"Is there a young man in the family?"

"Yes."

"Well, I want to know him. Find a way of presenting me to him, will you?"

Sam's amazement was amusing.

"You want an introduction to Israel Rosenthal?"

"I have said so."

"Well, everyone to his taste. I'll procure you one this evening at the theatre. He's a great patron of the Lyceum."

"And are you going there?"

"As soon as you release me."

"Very good; expect to find me in the lobby after the first act."

"I'm obliged to you." This because I had moved out of his way. I have seen Sam when he was personally more agreeable to me.

It would be impossible for me to say what play I saw that night. It was one of the well-known successes of the season, but it meant nothing to me. All my mind and attention were on the young man I had come there to see.

He was in one of the boxes; this I found out before the first act was over; and though I caught flitting glimpses of his face, I did not see him closely enough to form any judgment of his temper or disposition. When the first act was over I went into the lobby, but Sam did not join me there till it was nearly time for the curtain to rise again. Then he came alone.

"He'll be out at the end of the third act," he remarked. "The wait is a long one and he will be sure to improve it in the usual way."

I nodded and Sam went back. Strange to say, he was interested in the play, if I was not.

I had no intention of forcing an immediate disclosure from Mr. Rosenthal. Neither the time nor place was propitious for that. When, therefore, the anticipated moment arrived and Sam sauntered out from one aisle and Rosenthal from another, I merely pulled myself together to the point of making myself agreeable to the rather unpromising subject of my present interest. We were introduced offhand by Sam, who, if he did not like the job (and it was very evident he did not), at least went through his part in a way not to disturb the raw pride of my new acquaintance. Then we began to talk, and I thought I saw more than ordinary satisfaction in the manner with which young Rosenthal received my advances, a satisfaction which led me to mentally inquire whether his pleasure rose from gratification at Underhill's attention or from any erroneous idea he may have had of my being a stepping-stone to certain desirable acquaintances. Or, more important still, was he, for reasons I was not as yet ready to dwell upon, glad to know a man whom all recognised as an important witness in the great affair whose unsolved mystery was still the theme of half the town? I curbed my impatience and was eagerly pursuing the conversation towards a point which might settle this disturbing question, when, presto! the curtain rose on the fourth act and he flew to regain his box.

But not before Sam, with a self-denial I shall not soon forget, had asked him round to our apartments after the play; which invitation young Rosenthal seemed glad to accept, for he nodded with great eagerness as he disappeared around the curtains of the doorway.

"So much to humour a friend!" growled Sam, as he, too, started for his seat.

I smiled and went home.

At about midnight Sam came in with my expected guest, and we had a rarebit and ale. In the midst of the good feeling thus established, Rosenthal broke forth in the very explanation I had been expecting from the first.

"I say! you were with old Gillespie when he died."

"The fact is well known," I returned, refraining from glancing at Sam, though much inclined to do so.

"Well, I've a mighty curiosity about that case; seems somehow as if I had had a hand in it."

There was champagne on the table; I pushed the bottle towards Sam, who proceeded to open it. While this was going on I answered Mr. Rosenthal, with all the appearance of surprise he doubtless expected:

"How's that? Oh, I think I understand. You are a neighbour. All who live near them must feel somewhat as you do."

"It isn't that," he protested, draining his glass, which Sam immediately refilled. "I have never told anyone,—I don't know why I tell you fellows,—but I was almost in at that death. You see, the windows of my room look directly down on the little den in which he died, and I chanced to be looking in its direction just as—"

Here he stopped to enjoy his second glass. As the rim slowly rose, obscuring his eyes, I caught an admiring Hm! from Sam, which filled, without relieving, this moment of suspense. As the glass rang down again on the table, Rosenthal finished his sentence:

"—just as Mr. Gillespie lifted his window to empty out a glass of something. Now, what was that something? I have asked myself a dozen times since his death."

"But this is evidence! This is a fact you ought to have communicated to the police," broke in Underhill, with momentary fire. Perhaps it was a real one, perhaps it was the means he used to draw Rosenthal out.

"And be dragged up before a thousand people, all whispering and joggling to see me? No, I have too much self-respect. I only speak of it now," said he with great dignity, "because I'm so deuced curious to know whether it was poison he threw out, a dose of chloral, or just plain wine. It might have been any of these three, but I have always thought it was the first, because he seemed so afraid of being seen."

"Afraid of being seen drinking it or of throwing it out?"

"Throwing it out."

"Oh!"

Sam and I stopped helping ourselves to wine and left the bottle to him.

"Do you know what time this was?" I asked.

"No; how should I? It was before ten, for at ten he was dead."

"It could not have been poison he threw out or even the remains of it," I remarked, "for that would imply suicide; and the verdict was one of murder."

Mr. Rosenthal was just far enough gone to accept this assertion.

"That's so. I wonder I never thought of that before. Then it must have been wine. Now, I wouldn't have thought so badly of Mr. Gillespie as that. I always considered him a sensible man, and no sensible man pours wine out of a window," he sapiently remarked, raising his glass.

It was empty, and he set it down again; then he took up the bottle. That was empty, too. Grumbling some unintelligible words, he glanced at the cabinet.

We failed to understand him.

"There are but two excuses for a man who deliberately wastes wine," he proceeded, in tipsy argument with himself. "Either he has had enough—hard to think that of Mr. Gillespie at so early an hour in the evening—or else the liquor's bad. Now, only a fool would accuse a man like Mr. Gillespie of having bad liquor in his house, unless—unless—something got into it—Oh!" he suddenly exclaimed, with the complacency of one who has unexpectedly made a remarkable discovery, "there was something in it, something which gave it a bad taste. Prussic acid has a bad taste, hasn't it?—and not liking the taste he flung the wine away. No man would go on drinking wine with prussic acid in it," he mumbled on. "Now, which of those fellows was it who poured him out that wine?"

We sat silent; both bound that he should supply his own answer.

"I ought to know; I've read about it enough. It was the slick one; the fellow who goes by me as if I were dirt—Oh, I know; it's Leighton! Leighton!" And he stumbled to his feet with a sickening leer.

"I'm going down to the police station," he cried. "I'm going to inform the authorities—"

"Not to-night," I protested, rising and speaking somewhat forcibly in his ear. "If you go there to-night they will shut you up till morning—jail you!"

He laughed boisterously. "That would be a joke. None of that for me. I'll see them dashed first." And he looked at us with a sickly smile, the remembrance of which will make me hate him forever. Suddenly he began to search for his hat. "I think I'll go home," he observed, with an air of extreme condescension. "Leighton Gillespie, eh? Well, I'm glad the question is settled. Here's to his health! and yours—and yours—"

He was gone.

We were both on our feet ready to assist him in his departure. But he got away in good shape, and when the lower door slammed we congratulated each other with a look. Then Sam seized the bottle and I the glass from which this fellow had drunk, and both fell crashing into the fireplace. Then Sam spoke:

"I fear Leighton Gillespie will sleep his last sound sleep to-night."

"You must consider the drivel we have just listened to as of some importance, then," I declared.

"Taken with what Yox told us, I certainly do," was Sam's emphatic reply.

The sigh which escaped me was involuntary. If this was Sam's opinion, I must prepare myself for an interview with Hope. Alas! it was likely to bring me sorrow in proportion to the joy it brought her.

CHAPTER XXIII

IN MY OFFICE

It was with strange reluctance I opened the paper next morning. Though I had no reason for apprehending that my adventure of the day before had been shared by anyone likely to give information in regard to it, the consciousness of holding an important secret is so akin to the consciousness of guilt, I could not help dreading some reference to the same in the sheet I now unfolded. I wished to be the first to tell Miss Meredith of the new direction in which suspicion was pointing, and experienced great relief when, upon consulting the columns usually devoted to the all-engrossing topic of the Gillespie poisoning case, I came upon a direct intimation of the necessity, now universally felt, of holding Alfred accountable for his father's death, as the only one of the three who had shown himself unable to explain away the circumstantial evidence raised against him.

This expression of opinion on the part of the press had been anticipated too long by Miss Meredith for it to prove a shock to her. I therefore did not commit myself to an early interview, but went at once to my office, where important business awaited me.

I was in the midst of a law paper, when I was warned by a certain nervous perturbation fast becoming too common with me, that someone had been admitted to my inner office and now stood before me. Looking up, I saw her.

She wore a thick veil, and was clad in a long cloak which completely enveloped her. But there was no mistaking the outlines of the figure which had dwelt in my mind and heart ever since the fateful night of our first meeting, or the half-frightened, half-eager attitude with which she awaited my invitation to enter. Agitated by her presence, which was totally unexpected in that place, I rose, and, with all the apparent calmness the situation demanded, I welcomed her in and shut the door behind her.

When I turned back it was to meet her face to face. She had taken off her veil and loosened her cloak at the neck; and as the latter fell apart I saw that the left hand clutched a newspaper. I no longer doubted the purpose of her visit. She had seen the article I have just quoted, and was more moved by it than I had expected.

"You must pardon this intrusion," she began, ignoring the chair I had set for her. "I have seen—learned something which grieves—alarms me. You are my lawyer; more than that, my friend—I have no other— so I have come—" Here she sank into a chair, first drooping her head, then looking up piteously.

I tried to give her the support she asked for. Concealing the effect of her emotion upon me, I told her that she could find no truer friend or one who comprehended her more intuitively; then with a gesture towards the paper, I remarked:

"You are frightened at the impatience of the public. You need not be, Miss Meredith; there are always certain hot-headed people who advocate rash methods and demand any bone to gnaw rather than not gnaw at all. The police are more circumspect; they are not going to arrest any one of your cousins without evidence strong enough to warrant such extreme measures. Do not worry about Alfred Gillespie; to-morrow it will not be his name, but—"

With a leap she was on her feet.

"Whose?" she cried, meeting my astonished gaze with such an agony of appeal in her great tear-dry eyes, that I drew back appalled.

It was not Alfred, then, she loved. Was it the handsome George, after all, or could it be—no, it could not be—that all this youth, all this beauty, nay, this embodiment of truest passion and self-forgetting devotion, had fixed itself upon the unhappy man whom I had just decided to be unworthy of any woman's regard.

Aghast at the prospect, I plunged on wildly, desperately, but with a certain restraint merciful to her, if no relief to me.

"George, too, seems innocent. Leighton only—" Yes, it was he. I saw it as the name passed my lips, saw it even before she gave utterance to the low cry with which she fell at my feet in an attitude of entreaty.

"Oh!" she murmured, "don't say it! I cannot bear it yet. No schooling has made me ready. It is unheard of—impossible! He is so good, so kind, so full of lofty thoughts and generous impulses. I would sooner suspect myself, and yet—oh, Mr. Outhwaite, pity me! Every support is gone; everything in which I trusted or held to. If he is the base, the despicable wretch they say, where shall I seek for goodness, trustworthiness, and truth?"

I had no heart to answer. So it was upon the plainest, least accomplished, and, to all appearance, least responsive as well as least responsible, of Mr. Gillespie's three sons she had fixed her affections and lavished the warm emotions of her passionate young life. Why had I not guessed it? Why had I let George's handsome figure and Alfred's lazy graces blind me to the fact that woman chooses through her imagination; and that if out of a half-dozen suitors she encounters one she does not thoroughly understand, he is sure to be the one to strike her untutored fancy. Alas! for her when, as in this case, this lack of mutual understanding is founded on the impossibility of a pure mind comprehending the hidden life of one who puts no restriction upon the worst side of his nature.

These thoughts were instantaneous, but they made a dividing line in my life. Henceforth this woman, in all her alluring beauty, was in a way sacred to me, like a child we find astray. Raising her from the appealing posture into which she had sunk, I assured her with as much gentleness as my own inner rebellion would allow:

"You have not trusted him yourself, or you would let no newspaper report drive you here for solace."

She cringed; the blow had told. But she struggled on, with a feverish desire to convince herself, if not me, of the worth of him she loved so passionately.

"I know—it was my weakness—or his misfortune. He had given me no cause—no real cause—his eccentricities—my uncle's impatience with them—my own difficulty in understanding them—little things, Mr. Outhwaite, nothing deep, nothing convincing—I cannot explain—shadows—memories so slight they vanish while I seek them—I would have given worlds not to have been shaken in my faith, not to have included him for a minute in the accusation of that phrase, 'one of my sons'; but I am over-conscientious, and because the one I trusted—lived by, had not been exonerated by his father, I did not dare to separate him from the rest, in the doubts his father's accusation had raised. It would have been unjust to them, to the two who cared most for me—the two—" Here her voice trailed off into silence, only to rise in the sudden demand: "What has occasioned this change in public opinion? What have the police discovered, what have you discovered, that he should now be singled out—he against whom nothing was found at the inquest—who has a child—"

"Yet who allows himself to lead a double life."

I said this with a purpose. I knew what its effect must be upon so pure a soul, and I was not surprised at the emotion she displayed. Yet there was something in her manner as she pressed her two hands together which suggested the presence of a different feeling from the one I had expected to rouse in launching this poisoned arrow; and, hesitating with new doubt, I went falteringly on:

"Some men show a very different face in their homes and before their friends than in haunts where your pure imagination cannot follow them. The life lived under your eye is not the one really led by the melancholy being you have watched with such sympathetic interest."

She did not seem to follow me.

"What do you mean?" Her indignation was so strong that she leaped to her feet and eyed me with a manifest sense of outrage. "You speak as if you meant something I should not hear. He! Claire's father—"

It was a difficult task. Surely my lines had fallen in untoward places. But there was no doubt about my duty. If her fresh, unspoiled heart had made its home in a nest of serpents, it was well she should know her mistake before the shame of the discovery should overwhelm her.

Turning aside, so that I should not seem to spy upon her agitation, I answered her as such questions should be answered, with the truth.

"Miss Meredith," said I, "when I undertook to sift this matter, and if possible bring to light some fact capable of settling the doubt that is wearing away your life, I hoped to relieve your heart and restore your faith in the one cousin most congenial to you. That I have failed in this and find myself called upon to inflict suffering rather than to bring peace to your agitated heart is a source of regret to myself which you can never measure. But it cannot be helped. I dare not keep back the truth. Leighton Gillespie is unworthy your regard, Miss Meredith, not only because he lies under suspicion of having committed the worst sin in the calendar, but because he has deceived you as to the state of his own affections. He—"

"Wait!" Her voice was peremptory; her manner noble. "I wish to say right here, Mr. Outhwaite, that Leighton Gillespie has never deceived me in this regard. I have cared for him because—because I could not help it. But he has never led me into doing so by any show of peculiar interest in myself. George has courted me and Alfred nearly has, but not Leighton; yet to him my whole heart went out, and if it is a shame to own it I must endure that shame rather than injure his cause by leaving you under the influence of a prejudice which has no foundation in fact."

Before the generosity of this self-betrayal I bowed my head. Her beauty, warm and glowing as it was at this moment of self-abandonment, did not impress me so much as the mingled candour and pride with which she exonerated this man from the one fault of which she knew him to be innocent. It gave me a new respect for her and a shade more of forbearance for him, so that my voice softened as I replied:

"Well, well, we will not charge him with deliberate falsehood towards you, only with the madness which leads a man to sacrifice honour and reputation to the fancied charms of an irresponsible woman. He is under a spell, Miss Meredith, which I will not attempt to name. The object of it I have myself seen, and it was from her hand (possibly without her understanding the purpose for which he wanted it, as she has no appearance of being a really wicked woman) that he obtained the poison which did such deadly work in your uncle's house."

The worst was said; and the silence that followed was one never to be forgotten by her or by me. When it was broken, it was by Hope, and in words which came in such starts and with such pauses, I could only guess their meaning through my own identification with her shame and grief.

"Calumny!—it cannot be!—so good—so thoughtful in his bringing up of Claire—that day he pulled her aside lest she should stumble against the little boy with the broken arm. It is a dream! a horrible dream! He depraved? he a buyer of poison?—no, no, no, not he, but the evil spirit that sometimes possesses him. Leighton Gillespie in his true hours is a man to confide in, to regard with honour, to—to—to—"

I no longer made an effort at listening. She was not addressing me, but her own soul, with which for the moment she stood apart in the great loneliness which an overwhelming catastrophe creates. She did not even remember my presence, and I did not dare recall it to her. I simply let her lose herself in her own grief, while I fought my own battle, and, as I hope, won my own victory. But this could not last; she suddenly awoke to the nearness of listening ears, and, flushing deeply, ceased the broken flow of words which had so worn upon my heart, and, regaining some of her lost composure, forcibly declared:

"You are an honest man, Mr. Outhwaite, and, I am told, a reliable lawyer. You have too much feeling and judgment to malign a man already labouring under the accusation which unites this whole family in one cloud of suspicion. Tell me, then, do you positively know Leighton to have done what you say?"

"Alas!" was my short but suggestive reply.

Instantly she ceased to struggle, and with a calmness hardly to be expected from her after such a display of feeling, she surveyed me earnestly for a moment, then said:

"Tell me the whole story. I have a reason for hearing it, a reason which you would approve. Let me hear what you learned, what you saw. It is not to be found in the papers. I have only found there a general allusion to him calculated to prepare the mind for some great disclosure to-morrow—" And her hand tightened upon the sheet which I now discovered to be the one morning journal I had failed to see. "You will pay no attention to my feelings—I have none—we are sitting in court—let me hear."

Respecting her emotion, respecting the attitude in which she had placed me, I did as she requested. With all the succinctness possible, I told her how I had been led to go to Mother Merry's and what I had discovered there. Then I related what we had learned from Rosenthal. The narrative was long, and gave me ample opportunity for studying its effect upon her.

But she made no betrayal of her feelings; perhaps, as she had said, she had none at this moment. With her hand clenched on her knee, she sat listening so intently that all her other faculties seemed to have been suspended for this purpose; only, as I approached the end, I noticed that the grey shadow which had hung over her from the first had deepened to a pall beneath which the last vestige of her abounding youth had vanished.

My own heart grew heavy as the gladness left hers, and I was nearly as desolate as she when I made this final remark:

"That is all, Miss Meredith. I as truly believe that Leighton Gillespie bought the bottle of poison from the girl he called Mille-fleurs as if I had seen him laying the money down before her. But Rosenthal's admissions you must take at your own valuation. He says he saw your uncle, with backward looks and signs of secret fear and disturbance, pour out something from a glass on to the grass-plot underneath his open window. Was it the wine which had been given him by Leighton, and did he do this because of the drug he had detected in it?—a drug, alas! so fatal, it was not necessary for him to drink the full glass in order to succumb to it? That is a question you must answer in your mind from the knowledge you have of your uncle and his family."

There was a hope held out in this last phrase which I expected to see her embrace. But she did not; on the contrary, her depression remained unchanged and she said:

"I knew my uncle well. He was a just man, and, in times of great danger, a cool one. He would never have written for my eyes those four words—'one of my sons'—unless some new fact had added certainty to his former conviction. The drug was in the wine handed him by Leighton; we must accept that fact whatever it may cost us."

Her calmness amazed me. For the last few minutes she seemed upborne by some secret thought I could neither fathom nor understand.

But suddenly her old horror returned with the recurrence of some old memory. "Then it was his hand that stole towards my uncle's glass in the dark!" she cried; "that murderous, creeping hand, the vision of which has haunted me night and day since I heard of it. Oh, horrible! horrible! What a curse to fall upon a man! It is the work of the arch-fiend. Poor Leighton! poor Leighton!" she cried in her agony.

Bowing her head, she sobbed bitterly, while I surveyed her in amazement. I did not understand her. She seemed to be weeping for Leighton, not for herself; at all events she did not show the repulsion I expected from her in face of such monstrous depravity. Was the fascination he exerted over her so great that she could not weigh at their proper value characteristics so entirely evil? It did not seem possible. Yet there she sat mourning for him, instead of crushing the very thought of him out of her heart.

"I think I comprehend it all now," she finally whispered, half to herself and half to me. "I have had the thought before; it has come when that bewildering look of mad uneasiness has crossed his face and he has left us to be gone days, sometimes weeks, without notice or explanation. It is a strange idea, a secret, almost an uncanny one; but it is the only one that can explain a crime for which one and all of my cousins seem to lack the inherent baseness. Dare I breathe it to you? It may be the saving of Leighton, if true; God knows it is my only excuse for clinging to him still."

"And you do cling to him still?" I asked, knowing what her answer would be, but hoping against hope.

The look she gave recalled all her old beauty. Would that I might have been the cause of it! or that a woman would love where she was loved and not where her heart must encounter disgrace and bitter suffering.

"I cannot help doing so," she murmured. "He will soon need my aid, if not my comfort; for I know what these horrible contradictions mean. I understand them, understand him, and even the revolting crime of which he may have been guilty. Hypocrisy does not explain it; depravity does not explain it; his good acts are too real, the nobility of his nature too unmistakable. Disease alone can account for it. He is the victim of double consciousness, and he leads two lives—your own expression—because the two hemispheres of his brain do not act in unison. Wickedness is not his normal condition. His normal condition is a noble one. By nature he is a God-fearing man, devoted to good works and high thoughts. When he goes astray it is because the balance of his faculties has been disturbed. This is no new thing to the psychologist. You yourself have heard of men so afflicted. Leighton Gillespie is one."

Was her own brain turned by her terror, anxiety, and wonder? Surely she was either mad or playing with my common sense. But the calm dignity of her manner proved that she had advanced this astonishing, this fantastic explanation of Leighton Gillespie's contradictory actions in good faith. Despair seized me at this proof of his tenacious hold upon her, and I could not quite restrain a touch of irony.

"You would make him out a sort of Jekyll and Hyde," I ventured. "Alas! I fear the courts do not take into account the theories of the romancer in their judgment of criminals."

The sarcasm passed unheeded. Growing more and more beautiful as her earnestness increased, she said with simple confidence:

"Talk to Dr. Bennett; he has known my cousin almost from his birth. Ask what these sudden changes mean in a man whose primal instincts have always been good. Ask why this devoted father, this kind son, suddenly loses himself, it may be at table, it may be while sitting with his own child by the fire, and, deaf to all remonstrance, blind to the most touching appeals of those about him, goes suddenly out and does not come back till he can be himself again in the presence of his family and under the eye of his friends. Previous to that awful morning when my uncle unsealed to my eyes the horrible secret that rested like a cloud over the household, I used to give another explanation to these varying moods, and see in them a promise of more personal hopes and an augury of my own future happiness; so easy is it for a woman to deceive herself when she worships a man without fully comprehending him. I thought—" Here her calm candour grew almost heroic in the effort she made to impress me with the reasons she cherished for her belief, "I thought he was jealous of George or angry with Alfred, and was driven away by his fears of self-betrayal or his dread of being led into making unworthy reprisals. But now I see that it was his abnormal nature which had come into play, a nature of which he may be ignorant when in full health, and for the manifestations of which he may be no more responsible than we are for the vagaries we commit in dreams."

"You have not read the latest discoveries in hypnotism," I rejoined. "A man can be driven into no act for which he lacks the natural instinct. But I do not want to be cruel, Miss Meredith. I am too sincere in my desire to save you unnecessary pain and heartache. Since you wish it, I will see Dr. Bennett, but—"

My smile seemed to unnerve her.

"But you do not think he will agree with me in my interpretation of this crime and Leighton's connection with it?"

"I do not, Miss Meredith."

"Then," she cried, with a high look and a gleam of quiet resolve that made me realise how small was my influence in face of her overpowering love for this man, "God's will be done! I shall believe in what I have said till he whom I have trusted is proved the heinous malefactor you consider him. When that hour comes, I perish, killed by the greatest shame that can overwhelm a woman. To love one who has never sought your affection may cause the cheek to burn and the heart to recoil upon itself; but to have given all one's youth and the most cherished impulses of the heart to a man who is no more than a whited sepulchre of deceit and revolting crime—that would be to sap life at its spring and tear up the heart by its roots. Oh, Mr. Outhwaite, forgetting all womanly delicacy, forgetting everything but your forbearance and the confidence with which you inspire me, I have poured out my soul before you. Prove to me that this man is good—moral in his instincts, I mean, except when the evil spirit has a grip upon him—and I will bless you as the saviour of my self-respect. But if you cannot,—" here she turned pale and tottered,—"then do not expect me to survive. I—I—could not."

The alternative was a bitter one. I did not see at that moment how she could expect, still less how I could perform, such a miracle. But I could not see her depart without some gleam of encouragement, and so I told her that if the tide turned so as to free Alfred from suspicion and land Leighton in the courts, I would embrace the opportunity thus offered to do all that lay in my power to prove her theory a true one.

And with this understanding between us she went away, leaving me to take up, with what courage I could, my own broken and disjointed life.

CHAPTER XXIV

AN OLD CATASTROPHE IS RECALLED

This idea as advanced by Hope was fantastical to a degree; yet it made its impression upon me and was still in my mind when I opened the evening paper for the latest news concerning the Gillespie murder. The first paragraph I encountered proved that I had not warned her an hour too soon of Leighton Gillespie's position.

"Fresh disclosures in the Gillespie Poisoning Case. Leighton Gillespie, long regarded as the most respectable and hitherto best-esteemed son of the murdered man, discovered to have been for years the owner, and at times the occupant, of a little house in one of the Oranges, where, unknown to the world at large—"

Here followed some open allusions to Mille-fleurs.

Other statements were added to this, among them a résumé of the facts advanced to me the evening before by Rosenthal. At the end were these lines:

"The District Attorney has the whole matter in charge, and the public is promised some decided action to-morrow."

I folded the paper, put it in my pocket, and went directly to Dr. Bennett's office.

I had not seen the good physician since the inquest, and naturally the sight of his face recalled the strange and moving incidents which had first brought us together. But I made no allusion to these past experiences, and his first remark was wholly professional.

"I hope it is not as a patient I see you, Mr. Outhwaite?"

With a shake of the head I took out the newspaper I had been careful to bring with me, and pointed out the paragraph concerning Leighton and Mille-fleurs.

"Is this news to you?" I asked. "I make the inquiry solely in the interests of Miss Meredith, who has hitherto had unbounded confidence in this cousin."

He glanced at the lines, frowned, and then with a pained look, replied:

"I do not believe this of Leighton. He of all Mr. Gillespie's sons is the furthest removed from the suspicion connecting them with the crime which has wrecked their good name. He is incapable of any serious wrong-doing; incapable even of what these lines suggest. I have known him from his birth."

I would gladly have left this kind-hearted physician in undisturbed possession of this confidence, but the situation was too serious to trifle with.

"He enjoys a good name," I allowed, "and has even been known to exert himself in many acts of benevolence towards the unfortunate and the suffering. But some natures, and they are frequently those from which most is to be expected, have a reverse side, which will not bear the scrutiny either of their friends or the world at large. Leighton Gillespie has one of these natures. This story of the little house is true."

The doctor, who was evidently heart and soul with this family, showed a distress at this avowal which spoke well for the hold which this especial member of it had upon his affections.

Seeing that, while not ready to question my word, he was anxious to know the sources of my information, I was about to enter upon the necessary explanations, when he forestalled me by saying:

"There have always been unexplained traits in this man. He stands alone among the other members of the family. He has neither the social qualities of George nor the luxurious tastes of Alfred. Nor is he like his father. I, who knew his mother well, have no difficulty in attributing to their correct source the religious tendencies which form so distinct a part of his character. But the melancholy which pervades his life is not an inheritance, but the result of nervous shock incident upon an extreme grief in early life, and while I do not profess to understand him or the many peculiarities to which his father rightfully raised objection, I am positive that he will never be found guilty of a depraved act. I am ready to stake my reputation on it."

"You should talk with Miss Meredith," I suggested. "She believes, or endeavours to believe, in him also. But even she finds herself forced to accept the truth of this report. The facts favouring it are too unmistakable. I can myself supply evidence enough to make his guilt in this regard quite sure."

And, without preamble, I entered upon a detailed account of the discoveries made by me at Mother Merry's. They were, as you well know, convincing in their nature, and allowed but two conclusions to be drawn. Either Leighton Gillespie was a monster of hypocrisy or he was the victim of the mental derangement so fondly suggested by Hope.

This last explanation I left to the perspicacity of the trained physician. Would he seize upon it as she did? Or would he fail to see in these results any symptoms of the strange mental malady alluded to by Hope? I watched him anxiously. Evidently no such explanation was likely to suggest itself to him unaided. Indeed, his next words proved how far any such conclusion was from his mind.

"You overwhelm me," said he. "It was hard enough to look upon George or Alfred as capable of a crime so despicable, but Leighton!—I shall have to readjust all my memories and all my fancied relations with this family if he is to be looked upon with suspicion. Then there is Claire!"

"Pardon me," I ventured, in vague apology for an interruption which seemed out of place from a stranger. "Have you looked upon Leighton as a well man? You speak of a great grief—"

"The loss of his wife."

"I supposed so. Now, could this grief have disturbed the even balance of his mind so as to make these abnormal developments possible? Did he show the inconsistencies you mention prior to the event you speak of? It might be well to inquire."

"Insanity?" he intimated. "Will that be the plea?"

"Do you think it can be advanced? He has not yet been arrested or even openly accused, but I am confident he will be, and soon, and it is well for his friends to be prepared."

"That is a question I cannot answer without serious thought," rejoined the doctor, restlessly pacing the room. "Intimately as I have been associated with him I have never for a moment felt myself called upon to doubt his perfect sanity. Does Miss Meredith regard his eccentricities in this light?"

"Miss Meredith's inherent belief in the goodness of this favourite cousin leads her to give him the benefit of her doubts. She regards him as a man cursed by recurrent aberrations of mind; in other words, a victim of double consciousness."

"Hope does? What does she know about the nice distinctions governing this peculiar condition? She must have brought all her imagination to bear on the subject, to find such an excuse for his contradictory actions. This argues a great partiality for him on her part. She must be in love with Leighton."

I was silent.

The doctor's amazement was very genuine.

"Well, I never suspected her of any such preference. I have had an idea at times that she favoured Alfred rather than George, but I never thought of her being caught by Leighton's melancholy countenance and eccentric ways. Well! women are an incomprehensible lot! The only widower amongst the three! The only one not likely to be affected by her partiality. But that's neither here nor there. It's her theory we are interested in. A strange one! A very strange one!"

Suddenly he grew thoughtful. "But not an impossible one," was his final comment. "The shock he sustained might account for almost anything. Such restrained natures have great depths and are subject to great reactions! I must study the case; I can give no offhand opinion upon it. The contradictions observable in his conduct are not normal and certainly show disease. What was the question you asked me?" he suddenly inquired. "Whether he showed his present peculiarities prior to the death of his wife? I don't think he did; really, I don't think he did. He was reserved in his ways, unhappy, out of tune with his father because that father failed to appreciate the daughter-in-law he had foisted upon him, but he showed these feelings naturally and not at all as he showed them later. Have you heard the current gossip concerning his marriage?"

"Not at all, save that it was an unfortunate one and created, as you say, a certain barrier between him and his father."

"Yes, it was an unfortunate one; the whole thing was unfortunate. So much so that his friends felt a decided relief when young Mrs. Gillespie died. But her husband regarded this loss as an irreparable one; he was wrapped up in her when she was alive, and, as you now call to mind, has never been the same man since her death. Perhaps it was because he had no outlet for his grief. His father would not hear her name mentioned, and little Claire was too young to even remember her mother. Fortunately, perhaps."

The last words were said in his throat, and opened up a wide abyss of possibilities into which I had not the curiosity to penetrate. I only felt impelled to ask:

"Was her death attended with any unusual circumstance that you speak of his sorrow as a shock?"

For reply he went to his desk, and after some fumbling brought out several slips of paper, from among which he chose one which he passed over to me.

"I have kept this account of a very tragic occurrence, for reasons you will appreciate on reading it."

I took the slip and perused it. With no apology for its length, I introduce it here. As you will see, it is an engineer's account of the extraordinary accident which took place on the B., F. and D. road some half-dozen years ago. It begins abruptly, the extract having been closely clipped from the columns of the paper containing it:

Big Hill is only twelve miles long and has a grade averaging 140 feet to the mile, and the principal part of the grade is in spots. Six loaded cars made a train up this hill, and the train of six cars was hauled and pushed up the grade by two engines. My engine was stationed permanently on the hill, and its duty was to couple to the back end of one of these trains and help it up the grade.

At the top of the hill was a side-track called Acton, but no telegraph operator was stationed there. At the foot of the grade was Buckley, a telegraph office in the centre of a big side-track system used for breaking up trains before sending them up the grade in sections. Eight miles below Buckley was an abandoned mining town named Campton. Here was a set of side-tracks and switches and a dozen unoccupied miners' shanties, while the disused telegraph office was occupied by a one-legged pensioner of the company—a flagman—and his nineteen-year-old daughter. Twelve miles further down the line was Mountain Springs, now one of the foremost summer resorts in the mountains, and even twenty years ago much frequented by Eastern health-seekers. I explain this so that you will readily understand what happened.

We had run No. 17 up the hill and were ordered on to the side-track at Acton to get out of the way of No. 11, the through train from the South that was coming North as a double-header, and with a third big engine pushing her. No. 11 was a regular, but was making this trip as an excursion train, and was made up of eight coaches, crowded with people from Mountain Springs.

As the freight we were shoving came to a stand-still, my fireman leaped to the ground and uncoupled the engine from the last car, and I backed down over the switch and then ran ahead on the side-track. While this was being done, a brakeman had cut the train in front of the last two cars, and the regular engine in front had started ahead with the other cars towards the north switch to back the four cars in on the spur.

As I shut off steam and centred the reverse lever I saw that the two cars were moving slowly down the hill, and I watched them only long enough to see the rear brakeman clamber up the side-ladder and seize the brake-wheel. Then I tried the water in the boiler, started the injector, and again glanced at the cars. Evidently the brake on the first car was out of order, as the cars were moving more rapidly, and the brakeman was hastening towards the brake on the second car. He grasped it and swung around, and nearly fell to the ground. The brake-chain was broken, and there was nothing to hold the cars.

In an instant the picture of an awful horror flashed before my eyes. No. 11, crowded with passengers, was coming, and those cars, running at terrific speed, would crash into the train, carrying death and destruction to scores, if not hundreds. The scene at the moment the realisation of the impending disaster came over me is before me now as plainly as on that day, nearly five years ago,—the moving cars, the brakeman stumbling towards the side-ladder to descend, the fireman, who was more than a little deaf, walking away without seeing or hearing what had occurred, and, in his place, a man (I had almost said a gentleman) standing by the switch-staff and gazing towards the cars with eyes that reflected the horror in my own; while thirty miles below, on the line of the twisted, winding track, a faint blur of smoke that told me No. 11 had left Mountain Springs.

Before the moving cars crossed the switch we all knew what must be done. The man, who for all his good clothes, must have been some fireman off duty, had thrown the switch, and then, seeing that my own man was too far off to meet this emergency, had swung himself on to the foot-board back of the tank; and old 105 was in pursuit of the runaways.

The brakeman remained to close the switch and the stranger was bracing himself to couple the engine to the swift-moving cars when we should approach them.

No steam is ever used going down that hill; at the top of the incline the throttle-valve is closed and the speed of the train is controlled by the air-brake. But, as the stranger who had boarded the engine took his stand on the foot-board, I opened the throttle wide to give her a start, then put on the air until I had her under control, and then away we went. The runaway cars were fully one hundred yards ahead as we crossed the switch, and were moving apparently at the rate of eight or ten miles an hour with rapidly increasing momentum. In sixty seconds old 105 was running fifty miles an hour, and in thirty seconds more we were close to the cars. I heard the voice of the man in front shouting something, and knowing that it was to slow down in order to approach the cars without a crash, I applied the air. A slight jolt told me that the engine and car had come together, and after waiting an instant to give my unknown assistant time to drop the pin in place, I pulled the air-valve to lessen the speed. As the engine slowed under the pressure of the brake, I saw the cars glide away from us. He had missed the coupling. Again engine and cars came together and again I applied the air, with the same result.

We were running now at a speed of sixty or seventy miles an hour, and when you consider that the track on the hill is the crookedest ever surveyed by an engineer, cut up by deep ravines and canyons, and leading along high precipices, you can appreciate the danger of the run. Down the hill we thundered, swinging through deep cuts and around sharp curves, the engine swaying and swinging on her springs as if struggling in an effort to dash herself into one of the gorges lining the track. The engine was surrounded by rolling clouds of dust, through which at times I caught glimpses of the cars pitching and tossing like some dismantled vessel in a storm at sea. I knew the cars might jump the track at any moment and ditch the locomotive, sending the fireman and myself to quick death; but we must take the chances so long as there was a possibility of stopping the runaways.

Again and again we tried to make the coupling, but failed each time. I did not know, until all was over, the difficulties which the stranger was experiencing. The drawhead in the car was the old-fashioned single-link bumper,—a man-killer we call it now,—and was so loose in its socket that it had to be raised six or eight inches and held in position while the link was being put in place. This required two hands, and as he could not maintain his position on the swaying foot-board without using one hand to cling to the handrail, he could not get the link in place and drop the pin through it.

By this time we were within three miles of Buckley. As the locomotive and fleeting cars dashed across a trestle one hundred feet high, I caught a glimpse of the little telegraph shanty down in the valley, surrounded by a network of rails. I opened the whistle and kept it shrieking until we were within two hundred yards of Buckley, but no one appeared on the station platform; and as we flashed past the telegraph office the white face of the operator, his eyes wide open with alarm and horror, appeared at the window for the fraction of an instant.

As we dashed past the telegraph office the long arm of the signal-board pointed down, and I thanked God that the next block was still open, and that we had another chance for life. We had eight miles of clear track and might yet prevent a disaster. The only hope, however, was in catching the runaway cars, as there was no telegraph office at Campton and No. 11 had left Mountain Springs and was booming towards us as fast as three big engines could send her, and without a stop ahead.

We crossed the half-mile of side-tracks at Buckley so fast that there was an unbroken rattle of clanking rails, and swung around the point of the mountain and down the winding track towards Campton. Over swaying bridges, through cuts, old 105 jolted us along at the rate of seventy or eighty miles an hour. In two minutes after crossing the yards at Buckley we were within sight of Campton, nestling below us in the valley. The man on the foot-board had been silent seemingly for hours, and whether he was still at his post or had fallen on the rails and been ground to pieces, I did not know. I realised now that there was no longer a possibility of stopping the cars by coupling to them, and what my hope was, if I had any at all, I do not know; there was only a mad determination to follow those runaway cars to the end and die with the rest.

As the roofs of Campton came into view the whistle began to sound again. Three miles below lay the half-deserted mining camp; now I could see the rough board station, the red and white switch targets, and the dark spots on the mountain-side that marked the abandoned test-shafts. Then I distinguished a form on the station platform, a slender form in dark calico and wearing a sun-bonnet. The woman's back was towards me, but I knew her to be Nettie Bascom, the daughter of the one-legged flagman. It was ten seconds, perhaps, before the girl heard the whistle; then she turned slowly, looking an instant towards us, and, with a quick spring, was at a switch-stand and had thrown the lever, and the white of the target turned to red and we were safe. But not so the passenger train. The cars had passed over the switch before it could be turned, and in another moment the sound of its bounding wheels, our own cries, and all the other noises of the dreadful moment, were drowned by an explosion that lifted old 105 off the rails and laid everyone within sight insensible on the road. Those cars which we had chased unavailingly for thirty miles or more were laden with dynamite, and when they crashed into that train—

Do you ask about the man who shared my peril, and all to so little purpose? I can tell you nothing about him. Whether my former conclusion was correct and he had been shaken from his narrow hold into some ditch or gully, or whether he was hurled to destruction at the time of the explosion, I cannot say. I only know that I never saw him again alive or dead.

Below was added a line by the editor:

This is an offhand relation of the catastrophe in which Mrs. Leighton Gillespie lost her life. She will be remembered by New York aristocracy as the brilliant, if eccentric, daughter-in-law of Archibald Gillespie, the multi-millionaire.

I returned the slip to Dr. Bennett. The excitement of that wild ride was upon me, and I seemed to have been present at the catastrophe it was intended to avert.

"Mountain Springs is in the West, I judge. How came the Gillespies there, and why was she the sole sufferer? Was he not on the train with her?"

"That is one of the peculiar features of the affair. He was not on the train, but he turned up at the wreck. Those who saw him there say that he worked like a giant, nay, like a Titan, amongst those ghastly ruins. Finally he found her. She was quite dead. After that he worked no more. It is a story of unmitigated horror, and the agonies of that awful finding might well leave an indelible impression on his brain."

"I am glad you recognise this possibility. The effect of such a scene, even where no personal interests are involved, often leaves a man's nerves in a shaken condition for years. Besides—forgive me if I press my theory beyond all reason—another possibility has been suggested to me by this engineer's tale. I will not broach it just yet, but inquire first how Leighton Gillespie was able to reach the scene of the wreck so quickly. Did he hasten down from the Springs, which seem to have been some miles away, or was he in the vicinity of the accident when it occurred?"

"That is a question I have never heard answered. But I long ago concluded that he was not far from the place where the collision occurred, for he was seen there as soon as the smoke lifted. Why, what now? You seem moved—excited. Has any new idea been suggested to you?"

I exerted myself to speak calmly, but did not succeed.

"Yes," I cried, "a strange, a thrilling idea. What if the man who shared this engineer's awful ride was Leighton Gillespie, and what if he knew through all that headlong rush, that the wife he so much loved was in the train he was risking his life to save from destruction?"

CHAPTER XXV

A SUMMONS

The doctor's emotion equalled mine.

"It may have been so," he admitted. "There was always some unexplained mystery in connection with his presence at the wreck and the reticence he maintained in regard to it. If what you suggest is true and he was the man who shared the engineer's ride down those precipitous slopes to the rescue of a train on which he knew his wife to be, it will be easy enough for us to start a plea of mental derangement. No one could go through such an adventure, with its overpowering excitement and unspeakable suspense, without some injury to his mental or physical health. But it is hard to conceive how Leighton Gillespie should have been wandering on the mountain-side that day instead of taking the excursion with his wife."

"I don't advance this explanation as a fact, only as a possibility," I replied. "The shock of his wife's sudden death would be enough in itself to change the man."

"Yes, and it did change him; to that I can swear."

"How long a time elapsed after this catastrophe before you saw him?"

"Just two days. He telegraphed for me, and I went West to assist him in bringing home the remains of his young wife. I remember finding him in a strained, nervous condition; this was natural enough; but his worst symptoms disappeared after the funeral."

"Do you mind telling me where this funeral took place?"

"In a small place up the Hudson River, where the Gillespies have a country home. Mr. Gillespie carried his feeling against his daughter-in-law so far as not to wish to have her buried from his New York house."

"I suppose so; another reason, perhaps, why Leighton has never recovered from this blow. And little Claire? You have not mentioned her. Was she with her parents when this disastrous event occurred?"

"She was but an infant, and from her very birth was given into the charge of her grandfather. She never knew her mother."

It would have been a satisfaction to me to have learned the cause of the determined hostility on the part of a man seemingly so just as Mr. Gillespie; but the doctor gave me no encouragement in this direction, and I merely said:

"We have made a start in case the necessity arises for proving him to be no longer responsible for his actions. But only a start. The direction taken by his mania is perilously like the excesses of a discouraged and reckless man."

"I am not so sure of that. In his sane mind, Leighton Gillespie is a great respecter of the rights of other people. I shall look into this subject, Mr. Outhwaite; I shall look into it at once. A half-hour's talk with him will satisfy me whether he is a victim of disease or the prey of unbridled passions and murderous instincts."

The good doctor rose with every appearance of starting forth then and there.

"But you have had no dinner," I suggested.

"I want none."

I accompanied the doctor out, but parted with him at the corner. I would have given much for the privilege of going with him to the Gillespie house, but as this was not to be thought of, I resolutely turned towards my apartments, which were in quite a different direction.

How was it, then, that by the time the lights began to be lit in the streets I found myself circulating restlessly in the vicinity of the very house I had determined to avoid? Had the exciting incidents of the day been too much for me? It certainly looked so. Surely I had not wandered hither through any act of my own volition or for any definite purpose I could name. Yet now that I had been so led; now that I was within sight of the house where so important an interview was going on, I surely might be pardoned for taking advantage of this proximity to note the doctor when he came out and see, if possible, from his manner and bearing the result of a visit upon which such serious issues hung.

It had threatened storm all day, and during the last few minutes the atmosphere had become permeated with a drizzle which made further tramping over wet pavements undesirable. I therefore looked about for refuge, and perceiving a building in process of construction on the opposite side of the way, I glided amid its shadows, happy both at the protection it offered and the full view it gave me of the Gillespie front door.

That this was the act of one bent on espionage I am ready to acknowledge, but it was espionage undertaken in a good cause and for justifiable reasons. At all events I was engaged in inwardly persuading myself to this effect, when an event occurred which drew my attention from myself and fixed it with renewed interest on the door I was watching.

A boy of whose proximity I had had some previous intimation suddenly darted out from the space behind me, and went flying across the street to the Gillespie house. He had a missive in his hand, and seemed anxious lest he should be caught and stopped.

This roused my curiosity, so that no detail of what followed escaped me. I noted the furtive way in which he thrust the letter into the unwilling hand of the old butler, who answered his frightened ring at the bell. Also the misgiving shake of the head with which the latter received it, and the doubtful looks they both cast at someone back in the hall. Who was this someone, and what lay behind old Hewson's agitated demeanour? The door closed on my curiosity, and I was left to ponder this new event. But not for long; scarcely had my eyes returned from following the escaping figure of the boy, when the door on the opposite side of the street unclosed again and Dr. Bennett came out.

Now, as I have taken pains to say, I had posted myself there in order to note how this gentleman looked on leaving Leighton Gillespie. But now that this opportunity had come, I not only failed to avail myself of it, but found my whole attention caught and my interest fully absorbed by a glimpse I had received of the latter gentleman standing back in the hall reading the letter I had just seen delivered in such a surreptitious manner.

His attitude, the gestures he unconsciously made, argued sudden and overwhelming emotion, an emotion so sudden and overwhelming that he could not conceal it, though he evidently would have been glad to do so, judging from the haste with which he thrust the letter in his pocket and turned—But here the door closed, as frequently happens at critical moments, and I found my eyes resting upon nothing more exciting than the figure of the doctor feeling his way with due care down the damp steps.

Had I not been witness both to the peculiar actions of the urchin who brought this letter, and to the strange manner in which Leighton received it, I might not have considered it decorous to make my presence known to the doctor at a moment and in a place so suggestive of a watch upon his movements. But as everything affecting Leighton was as interesting to this, his best friend, as it was to me, I crossed the street, and, with scant apology for the seeming intrusion, told the good doctor what had just come under my observation.

He seemed surprised, if not affected, by what I had to say. He had seen no letter and no evidences of disorder on the part of Leighton. To be sure, he had left before any letter had been received.

"Indeed, you astonish me," he declared. "Seldom have I seen my young friend in a more equable frame of mind. He talked evenly and with discretion about the most exciting subjects; and, though I could wish him to have been more open, he showed a self-control hardly to be expected from a man placed in such a disturbing situation. The detective, who appeared to have full range of the house, hardly looked our way once. The letter which you say he received just as I left him must have contained very agitating news. I wonder if we will ever know what."

"Were you able to settle in your own mind the question just now raised between us at your office?" I asked, after a momentary silence. "It may not be in order for me to ask, and you may not feel at all ready to answer me. If so, do not hesitate to rebuke my importunity, which springs entirely from my excessive interest in the matter."

"I will the more readily excuse you," was his reply, "because my answer must dash your client's hopes. Leighton Gillespie is not a victim of double consciousness. If he were, he would not remember in one state what passes in the other. Now, he does remember. Though he gives no explanation of what allures him into haunts so out of keeping with his usual associations, I caught the glint in his eye when I mentioned certain names. Leighton cannot deceive me. Moreover, Mr. Outhwaite, I cannot professionally state that in my opinion he is otherwise than completely sane, notwithstanding the tragic experience he once went through. I say tragic, because the surmise you indulged in concerning him was true. He was the man who flung himself upon the foot-rail of that plunging engine. He acknowledged it to me just now, and acknowledged, also, that he knew that those cars contained dynamite. A great and wonderful act for a man who had had no experience outside the club-room and the gymnasium."

"I respect heroism wherever I meet it," said I, slightly lifting my hat.

"And I," echoed the doctor; then as we turned down the street; "I do not comprehend Leighton or what has led him into this course of duplicity if not crime. A hero at one period of his life; a scamp, if not worse, at another! What are we to think of the man whose nature admits such contradictions! What are we to think of human nature itself! I declare I am sometimes baffled by its operations, and heartily wish that in this present instance I could ascribe them to an unsound mental condition."

I had no answer for this ebullition of feeling, so walked on silently till our ways divided. As he turned towards home, I took the shortest route to my apartments. But before entering them I dined in the café below, so that it was eight o'clock at least before I mounted to my rooms.

A man was sitting on the stairs waiting for me. As I stooped to unlock my door, he made known his errand. He was an officer in plain clothes, and he came to tell me that I was wanted at the earliest possible moment at the District Attorney's office.

CHAPTER XXVI

FERRY LIGHTS

There could be but one reason for this message from the District Attorney. I had identified myself too closely with the Gillespie case not to have attracted the notice of the police. I was about to be called upon to explain; and, while I shrank from the task, I could not but acknowledge to myself that the time for such explanations had come; that the burden then weighing upon me was too heavy to be borne any longer unassisted.

But the explanations I have thus alluded to would cost me Hope. Never would she forget through whose instrumentality the man she loved had been betrayed to his doom.

It was now raining hard, and the chill which this gave to the atmosphere was sensibly felt by us both as we stepped out into the air. At the suggestion of the officer accompanying me, I had provided myself with a heavy overcoat. It stood me in good stead that night, much more so than I had any reason for anticipating when I donned it.

The ride down-town was hurried and without incident. I entered the District Attorney's office about nine o'clock, and found him in close conversation with Mr. Gryce. Both showed relief at seeing me. This did not add to my satisfaction, and when the detective rose and I noticed his composed aspect and the somewhat startling fact that the wrinkle which I had so long observed between his brows had entirely disappeared, I experienced a strange sensation of dread only to be accounted for by the delicate nature of the sympathy which bound me to Hope Meredith. For the moment I was Leighton Gillespie, conscious of guilt and quailing under the quiet eye of this old detective.

This sensation, odd and thrilling as it was, did not cease with the first sight of this man. It followed me with more or less insistence through the whole of this memorable night, occasioning me, I have no doubt, a more poignant anguish and a more intolerable share in the grief and suspense of the woman most affected than Leighton Gillespie himself would have felt or did feel when the whole power of the law was brought to bear upon him.

But these feelings, with all their sub-consciousness of another's suffering, did not interfere with my outward composure; and I may here remark in passing that I learned a lesson from this experience which has proved of great use to me in my profession. However true it may be that sudden shock reveals the hidden motions of the heart, it is also true that a man, if he is a man, may be the victim of the keenest internal struggle without abating a jot of his natural manner, or showing by look or gesture the wild contention raging within him. This I have learned, and I no longer gauge a man's internal sensations by his outward appearance.

The District Attorney was not slow in making me understand what he wanted of me.

After the necessary civilities had passed, he told me bluntly that he had heard of my visit to Mother Merry's and of the conversation I had held there with a young woman against whom a warrant of arrest had for some time been made out. As by this interview I had been rendered competent to identify her, would I be good enough to accompany the officers who were about to attempt her arrest? A failure in seizing the right girl would at this stage of the affair be fatal to the successful progress of the important matter at present engaging them.

What could I say? My position at the best required explanation, and any hesitation I might show towards aiding the police in their legitimate task, might easily be construed not only to my own disadvantage, but to that of the man in whose behalf I showed resistance. Indeed, there was nothing left for me but acquiescence, hard and uncongenial as I found it.

"I am at your service," I returned. "But, first, I should like to explain—"

"Pardon me," interposed the District Attorney. "Explanations will come later. Mr. Gryce says he has no time to lose, the woman being a very restless one and liable at any moment to flit. Her name is Mille-fleurs; or, rather, that is the name by which she is known on the police books. You have seen her, and have only to follow Mr. Gryce; he will explain the rest."

I bowed my acquiescence, and joined the old detective at the door.

"It will be a rough night," that venerable official remarked, with a keen glance at my outfit. And with just this hint as to what was before us, he stepped out into the street, where I hastily followed him.

We did not carry umbrellas, Mr. Gryce looking upon them as a useless encumbrance; and as I waited there in the wet while my companion exchanged some words with a man who had stepped up to him, I marvelled at the impassibility of this old man and the astonishing vigour he showed in face of what most young and able-bodied men would consider the disadvantages of the occasion. Short as was the whispered conference, it seemed to infuse fresh life into the rheumatic limbs I had frequently seen limping along in much more favourable weather, and it was with a gesture of decided satisfaction he now led the way to a cab I had already seen dimly outlined through the mist which now enveloped everything in sight.

"We shall have to cross the city," he announced, as he followed me inside. "It's a bad night and gives promise of being worse. But you are young, and I—well, I have been younger, but, young or old, have always managed so far to be in at the finish."

"It is the finish, then?" I ventured, with that sinking of the heart Leighton might have felt had he heard his own doom thus foreshadowed.

The old detective smoothed out the lap-robe he had drawn over his knees.

"There is reason to think so, unless some mistake or unforeseen misfortune robs us of success at the moment of expected triumph. Is your interest a friendly or a professional one? The affair is one which warrants either."

It was a question I was surely entitled to evade. But I had already decided to be frank in my explanations to the District Attorney, and why not with the man most in his confidence?

"I am a friend of Miss Meredith," said I; "in other words, her lawyer. She is more than a friend to the Gillespies, as her relationship demands. To serve her interests I have meddled more in this matter than was perhaps judicious. I was anxious to prove to her that her cousins' lives would bear scrutiny."

"I see, and discovered that one of them, at least, would not. Poor girl! she has my sympathy. You are without doubt a man we can rely on, no matter into what complexities our errand takes us?"

"I don't know; I have never undergone any great test. I am willing to assist you in the identification of this girl; but I would rather not be present at her arrest."

We were crossing Broadway. He looked out, gave one rapid glance up and down the busy street,—busy even at that hour and in the wet,—and quietly remarked:

"Or at his, I suppose?"

The jolting of the cab over the car-tracks struck my nerves as his question did my heart. To this day I never cross a street track in a carriage, but the double anguish of that moment comes back; also the mist of lights which dazzled down the long perspective as I cast a glance through the dripping windows.

"His?" I repeated, as soon as I could trust my voice.

"Yes, Leighton Gillespie's. We expect to take him to-night in her company," he added.

That last phrase startled me.

"You are going to take him in the presence of Mille-fleurs!" I exclaimed. "Why, I saw him an hour ago standing in his own hall in Fifth Avenue."

"No doubt, but if you have made a study of Mr. Gillespie's habits, you have learned that he is given to sudden sallies from his home. He will be found, I assure you, in the same house as Mille-fleurs. I hope we may make no mistakes in locating this house correctly. I hardly think we shall. The men I have chosen for the job are both keen and reliable; besides, for a gentleman of his antecedents, Mr. Gillespie shows a startling indifference to the result of his peculiar escapades. A strange man, Mr. Outhwaite."

"Very," I ejaculated abstractedly enough. My thoughts were with a possibility suggested by his words. Pursuing it, I said, "The letter I saw Mr. Gillespie read was from her, then? I noticed that it caused him great agitation, even from where I stood on the other side of the street."

The old detective smiled instinctively at my reckless betrayal of the part I had played in this scene, but made no reference to the fact itself, possibly because he was as well acquainted with my movements as I was myself. He only gave utterance to an easy-toned, "Exactly!" which seemed not only to settle this matter, but some others then inflaming my curiosity.

"We have been waiting a long time for some such communication to pass between them," he presently resumed, with a benevolent condescension, springing, perhaps, from our close contact in that jolting cab. "Otherwise, we should have taken him to-day, and in his own house. We have had great difficulty in holding the reporters back and even in keeping our own men quiet. It was desirable, you see, to take them together."

"And couldn't she be found? Wasn't she at Mother Merry's?"

"Not lately. No one answering to her description has shown up there for days. She seems to have fled from that place, alarmed, no doubt, by the interest shown in her by the young gentleman who got speech with her at the cost of a couple of silver dollars."

I began to note the corners as we passed them.

"Then we are not going to Mother Merry's?" I observed.

"No, we are not going to Mother Merry's."

"Yet we are not far from the docks," I remarked, as I caught transitory glimpses of the unmistakable green and red lights of the ferry-boats shining mistily on the left.

"No, our errand takes us in the region of her old haunts. I hope you feel no concern as to your safety?"

"Concern?"

"Oh, there's cause enough, or would be, if we were not in force. But our preparations have been made very carefully, and you can trust us to bring you out all right."

I signified my entire satisfaction. The prospect of physical struggle or some open adventure was welcome to me. My inner excitement would thus find vent.

"Do not bother about me," said I. "What I dread most is the possibility of meeting that unhappy woman's eye. Seeing me with you, she may think I have betrayed her. And perhaps I have; but it was done without intention. She did not strike me as a wicked woman."

"So much the less excuse for the man who has made her his accomplice," came in quiet rejoinder.

This ended our conversation for the time.

We were now making our way up-town through upper West Street. As I came to what I knew must be Canal Street from the cars that went jingling across our path, the difficulties of advance became more marked, and finally the cab stopped.

"What is going on here?" I asked, as carriage after carriage rolled into our course, till the street was blocked and we found it impossible to proceed.

"It's a Cunarder going out. The tide sets late to-night."

Here a coach, with a sweet-faced girl, drew up along-side us. I could see her happy smile, her air of busy interest, as she bent her head to catch a glimpse of the steamer upon which she was perhaps about to take her first voyage abroad. I could even hear her laugh. The sensation was poignant. Wrapt up in the thought of Hope, whom I had not forgotten for one moment during this wild ride, the sight of joy which might never again be hers came like a glimpse into another sphere, so far removed did I feel from everything bespeaking the ordinary interests of life, much less its extraordinary pleasures and anticipations.

Mr. Gryce in the meantime was fuming over the delay.

"We might better have come up — Street," he said. "Ah! that's better. We will arrive at our destination now in less than ten minutes."

We had passed the Cunarder's wharf, and were now rolling rapidly northward.

Suddenly the cab stopped.

"Again?" I cried.

Mr. Gryce replied by stepping out upon the sidewalk.

"We alight here," said he.

I rapidly followed him.

The rain dashing in my face blinded me for a moment; then I perceived that we were standing on a corner in front of a saloon, and that Mr. Gryce was talking very earnestly to two men who seemed to have sprung up from nowhere. When he had finished with what he had to say to them, he turned to me.

"Sorry, sir, but we shall have to walk the rest of the way. There are alleys to explore, and a cab attracts attention."

"It's all one to me," I muttered; and it was.

He turned east and I followed him. At the first crossing, a man glided into our wake; at the second, another. Soon there were three men sauntering behind us at a convenient distance apart. Each held a policeman's club under his coat; and walked as if the rain had no power to wet him. Suddenly I felt myself wheeled into an alley-way.

It was pouring now, and even the street lamps shone through a veil of mist, which made them all look like stars. The alley was dark, for there were no lamps there; only at the remote end a distant glimmer shone. It came from the murky panes of some shop or saloon.

Towards this light we moved.

Suddenly the figure of a man stepped out before us. It was too dark to see his face, but his voice had a familiar sound as he said:

"It's all right. He's there. I saw him go in a half-hour ago."

"Very good. My man, Sweetwater," explained Mr. Gryce, turning for an instant towards me; then, in hurried tones to the other, "Do you know on which floor he is to be found; and whether the man at the bar suspects what's up?"

"If he does, he's pretty quiet about it. All looks natural inside. But you can't tell what whispers have gone about. As for him, he's chosen his place with his usual indifference to consequences. He's in one of the attic rooms, sir, well back, and can be reached from the outside by means of a shed that slopes up almost to the window-ledge. If he wanted to escape, he could easily do so by a drop of only four feet. But I have left a man on watch there and our young gentleman would fall into arms that wouldn't let him go in a hurry. Will you come around that way? There's a light in the window and there's neither curtain nor shade to hinder a man's looking in. If you wish, I can crawl up on the roof I spoke of and take a peep at our doves before we venture upon disturbing them."

"It can do no harm," rejoined the older detective; "and if the girl is where she can be seen, this gentleman can go up afterwards and identify her. It will mean surer and quieter work than approaching them by the stairway. The house is full, I suppose?"

"Chuck." And with this characteristic word Sweetwater melted from before us as if he had been caught up in one of the swirls of wind and rain that ever and anon swept through the alley, dashing our faces with wet and making our feet unsteady on the slippery pavement.

I began to feel strange and unlike myself. The night, the storm, the uncongenial place, our more than uncongenial errand, were having their effect, lending to that dark entrance into one of the worst corners of our great city a sense of mysterious awe which has caused it to remain in my memory as something quite out of the ordinary experiences of life. It was not a long alley, and we soon reached the light I have mentioned. We could hear voices now, loud voices raised one moment in contention, the next in drunken cheer; and, thrilling through it all, a woman's tones singing some bewildering melody. It was not the voice of Mille-fleurs. I could never have mistaken that—but it was a young voice, and did not lack sweetness in the low notes. As I was listening to it, something flew flapping into my face. It was a piece of damp paper peeled from some billboard by a wandering gust and sent scurrying through the air. I tore it away from my eyes, drawing a deep breath like a person suddenly released from suffocation; but I shall not soon forget the effect of that cold slap in the face at the moment when my every nerve was on tension. Mr. Gryce, who had seen nothing,—it was hardly possible to see in the deluge which now swept down upon us,—gave me a pull which drew me from before the swinging door I was unconsciously making for, into a corner where I found myself more or less shielded from the wind if not from the rain. The alley had an L, and leading down from this L was a narrow passage, within which we now stood, surrounded by reeking walls and facing (whenever the fury of the storm abated sufficiently for us to look up) an opening into what might be called a labyrinth of back-yards. As I was bracing myself to meet all alarms, real or imaginary, associated with this noisome place, I beheld a sudden figure emerge from the opening and hastily approach us. It was Sweetwater again. He had just descended from his clamber over the roofs, where he seemed to be as much at home as a cat.

"Lucky that it rains so," he panted; "keeps the kids in. Otherwise some of us would have been spotted long ago. There are about fifty of them in this one house." Then I heard him whisper in the ear that was necessarily very near mine:

"It's all right up there. I can see his figure plainly. He's sitting with his back to the window, but there's no mistaking Leighton Gillespie. He's in dinner dress, just as he came from his own table in Fifth Avenue. The girl—"

"Well, what of the girl?"

"Is in one of her heavy sleeps. I could not see her face, only her hair, which hung all about her—"

"I would know her hair," I put in.

The two men drew a step aside and whispered together. Then Mr. Gryce came back, and, putting his mouth to my ear, asked if I had enough agility to mount the shed as Sweetwater had done. "He says the wood is slippery, but the climb up quite practicable for an agile man. He had no difficulty, and if you will catch hold of the window-casings as you go along—"

"Let me see the place," said I.

Sweetwater at once drew me down the passage into the open place in the rear. Here wind and storm had their will again, and for a moment I could neither hear nor see anything but a vast expanse of hollow darkness, lit here and there with misty lights, and reverberating with all sorts of sounds, among which the shrieking wind wailed longest and most furiously.

"Up there!" called a voice in my ear, and then I became aware of an arm pointing over my shoulder towards a dark incline running up over a flight of stairs, upon the lower step of which I had almost stumbled. "That's your road. Can you take it?"

Jamming my hat over my head, I looked up. A lighted square met my eyes in the blank side of the wall, against which this none too desirable road, as he called it, ran up.

"The window is wide open," said I.

"As you see," said he.

"I shall make a noise; he will hear me—"

"He didn't hear me—"

"That's no proof he won't hear me. But I forget the gale, and that sound—what is it?"

"Tin cans rattling; loose in some gutter, I suppose—"

"It is infernal." Then with sudden resolution—a resolution I hardly understand, for I certainly did not feel called upon to risk either self-respect or safety in this cause—I cried out: "I'll try for it; though it's long since I put my agility to the proof. But how am I to get onto the roof?"

For reply, Sweetwater uttered a low but peculiar call, and a shadow near by became a man.

"Lend your back to this gentleman," said he; and as I took advantage of the assistance thus afforded me and worked my way up onto the ledge over his head, he softly added:

"Catch hold of everything that offers, and be careful your feet don't slip. When you're up, give one look and come down. We will be on hand to catch you when you get to the edge of the roof."

The rain was dripping from my hat to such an extent that it nearly blinded me. I tore it off and flung it at their feet; then I started on my perilous climb.

It was a difficult one, but not so difficult as I had expected; and in two minutes I was under that open window. A tangle of ropes struck my head—clothes-lines, I suppose. Laying hold of them, I steadied myself before looking in. As I did so, a consciousness of my position made the moment a bewildering one. I thought of Hope and what her surprise would be could she see me in my present situation on the peak of this sloping roof, thirty feet above the ground. Hope! the word brought resolution also. I would look in upon this man with eyes schooled to their duty, but unsharpened by hate. If there was forbearance due him, I would try and exercise that forbearance, remembering always that he was an object of affection to the woman I loved.

Was this why I, for the first time, saw him as he may have looked to her and probably did? He was seated in such a way that only his profile was visible beyond the casing around which I peered. But that profile struck me forcibly, and, forgetting my errand, I allowed myself a moment's study of the face I had never rightly seen till then.

I was astonished at the result; astonished at the effect it had upon me. Leighton Gillespie seen with his brothers was not the Leighton Gillespie I looked upon now. Beheld thus by himself he was an impressive figure. Lacking George's height and Alfred's regularity of feature he was apt to be regarded by superficial or prejudiced observers as the one plain man in an exceptionally handsome family. But I saw now that this was not so. He had attractions of his own which could bear comparison with those of most other men; and, relieved from too close comparison with these two conspicuous personalities, the traits of his dark, melancholy countenance came out, and in the regard of his sad and preoccupied eye was felt a charm which might have ripened into fascination had no dark secret beclouded their depths or interfered with the natural expression of feelings that must once have been both natural and spontaneous. Had he been more fortunate in his tastes or more able to put restraint upon his passions, he might, with that eye and smile, have been one of those men whose influence baffles the insight of the psychologist, and from whose magnetic personality spring innumerable benefits to those of his day and generation.

All this was forcibly impressed upon me as I knelt in the pouring rain, looking in upon his face at this momentous crisis of his life, and, had I known it, of my own also.

I had feared to advance my head too far lest he should be attracted by the movement and so detect my presence at the window. Consequently I had seen as yet nothing of Mille-fleurs, and but little of the room. This would not do, and I was just preparing to extend my view further when the face I was watching sank forward out of sight and a groan came to my ears so thrilling and heartbroken that my own heart stopped beating in my bewilderment and surprise. From whose lips had this expression of anguish sprung? From hers? It had not sounded like a woman's voice. Could it be—

Again! What could it—did it, mean? Had Leighton Gillespie received some warning of the fate which at this moment hung over him, and was it his voice I heard lifted in these heartbroken accents? I was willing to risk everything to see. Thrusting my head forward, I looked boldly into the room, and momentary as the glance was, or seemed to be, I have never forgotten the dolorous and awe-compelling picture upon which it fell.

By the light of a guttering candle, whose blowing flame threatened every minute to go out, I saw a wretched pallet drawn up against a dirty and mouldering wall. On this pallet lay a woman, with just a ragged counterpane covering limbs I had so lately seen moving in rhythmical measure. Her hair—those bewildering curls, the like of which I had never before seen and would never see again, lay about her wherever those faded rags failed to reach. It hid her arms, it framed her temples, and, flowing away, coiled in great masses over the side of that pallet and onto the floor it seemed to richen with its wealth. But it did not hide her face. Either she had moved or her locks had been drawn aside since Sweetwater crouched in my place, for now her features were plainly visible and in those features I had no difficulty in recognising—Mille-fleurs.

Beside her, and drawn up so close that the rich broadcloth of his sleeve brushed the foul bed and lost itself among those overflowing curls, sat Leighton Gillespie, with his head in his hands, weeping as a man weeps but once in a lifetime.

There was no mistaking that grief. Real heart agony cannot be simulated; and, touched with awe for what I could not understand, I was about to slip away from my post, when he gave an impetuous start, roused himself, and glanced in sudden anger towards a door set in the wall directly opposite me. Another instant he was on his feet, with his hands held out across the prostrate figure before him, in an attitude of jealous love such as I have never seen equalled. What had he seen or heard? The door was closed, yet he seemed to fear intrusion. Whose? Not mine, for his eyes did not turn towards the window, but remained fixed upon this door. Had the sound of steps reached him from the hall? Probably, for, as I watched the door with him, I beheld the knob turn, then the door itself open, slowly at first, then more quickly, till it suddenly fell back, disclosing the quiet form and composed countenance of the old detective I had left behind me in the dark corner of the passage at the side of the house.

At the same instant a voice whispered from over my shoulder into my ear:

"Lie still; or slip silently down to the officers stationed below. You were so long that Mr. Gryce became impatient."

Up till then I had supposed that only a moment had elapsed since I first looked in.

"I will stay," I whispered back. I saw that Leighton was about to speak.

"Who are you?" I heard him demand of the intruder, in a passion so great he failed to note the identity of the man he thus accosted. "I have a right to this room. I have paid for it—Ah!" He had just recognised the detective.

With a quick turn he drew the coverlet over the face he seemed to guard so jealously, then with an air of command, which was at once solemn and peremptory, he pointed to the hat which naturally rested on Mr. Gryce's head, and said:

"Respect for the dead! You will uncover, Mr. Gryce."

"The dead?" repeated the astonished detective, striding hurriedly into the room. "The dead? Is this girl dead?"

But his doubt, if doubt it were, disappeared before the look with which Leighton Gillespie regarded him.

"Dead!" that gentleman declared. Then as Mr. Gryce instinctively bared his head, this strange, this incomprehensible man advanced a step, and in tones inconceivably touching and dignified, added this short sentence:

"To respect her is to respect me; this woman is my wife."

CHAPTER XXVIII

BY THE LIGHT OF A GUTTERING CANDLE

My amazement was unaffected, and so overwhelming I hardly understood myself. His wife, Mille-fleurs! Alas, then, for Hope, who, in her unthinking if generous love for this man, was prepared for any other grief than this! Yet why "alas"? Had she not told me that her greatest wish, her supreme desire, was to see his character restored to its old standing in her eyes, and had he not at this moment cleared himself of the one sin her womanly heart would find it hardest to pardon? The cry of "poor Hope!" with which my heart was charged changed to "happy Hope," and my composure, which had been sadly shaken, was slowly returning, when the insoluable mystery of the situation absorbed me again, and I glanced at Mr. Gryce to see how he had been affected by Mr. Gillespie's announcement.

This aged detective, who, when I last looked his way, was standing alone in the doorway, now had Sweetwater at his side,—that agile young man having bounded into the room before the words which had made so great a change in the situation had fully left Mr. Gillespie's lips; and the contrast of expression as seen in the two faces was noticeable. Sweetwater, young in experience, young in feeling, reflected in look and attitude the sensations of awakening sympathy and interest with which I own my own breast was full, while the older detective, with characteristic prudence, withheld his judgment, and, consequently, his sympathy, for the explanations which such an avowal from such a man certainly demanded.

Indeed, the situation might very naturally suggest to one so accustomed to the seamy side of human nature, that this sudden demise of an inconvenient witness chimed in too opportunely with the need of the man he had come there to arrest, for it to be viewed without suspicion.

There was, however, only a tinge of this feeling in his voice as he quietly remarked:

"I thought you buried your wife five years ago in Cornwall."

"And I thought so also," was Leighton Gillespie's quiet reply. "For many, many wretched weeks and months I believed this in common with all my friends. Then—but it is a long story, Mr. Gryce. Do you require me to relate it now and here?"

The reverence with which he allowed his hand to touch rather than fall on the breast he had so carefully covered from our curious gaze spoke volumes. At the sight of this simple action, both men bent their heads. I doubt if he noticed it. A stray lock which had escaped from the coverlet and now hung curling and glittering over the straw which protruded from the wretched pallet, had attracted his eye. Lifting it with a lingering touch, he put it softly out of sight; then he quietly said:

"I would like to have one fact made known to the public. My father was ignorant to the last that it was a stranger and not my wife we buried in Cornwall. There were reasons which made it difficult for me to tell him that Mrs. Gillespie still lived; and while I make no excuses for the silence I maintained towards him on this subject, I acknowledge that to it are due my present position and the misery I am now under of seeing the darling of my heart die in an attic where I would not house a dog."

The accents of heartfelt sorrow are not to be mistaken. The air of severity with which Mr. Gryce had hitherto surveyed this supposed criminal softened into a look more in keeping with his native benevolence, but he had no reply ready, and the silence became painful. Indeed, the situation was not an easy one for even so experienced a man as Mr. Gryce to handle, and, noting his embarrassment, I bounded into the room and took my place at his side, much as Sweetwater had done.

Mr. Gillespie scarcely remarked this new inroad upon his privacy. He doubtless took me for another police-officer, and as such not to be noted or counted. But the detectives showed some surprise at my intrusion, which seeing, I turned to Mr. Gryce and said:

"If you will excuse my presumption I should like to speak to Mr. Gillespie."

The latter started, possibly at my tone, and, wheeling about, gazed at my bare head and drenched figure with sharp curiosity in which a growing recognition soon became visible.

I at once bowed.

"You remember me," I suggested. "I am Mr. Outhwaite. If you will pardon my method of entrance and the proof which it gives of my connection with these men, I should like to offer you my assistance at this crisis. Mr. Gryce evidently wishes some conversation with you, which you rightly hesitate to accord him in a place made sacred by the presence of your dead wife. If you will have confidence in me, I will watch this room while you go below. No one shall approach the bed and no one shall enter the room, if Mr. Gryce will leave a guard at the door. Will you accept this service? It is sincerely tendered."

He stood perplexed, eyeing me with mingled doubt and astonishment; then, turning with an inexpressible look of longing towards the one object of his care, he cried:

"You do not understand or you would not ask me to leave her, not for a moment. I have not had her so near me, so near my hand, so near my heart, these many minutes in years. She cannot rise and run away from me now. She does not even wish to. This is a happiness to me you cannot appreciate, a happiness I cannot endure seeing cut short. Leave me, then, I pray, and come again when she has been laid in her grave. You will find me ready to receive you, ready to explain—"

"You ask the impossible," interrupted Mr. Gryce. "Some explanations will not bide the convenience of even so recent a mourner as yourself. If you do not wish to be taken immediately from this place, you will make some few things clear to us. What has this woman had to do with your father's death?"

"Nothing."

The fire with which Leighton Gillespie uttered this word made us both start. Aghast at what struck me as a direct falsehood, I instinctively opened my lips. But Mr. Gryce made me an imperceptible gesture, and I refrained from carrying out my inconsiderate impulse.

"I see," continued the unhappy man, "that suspicions which I had supposed confined to my brothers and myself have involved my innocent wife. This is more than I can bear. I will at once make known to you my miserable story."

Mr. Gryce drew up a chair and sat down. As there was no other in the room we knew what that meant. The damp air was beginning to tell upon the rheumatic old man. Attention being thus called to the open window, Sweetwater moved over and closed it. Never shall I forget the look which Leighton Gillespie cast towards the bed as that broken and ill-fitting sash came rattling down.

"See if the hall is clear," said Mr. Gryce.

The young detective crossed to the door. As he opened it and looked out, a gust of noisy laughter rose from below, mingled with the shrill sound of a woman's singing, the same, doubtless, which we had previously heard in front. These tones, heard amid brawl and shouting, seemed to pierce Mr. Gillespie to the heart. Mr. Gryce, who saw everything, motioned to Sweetwater to close the door as he had the window. Sweetwater complied by shutting himself out. This was an act of self-denial which I felt called upon to emulate.

"Shall I join Mr. Sweetwater?" I asked.

It was Mr. Gillespie who replied:

"No. I wish more than one listener; let the lawyer stay."

I was only too happy to remain. Wet as I was, I felt anxious to hear what this man so singled out by Hope had to say in explanation of his relations to the wretched woman he now acknowledged to be his wife.

He seemed in haste to make them.

"Seven years ago this fall," he began, "I met this woman, then a girl."

"Wait!" put in Mr. Gryce; "there is a point which must first be settled." And, advancing to the cot guarded so jealously by the man before him, he laid his hand upon the coverlet. "You will allow me," he said firmly, as with a gentle enough touch he drew it softly aside.

"How came this woman—pardon me, how came Mrs. Gillespie to die thus suddenly?"

The unhappy husband, after his first recoil of outraged feeling, forced himself into a recognition of the detective's rights, and, with apparent resignation, rejoined:

"I should have come to that in time. She died, as you can readily perceive, from exposure. Driven from Mother Merry's miserable quarters by some terror for which, perhaps, she had no name, she wandered in and out among the docks for two wretched days and nights, often dragging her feet through the ooze of the river, so that her garments were never dry and are not so yet. At last she came here, where once before she had found shelter in a biting storm. Here! But it is a better place than the wharves, and I am glad God guided her to even so poor a refuge. She was raving with fever when she came straggling into the room below. But after the warmth struck her and she had tasted something, she came to herself again, and then—and then she sent for me."

He paused. I did not yet understand him or the circumstances which made this situation possible, but a strange reverence began to mingle with my wonder,—not for the man—I could not feel that yet; but for a love which could infuse such feeling into the lightest allusion he made to this beloved, if wretched waif.

"There was a doctor here when I came," he speedily continued. "You can find him;—he will tell no different tale from mine—but no doctor could help her after those nights of bitter cold and exposure, and I paid him to leave me alone with her; and she died in my arms. May I tell you why this was everything to me? Why, the happiness of having received her last sigh is so great, that I have no room for resentment against you for this intrusion, and hardly feel the shame of being found in this place, with my dead darling lying in her miserable rags on this hideous pallet!"

"You may tell us," assented Mr. Gryce, replacing the coverlet over the face upon which was fast settling that look of peace which is Death's last gift to the living.

Mr. Gillespie's tone grew deeper; it could hardly have grown more tender or more solemn.

"I loved this woman. She was young when I first saw her. So was I. There were no haggard lines about her dancing eyes and laughing lips then. She was a vision of—well, I will not say beauty; she was never beautiful—but of—I cannot tell you what; I can only say that my life began on that day, not to end till she died, a half-hour ago.

"I married her. She was not a woman to take into my father's house; perhaps not into any family circle. The stage was her home, the stage from which I took her; but I did not know this; I simply knew that she was wild in spirit, and unused to household ways and social restrictions. But had I understood her then as I do now, I doubt if I would have acted any differently. I was headstrong in those days and quite reckless enough to grasp at what I felt to be my own, even if aware it would fall to nothing in my frenzied clutch.

"I took her into my father's family. I took this wild bird out of its native air, and shut it up behind the strict bars of a conventional household. One promise only I exacted from her as the price of this gracious act on my part. She was never under any pretext, not even in the event of my death, to return to the stage. Poor child! she has kept that promise. Perhaps it is all she has kept: kept it, though hungry; kept it when the wild craving for morphine tore at her breast and brain and she could have got the drug for one strain from her marvellous voice; kept it, though her veins burned with longing for the movement that was her life, and the weights on her tongue lay heavy on her heart, which beat truly only while she was dancing or singing. It was her dancing and singing which had won my heart; or, rather, the woman when dancing and singing; yet I cut her off from these natural expressions of the turbulent joy springing from her exuberant nature, and expected her to be satisfied with my love and the routine of a well-regulated household. This was my folly; a folly born of the delight I took in her simple presence. I thought that she loved me as I did her, and found in love's madness the recompense for what she had laid aside. But I had not read her nature. No man could fill her heart as she filled mine. She was a genius,—an untamable one,—and the restiveness of her temperament made demands which could only find relief in spontaneous song or rhythmic movement.

"My father, who loved quiet women—women like my mother, whose force lay hidden in such sweetness that she shines with almost a saint's glory in our memory—could not understand my wife's temperament; and, consequently, could not show even common patience towards her. He was not harsh in his treatment of her, but he failed to give her credit for so much as wishing to conform to his ways and the habits of the people she must meet in our house. When he came upon her, stealthily posing before our long mirror in the drawing-room, or caught floating down the stairs a faint echo of her magical voice in one of the tragic strains she best loved to sing, he showed such open shrinking and distaste that she flew for comfort to the one resource capable of undermining for me all hope of a better future. I allude to her use of morphine.

"She had taken it before our marriage, but the fact was kept from me. When I awoke to a realisation of the horror menacing my happiness, I devoted time, strength, and every means I then knew, to win her from this practice. But I only partially succeeded. She did not realise the harmfulness of this habit and could not be made to. Eluding my vigilance, she resorted more and more to the drug I could never succeed in keeping out of her grasp, and it fell to me to stand in the breach thus made and keep the knowledge of this crowning humiliation from my father and brothers.

"Meanwhile my father, who was strictness itself in all matters of propriety, insisted upon her sitting opposite him at the table and comporting herself in every way as the lady of the house. Just because he so dreaded comment and had so much pride in his own social standing and that of his sons, he kept her continually on view and carried her to parties and balls, thinking that his prestige would cause recognition to be given her by his friends. And it did—but grudgingly! Admired for what she was not, she was scorned for what she was. I have seen her petted by some would-be society fine lady till my blood boiled, then marked the smile of supercilious sarcasm which would be thrown back upon her when her beautiful shoulders were turned. Yet I had hopes, strong hopes of better days after the first strangeness of the new life should have worn away and her good impulses had had time to develop into motive powers for kind actions. But it was not to be; never was to be. The fiend whose power I had set myself to combat was far stronger than any force I could bring against him. She grew worse—appeared once in public as she never before had appeared outside her own room, and my father, who was with her, never attempted to hold up his head again in his former unmoved fashion. Claire, who came to us later, had no power to hold her mother back, and while she was still an infant, the inevitable occurred—my wife ran away from us.

"It was the first overwhelming shock my hitherto unfailing faith had had to sustain. She had slipped away at nightfall without money and almost without farewell. The merest note left on the piano in our little room on the third floor told me she had tried to be happy in a domestic life, but had failed; and begged me not to seek her, for she was stifling for air and freedom.

"And I have no doubt she was. Seeing, since, where she has found pleasure, and under what conditions the old gay smile has revisited her lips, I have no doubt that the very luxury we prized was oppressive to her. But then I only thought of the dangers and privations she must encounter away from my protection; and, confiding to no one the calamity which had befallen me, I rushed from the house and sought her in every place which suggested itself to me as a possible refuge. It was a frenzied search, and ended in my coming upon her, ten days after her disappearance, in a plain but decent lodging-house. Her money was gone, and she lay in that heavy sleep which has no such hallowing effect upon the beauty as this we look upon now.

"Some men's love would have sickened and failed them at this degrading sight. But though a change took place in the feeling which had held me in an entranced state ever since my marriage, it was a change which deepened, rather than deadened, the affection with which I regarded her. From a creature whose untold charm bewitched and bewildered me, she became to me a sacred charge for which I was responsible to God and man; and while she still lay there and I stood in a maze of misery before her, I vowed that, come what would, I would remain true to her and by means of this faith and through the unfailing patience it would call forth, make what effort I could to stay her on the brink of that precipice she seemed doomed to perish by.

"But I was to be tried in ways I had little foreseen. She was glad to see me when she woke, and readily consented to return to her home and her child. But in two months she was off again, and this time I did not find her so easily. When I did, she was in such a hopeless condition of mental and moral degradation that I took her to a sanitarium, where I had every reason to expect that a proper secrecy would be maintained as to her real complaint and unhappy condition. For my pride was still a torment to me, and an open rupture with my father too undesirable for me to risk a revelation of the true extent of the vagaries indulged in by his unwelcome daughter-in-law. Her escapades, serious as they were, had affected him but little. For I had so closely followed her in her sudden flittings that we were looked upon as having left home together on some hurried tour or at the call of some thoughtless impulse. He had believed us out of town, while I was engaged in hunting the city through for her.

"But after a week spent in the sanitarium, I perceived by the looks I encountered, on every side, that my secret was discovered; and was thus in a measure prepared when the door of my room opened one day upon the stern figure of my father. He had heard the true cause of my wife's condition, and a stormy scene was before me.

"It was then that I regretted that my early opportunities had been slighted, and that, instead of being independent of his bounty, I was not considered capable of earning my own living. Had my home been one of my own making, I might have stood up and faced him at that hour with a resolution to hold by my wife, which in itself might have ensured his respect. But I was tied hand and tongue by the realisation of all I owed him, was owing him, and was likely to owe him to the end of my days. I was not master of my own life; how, then, could I propose to be the master of another's?

"My father, whose favourite I had never been, could not be expected to know what was passing in my heart; but he was not without a realisation of what he might find in the adjoining room, and, casting a glance that way, he asked coldly:

"'Is she—Mrs. Gillespie—(he never called her by her given name) awake?'

"No question could have pierced my heart more poignantly. It was not the hour for sleep, and the use of the word had intention in it. But I subdued all signs of distress, and, calling her by name, bade her come out and greet father; after which I stood breathless, waiting for her appearance, conscious that it might be a smiling one, and equally that it might be—I dared not think what. She was not always to be depended upon.

"She did not appear at once. 'Sit down, father,' I begged. 'She may be dressing.'

"And she was. In a minute or two, as we stood watching, she threw open the door, and in an instant I saw that whatever hope I may have cherished of her creating a good impression in her partially recovered state, was an ill-founded one. She was not in one of her depressed moods, but, what was worse, perhaps, in one of her ecstatic ones. All her genius, and she had much, had taken fire under some impulse of her erratic brain, and she came into the room prepared to conquer in the only way she knew how. Still young, still beautiful in her own way, which was that of no other woman, she glided into our presence in one rapturous whirl, a scarf floating from her neck, and a wreath of wild vine about her head. I rushed to prevent her, but it was too late. She would dance, and she did, while my father, who had never seen her in this glowing state, drew me aside and watched with hard eyes, while she swayed and dipped and palpitated in what would have been a glorious ebullition of pure delight, had she not been my wife, and the man at my side as cold to her charm as the dew which stood out on my wretched forehead. When I could bear no more, I flung my arms about her and she stopped, panting and frightened, like a bird caught in full flight. 'Sing,' I whispered to her; 'sing that air from Ænone'. I thought the tragic pathos of her tones might make her dancing forgotten. And they did in a way. My father had never listened to any such dramatic rendering of a simple song before, and I saw that he was subdued by the feelings it awakened. But I gathered no hope from this. He had too little liking for public exhibitions of this kind on the part of women, for him to be affected long by any singing which was not that of the boudoir; and when, her first ebullition passed, she began to droop under the heavy reaction which inevitably followed these impulsive performances, I drew her into the other room, and shut the door. Then I came back and faced him.

"He was standing in the window of the large but unlovely room, drumming restlessly on the panes before him. As the light struck his head it brought to view the silver rapidly making its way through the dark locks he had been accustomed to pride himself upon, and a pang struck me at this sight, which made me quite dumb for the instant. I felt as if I, and not she, had been dancing over his heart. Then my ever-present thought of the woman I had sworn to cherish returned and held me steady while he said:

"'It is well that I have seen your wife once when the full spell was upon her. Now I know what has come into the Gillespie family. Leighton, do you love this woman?'

"'Enough to bear your condemnation if you choose to condemn us,' I assured him.

"'Then take her away out of my sight and from the possible sight of my growing grandchild. A dancing menad can be no mother to Claire.'

"'I will take her away,' I promised him. 'When this place has done all for her it can, I will carry her where she can offend no one but strangers.'

"'I would suggest an asylum,' he muttered. It was the only unjust thing I ever knew him to propose.

"'She is not insane,' I objected.

"'She is not sane,' he rejoined. 'No opium-eater is. But I will not force your conscience; only—let me never again see her in our home in Fifth Avenue. You will always be welcome.'

"I could not retort that I would enter no house from which she was thus peremptorily excluded. The house in Fifth Avenue was my home, the home of my child; and about it clustered every dear association of my heart save those connected with my unhappy love.

"'A man who marries for a whim must expect unpleasant results,' my father resumed. 'You shall have what money you need for her establishment elsewhere; but this hemisphere is too narrow to harbour both her and myself. Go to Europe, Leighton; there is more room there for your wife to dance in.'

"And I meant to follow this suggestion, but her health was not good enough for me to risk a voyage at this juncture, and we drifted West and put up at a place called Mountain Springs. It was during our stay there, that, so far as the world is concerned, the story of my married life ended. But for me it had only begun. The facts regarding my wife and her connection with that great catastrophe which robbed more than one household of wife and mother differed much in reality from those reported to the world and accepted by my own family. She did not perish in that wreck, though I thought she had, and mourned her loss for many months. She had merely taken advantage of the circumstances to effect another escape. How, I will endeavour to relate, hard as it is to disclose the failings of one so dear to me.

"My wife, whose natural longings had been modified rather than extinguished by her experiences at the sanitarium, soon awakened to the old sense of restraint and a desire to enjoy again the irresponsibilities of her early Bohemian life. But having gained wisdom by her past experiences, she allowed no expression of her feelings to escape her; and, relying on the effect produced upon me by her apparent content, merely asked the privilege of enjoying the sports indulged in by the other boarders. Fearing to cross her too much, I gave her all possible liberty, but when she begged to go on a certain excursion— the excursion which ended so disastrously for all concerned—I felt forced to refuse her, for I had made an arrangement that day which would prevent me from accompanying her. However, after repeated solicitation, I yielded to her importunities and gave her my consent, at which she showed much joy, and lavished many expressions of fondness upon me. Had my suspicions not been lulled by the undisturbed peacefulness of the last few months, these open demonstrations of affection might have occasioned me some alarm, for they were not without a suggestion of remorse. But I mistrusted nothing; I was too happy, and when I parted from her it was with the full intention of sacrificing for her pleasure the first real business engagement I had ever entered upon. But I did not carry out this impulse; I merely made arrangements for the train to stop for me at the little station on the mountains where my affairs led me. But I did not confide this plan to her till I was upon the point of leaving. Then I told her she might look for me on the train immediately after passing Buckley, and while I wondered at the way she received my words, I thought the embarrassment she showed was due to surprise. Alas! it sprang from much deeper sources. She had planned to leave me again, this time forever; and, baffled as she thought in the attempt, she succumbed for a little while to despair. Then her fertile brain suggested an expedient. Two trains left Mountain Springs that morning, one north and one south. She would take the southern train, and lest she should be prematurely discovered in her flight and so be followed before she had found a refuge, she prevailed upon a girl over whom she had some influence, to exchange garments with her and take her place among the excursionists. She little dreamed what lay before those excursionists. As little did I realise that it was in behalf of a stranger I entered upon that mad chase after the runaway cars I had seen slip from the engine and go crashing down towards the train on which I believed my wife to be. I knew those cars to be loaded with dynamite, for it was in connection with this fact I had come to this place, and the thought that they were destined to prove the destruction of the life I so much prized maddened me to such an extent that it was a mere matter of instinct for me to leap upon the engine I saw bounding to her rescue. Had time been given me to think, I might not have shown such temerity, for I knew nothing of a fireman's duties or what would be expected of me by the engineer. But I did not pause to think; I only stood ready to hazard my life for the woman I loved,—the woman whom I believed to be on the train I even then could see advancing up the valley. Of that ride, its swirl and whirlwind rush, I remember little; every thought, every fear, was engrossed in the one question, How were we to save that train? But two methods suggested themselves to me in my ignorance and isolation from the brave engineer. Either we must overtake the cars and by coupling to them stay their downward rush to the main track below—a trick I did not understand—or we must crush so fiercely into them as to explode the dynamite with which they were loaded before they had a chance to collide with the advancing train. That the latter catastrophe did not happen was not owing to any precaution on my part, for I do not remember that I had the least dread of personal destruction. As I have just said, my one thought, my only thought in that dizzy descent, was to save her. And I failed to do it; or so I had reason to think. As you remember, all our efforts were in vain; the unspeakable occurred, and wreck, death, and disaster met my eyes when, after a period of blank darkness, I rose from the ground where I had been hurled by the force of that dynamite explosion. Amid this wreck, in face of this death, I plunged in my search for her, and, as I believed, found her. A loving husband cannot be deceived in his wife's clothes, and the fragments I handled told their tale, as I thought, only too well. But, as you now know, it was not my wife who wore these clothes, though we buried her as such, and I mourned my lost love as no one who has not fixed his whole heart upon one object can possibly understand.

"My father, whose relief at this release can be readily imagined, endeavoured to calm my grief, not by sympathy, for that he could not feel, but by an unvarying kindness which assured me that, now that this obstacle to a right understanding between us had been removed, I might hope for the establishment of more cordial relations between us. I was older now, and he more considerate of my many uncongenial ways and habits; besides, Claire made a tender bond between us, and with one of her baby smiles healed many a breach that might otherwise have separated us.

"I began to be content, when, having some business in a strange quarter of the city, I chanced to walk down East Fourteenth Street. It was a holiday of some kind and there had been a procession. The stir in the streets was just what usually follows the breaking up of long lines of people. But this did not disturb me. Claire had been unusually engaging that morning, and I was just rejoicing in the memory of her innocent prattle, when the band in the far distance broke out into a merry strain, and I saw on the sidewalk before me a cluster of people separate into a sort of ring, in the middle of which a woman stood poised with swaying arms, so like the image that was day by day receding farther and farther into the deep recesses of my memory, that a species of faintness came over me and I drew back, sick and half-blinded, directly in the path of the people pressing in my rear. This caused me to receive a push from behind which effectually roused me and gave me strength to look again at one who could recall my lost Mille-fleurs. I expected—how could I expect anything else?—to be met by a strange face and an unknown smile. But it was her face, her smile; and the figure, clad in such clothes as I had never, even in my worst dreams, associated with the woman to whom I had given my name, was hers. Had God made two such women? Two with such eyes, such hair, such instincts, and such genius? Was this a sister of Mille-fleurs; a twin of my lost darling, of whose existence I had never heard? God grant not! I had buried Mille-fleurs, and with her, memories which this creature would only bring back to the destruction of my peace. I dared not give way for one instant to the thought that this likeness was anything but a passing illusion which the next moment would dispel. I dared not for my life. And yet I stood staring; hearing and not hearing the shouts of wild applause rising around me, and was looking, yes, looking directly into her eyes, when they suddenly turned my way in startled recognition. It was Mille-fleurs! Mille-fleurs! The woman I had buried was a stranger, and she who was making pastime for the passing crowd was my wife!

"I made no scene. I accepted the fact as we accept any unforeseen catastrophe that comes upon us unawares, tearing up our peaceful present and making a chaos of the future. As she was still dancing, though fitfully and with curious breaks, I stopped her by my steady look and held her so, till the crowd had melted away sufficiently for me to take her by the hand and lead her under the cover of the first small shop we came to. Then I questioned her closely, and, when I understood all, asked her if she would go with me and be clothed and fed. She answered with a startled look. 'I cannot!' she cried, and wearily drooped her head. 'I am not worthy.'

"God knows what passed through my mind then. I stood there in the wretchedness of this low shop, beside a counter from which the smell of stale tobacco rose in nauseous fumes, together with the sickening smell of partially decayed fruits—a flower in my button-hole (put there by little Claire), and before me this woman, loved as few of earth's best and worthiest have been, telling me with trembling lips what explained her rags, the degradation which had fallen on her beauty, and the whole pitiable downfall of a womanhood which once struck my heart as ideal and worthy of a man's unselfish worship.

"Drawing the flower from my button-hole, I crushed it in my hand. If I could have donned the clothes of some of the men lolling about us in greedy curiosity, I would have done so at that moment, if only the contrast between our outer selves might have been less apparent. But this was impossible, and I could only stand in silence in face of this wreck of bygone delights, and in one moment and under the gaze of a dozen pairs of eyes peering from behind the counter and gaping in at the doorway, live down my bitter humiliation at this untoward resurrection of a love I had learned to rejoice in as buried. For this was no wretched waif of the streets I could pity and leave. This was my wife, the mother of my child; the woman whom I had once vowed to hold in honour to the end, and to succour, no matter what her need or to what degradation she might come. Besides, there was an appeal in her drooping attitude and quivering mouth which touched my heart in spite of my judgment. I felt her misery as I had never felt my own; a misery all the more pronounced because of the joy so openly preceding it; and, feeling a fresh thrill in the old cord of union that had made our hearts one, I quietly asked her if she had lost all love for me. She gave me one quick look; and I saw her eye quicken as she softly faltered, 'No. Only,' she made haste to add, 'I cannot live in big houses under the eyes of people who think my ways odd and wrong. If you take me back to him I cannot help going wrong again. But I would like something pretty to wear and something good to eat.'

"I took her to an East Side hotel. I bought her clothes and gave her food, over which she laughed like a child. Then I told her what I meant to do for her. I would buy her a home in a pretty country place, where she need not fear intruding eyes. There she should live with some woman I could trust and who would be kind to her. A piano, music, flowers, books—she should have all, and if, in the course of time, she came to wish it, I would bring our child to see her. Did she think she could be contented in a home like this? Wouldn't it be better than the cold and squalor of the streets and these wild dances before unsympathetic eyes?

"She answered with a burst of affection which was real enough at the time; then asked if I was going to let my father know she was living. This brought to light the spectre which had stood over against us ever since I first recognised her as the woman I had sworn to love and cherish. Could I tell my father? Could I bring down again upon myself the old coldness, the old distrust, the old sense of a division that was gall to me because of the reverence and love I naturally felt for him?

"I could not; I recognised the cowardice of it, but I could not. I was ready to give her succour; I was ready to devote time, money, and care to her establishment and well-being; I could deny myself the pleasures and pursuits natural to men of my age, and even the uninterrupted enjoyment of the home I had come to prize, but I could not tell my father that the wild-eyed creature he was forcing himself to forget, still lived, and might any day bring down fresh humiliation upon him.

"She saw my doubt and smiled as in the early days of her untrammelled youth.

"'Better so,' she cried; 'then if I fail to be good it will not so much matter. And I may fail; it is in my blood, Leighton; in my unfortunate Bohemian blood. Oh, why did you ever care for me?'

"Such gusts of feeling and regret over the havoc she had caused were common to her. They made it impossible for me to hope in her ultimate restoration to respectability and a quiet life. But, alas! they were but gusts, and after a few months of peaceful harbourage in the rose-covered cottage I found for her, she fled from me again and was lost for years. But I never ceased searching for her. The unrest of knowing she was restless under the roof I had provided for her was nothing to the restlessness of not knowing where she was and in what misery and under what deprivation she was pining away in the dark holes where alone she could find refuge. I have sat hours under my father's eye, talking of stocks and bonds and railway shares, while my every thought and feeling were with her whom in my fancy I saw wandering from river to river, in dark nights and in cold;—rain on the pavements or slush in the streets,—drawing up to lighted doors for warmth or hiding her brown head with its flying curls under sheds a dog might be glad to fly from.

"It has happened to me often to be in the presence of women, at church or concert or festival, and with their eyes on my face and the perfume of their presence floating about me, to behold in my mind's perspective a solitary figure poised on the edge of some dock, in whose lifted arms and upstrained countenance I read despair, the despair that leads to death; and, forgetting where I was and to whom my words were due, have rushed out to do—what? Wander those down-town streets and the bleak places I had seen in my fancy, in the hope of coming once again upon the being who, unaccountably to myself, still held the cord whose other end was bound indissolubly to my heart. What wonder that I was looked upon as eccentric, moody, strange, or that my father, who naturally explained these freaks according to his own lights, showed displeasure at my unaccountable whims? Yet I went on with my search, and finally the day arrived when my perseverance was rewarded and I came upon her once again.

"She was in a low dance-hall, but she was not dancing. She was simply gazing at another woman attempting those dizzy whirls which, under the sway of her own genius, had once attracted the applause of a different crowd from this. There was infinite longing in her eyes, mixed with the sadness which will sometimes creep over those who are homeless through their own choice. When she saw me, and this was perhaps sooner than was best for either herself or me, I saw the old look of terror rise in her eyes, but mingled with it was a certain recognition of my faithfulness and self-forgetful care for her which melted the ice about my heart and reawakened the old hope for her. But she did not follow me when I beckoned her out; nor could I induce her to do so without risking a scene which would necessarily attract all eyes to us. But she promised, if I gave her money, to return the next day to the little house in New Jersey.

"And she did; but her stay was short, and it became a common thing for her to drift back there for a day or so, and then to flee away again, to return when the fancy seized her or the devils of discomfort drove her to seek a respite from the horrors which had now become for her synonymous with freedom.

"She always found something to reward her for these visits; some surprise in the shape of a new article or some fresh source of amusement. Money to me was only valuable as it gave me power to rivet another link to the chain with which I endeavoured to hold her to a better life; and though I knew the false construction which might be put upon these expenditures, not only by my father but others, I spared no means, stopped at no extravagance which might add one more allurement to the nest I had made for my weary and bedraggled one.

"The woman who had orders to keep this house in a continual state of readiness for its fitful visitant was as discreet as she was sympathetic. She may have surmised my secret, or she may have supposed all these efforts the result of an ill-conceived philanthropy.

"I could never tell by her manner. But I knew she treated my poor one well. Time after time has she opened the door to a disordered and dishevelled creature, whom next morning I found sitting in a bower of roses, fitted out in dainty cashmeres, and with her long locks combed till they shone and shone again. Nay, I have come upon her on her knees before the bruised and frozen feet upon which she was thrusting slippers of downy softness, which made my darling laugh until their very softness became a burden, and she threw them off to dance. I have never lingered over these sights, but I have imagined them over and over with tear-filled eyes, for, explain it as you will, every backward slip made by my darling toward the precipice I ever saw yawning for her strengthened the hold she had upon my heart, till the pity with which I regarded her filled my whole bosom to bursting.

"But the wild hawk cannot be tamed. She would vanish from our care just when we thought it was becoming dear to her, and my wild pursuit would begin again, to be followed by chance findings and renewed disappointments. She was not to be held, though in the hope of doing so I have spent many stolen hours in the little house, reading to her, talking to her, playing with her, sacrificing my good name and the regard of my relatives just to win back one innocent look to her face and keep her amused and contented without the help of the accursed drug. She slipped away from us in spite of all our efforts, and during this last year returned only once.

"Yet I think she has felt more drawn to me this year than in all the time of our marriage. But she felt her unworthiness more. She had listened to the hymns sung by the Salvation Army on some of the down-town corners, and, being susceptible to impressions of this nature, had followed the singers into their halls and heard some of the good words that are uttered there. Sometimes, I am told, she laughed at what she heard, but oftener was seen to cry, and once she herself sang till, as they said, the very heavens seemed to open. When I heard this, I could not keep away from these meetings, though I never came upon her at any one of them either on the East or West side. She seemed to anticipate my approach there as elsewhere, for often have I been assured that she had just that minute gone out, and must be somewhere near, though I never succeeded in finding her.

"This looked to me then like hate, but now I think it was simply shame; for when she knew that death was upon her she sent for me; and, seeing the old look of forbearance on my face, she threw up her wasted arms, and, panting like a child who has reached its mother's arms at last, turned her tired, tired face towards my breast with a feeble 'Forgive!' and died.

"You cannot know the heart of a man who has followed his lost lamb for years through tangled thickets and by headlong precipices, and it may seem strange for me to pour into ears so hardened and necessarily so unsympathetic the sacred secrets of my soul. But my position is a strange one and my story one that must be told in its entirety for you to understand why that smile upon her face is so much to me that my sole prayer at this time is to be allowed to remain in sight of it for one hour. She has loved me always; not as I loved her, not to the point of saving me one heartache or sparing me one erratic impulse of her ungoverned nature, but still better than I feared; better than her conduct would show. For when I came to lay her head down again upon its pillow, I found tied about her neck and fast clutched in her chilling palm, this.

"Our wedding ring," he murmured. "She might have pawned it for a dollar during any of the many crises of her miserable life."

He paused, put the token back in his breast, and added but one more word. "When she was alive and well, with vigour in her dancing foot, and a deathless unrest in her gypsy heart, she chafed at my presence and fled from my protection. But when the final shadow settled and she felt all other props give way, then her poor arms rose in recognition of the love which had never failed her." There was an indescribable tone of triumph in his tones. "She had need of me in her dying hours; she smiled—"

He paused, and his eyes, which had been fixed on her form, rose instinctively, not to the dingy rafters overhead, but to the heaven he saw above those rafters. For him her spirit had fled upward. Whatever we might think of her, to him she was henceforth a being blessed and gathered into a refuge from which she would nevermore seek or wish to escape.

It was hard to break into this calm hopefulness with words of stern or sinister meaning. But Mr. Gryce had no choice.

"What, then, is your special desire?" asked that officer.

Mr. Gillespie's eyes fell, and for a moment he stood thinking, then he said;

"I have retribution to make to her memory. I wish to take her to my own house and bury her from there as my wife. The humiliation from which my pride recoiled in the old days has been meted out to me ten-fold. I no longer wish to evade my responsibilities."

His expression as he said this was very different from the smile I had surprised on his face the night he stooped over his dead father. Yet the one brought up the other, and, in a measure, acted as a mutual interpretation. By means of it and the determination he had just expressed, I could comprehend the feeling of that moment, when with police in the house and the whole family subjected to a suspicion which involved it in the utmost disgrace, he contemplated the features of the man whose pride found the hemisphere in which he lived too small to hold both himself and the daughter whose worst fault was a proclivity to dance and sing.

Mr. Gryce, who had no such memories to reconcile, was meanwhile surveying the young man with a curious hesitation.

"I regret," said he, "the presence of an obstacle to your very natural wish to bury your wife from your own house. Mr. Gillespie, it is my duty to inform you that we are not here on a simple errand of surveillance: my orders were to arrest you on the charge of murdering your father."

CHAPTER XXIX

THE QUIET HOUR

I would rather have been spared the pain of that moment. Mr. Gryce had virtually promised that I should not be present at Mr. Gillespie's arrest, but I presume he forgot not only his promise but my very existence in the unexpected interest of this extraordinary situation. Mr. Gillespie, who at another time might have succumbed to the emotion of seeing himself singled out from his brothers on the charge which had hitherto involved them all, was already in a state of too much agitation to make much demonstration over this fresh humiliation. Nevertheless it became evident, from the droop of his arms and the general air of discouragement which crept into his whole bearing, that the iron had entered his soul and the climax of his many woes had been reached.

"I hoped for other results when I entered upon my long and painful story," he remarked. "Certainly you have found me able to account for much that has seemed anomalous in my relations to my father and the attitude I have been compelled to preserve towards society. I am surprised that anyone should continue to regard me as having had anything to do with my father's unhappy death. May I ask what special evidence you imagine yourselves to have against me? I may be able to refute it with a word."

This was more than Mr. Gryce could grant, and he said so, though with less imperturbability of manner than usual. "I am under orders to bring you into the presence of the District Attorney," he explained, "who will use his own discretion in the matter of having you detained. Will you accompany me quietly, leaving the care of your wife to Mr. Outhwaite, who, I am sure, will follow your wishes in the choice of such assistants as he may think necessary to employ?"

The look he received in return was eloquent in its appeal, but Mr. Gryce knew no relenting where his duty was concerned, and, recognising this, Mr. Gillespie took a fresh resolve and boldly said:

"You have discovered that I carried a bottle of prussic acid into my father's house the day before he died. Shall I tell you where I procured it? From the hand of her who lies here. I found it tied about her neck, when, after months of fruitless search, I was led to investigate Mother Merry's lodging-house. She was asleep when I discovered it; asleep in a way I always found it impossible to break, and the shock of finding her in quiet possession of what I instinctively knew to be poison maddened me to such an extent that I tore the phial away from her and put in its place a roll of bank-notes. These were probably stolen from her, as no proof remains of her having used them; but the bottle I carried away, having impulsively thrust it into my trousers' pocket at the first intimation I received of a raid being made upon the place by the police."

The explanation was so natural, and the manner in which it was made so convincing, that the detective's look and mine crossed, and I became assured that he as well as myself was beginning to give credence to this man.

"I can give no information of the use which was made of this drug after its introduction into my father's home, nor can I designate the hand which took it from my bureau where I placed it on emptying my pockets. My connection with it ended at the moment I speak of. I did not even think of it again till I came in from the meeting where I had vainly sought distraction, and found my father lying low and heard the cry of poison raised in the house."

"This would have been a welcome explanation at the time," commented Mr. Gryce. "Your delay has compromised you."

"So be it," was the short but proud reply which came from this singular man. "When you reflect that by the time I was able to satisfy myself that this bottle was missing from the place where I had left it, any attempt to exonerate myself would have been a virtual accusation of one of my two brothers, you will realise why I hesitated to speak then, and only bring myself to speak now under the compelling force of an interest greater than family pride or affection. In my desire to share the last offices which can be paid to my wife, I possibly show myself for the second time a coward."

Did he? Mr. Gryce did not seem to think so. The forehead of this aged detective was clearing fast, and he actually looked younger by ten years than when he entered this house. Yet his exactions remained the same, and Mr. Gillespie prepared to accommodate himself to them.

Meanwhile the incessant hammering of the rain on the roof had become less noticeable, and the drip, drip, on the sill without, less wearily persistent. There seemed, too, a diminution in the turbulence of the wind; the doors and windows did not rattle so loudly, and the worst noises in the yards below had ceased. Anxious to see if the storm was abating, I raised the window and looked out. Rushing clouds with great torn edges met my eye, and, below, a chaos of towering walls surrounding an abyss in which the imagination could picture nothing save a collection of foul yards and reeking alleys. Recoiling from a prospect which the condition of my mind and heart made more than usually gloomy, I turned back from the possible tragedies hidden behind those great walls to the actual one in which I had myself been forced to take so ungracious a part. Mr. Gillespie was waiting to speak to me.

"I am allowed to give you the names of such people as can best assist you in the removal of my wife," he remarked. "Here they are, together with the address in New Jersey where I wish her ultimately carried. Mr. Gryce will give you what further information you need—"

He placed a paper in my hand with a word of quiet thanks, to which I responded in the manner I felt would be most pleasing to Hope. Then he cast a glance at the detective.

"I have promised Mr. Gillespie the privilege of passing a moment in this room unseen and alone," observed that official, stepping towards the door.

I bowed and withdrew, shutting Mr. Gillespie in and ourselves out. Instantly all the noises in the house crowded clamorously to our ears. Laughter, singing, brawling, the screaming of children and the scolding of their distracted mothers, made a sort of pandemonium, which little harmonised with the mood induced by the pathetic story we had just heard. But it was not for us to be particular at such a moment, and I was glad that I had given no sign of my inward disturbance, when Mr. Gryce suddenly remarked:

"I am getting old." (His alert eye and attentive ear turned towards the room we had just left did not seem to indicate it.) "I find that such scenes make a deeper impression upon me than formerly. I no longer dwell on the skill it takes to bring them about, but rather muse upon the mistakes and woes of poor humanity which make them possible."

I wished to ask him what he thought of Mr. Gillespie's prospects, but he gave me no encouragement to do so, and we remained silent till the door reopened and Mr. Gillespie came out.

"I am ready now," he quietly informed us. "Mr. Outhwaite, I can trust you; and if Hope—" He stopped and looked the entreaty he dared not utter.

"I will tell her the whole story just as it has fallen from your lips. You wish me to?"

He signified his assent, but still looked wistful.

"When she has heard the true cause of the division which has taken place between you and other members of your family, she will act as her own kind heart will prompt her," I added.

He would have pressed my hand, but remembering his position as a prisoner, refrained.

"Let us go," he now said, in natural recoil from the noises which just then burst in renewed outcry from every quarter of the house.

Mr. Gryce gave a faint whistle. It was answered in the same guarded manner from below. At which the old detective turned to me with a few final directions, after which, with a promise to leave me well guarded, he made a gesture which Mr. Gillespie could not fail to understand. They began to descend. When Mr. Gillespie was half-way down, he gave one backward look at the door swaying between him and what he had loved best on earth; then he passed on, and I was left standing on that dingy landing, alone.

There was some clamour and no little jeering in the rooms below as the detectives passed through them with their well-dressed prisoner; but these tokens of class animosity speedily weakened to a sullen growl, amidst which I thought I heard the rattling of departing wheels.

With a heart as heavy as the silence which now filled the house, I turned and went back into that room.

It was filled with moonlight. The candle from which the winding-sheet had long ago melted and run upon the table, had flickered out, but its fitful flame was not missed. The clouds which had seemed so impenetrable a short time before, had thinned out and parted till they flecked, rather than covered, the white disk of the moon, now revealed for the first time in days.

That storm and that clearing have never left my memory. As the last lingering shred of cloud drifted away, leaving the face of the moon quite clear, I found courage to look once more towards the bed.

There was a change there. She lay, not as before, with her features quite concealed, but with her face exposed save where the loose curls had forced their way across her cheeks and forehead. The coverlet, drawn close under her chin, hung smooth and decent to the floor, and across it lay stretched one white arm, upon the hand of which shone the wedding-ring which Leighton Gillespie had taken from her neck and placed there.

CHAPTER XXX

AN UNEXPECTED ALLY

That night was a busy one for me; nevertheless I found time to send a message to Hope, in which I begged her to read no papers till she saw me, and, if possible, to keep herself in her own room. To these hurried words I added the comforting assurance that the news I had to bring her would repay her for this display of self-control, and that I would not keep her waiting any longer than was necessary. But it was fully ten o'clock before I was able to keep this promise, and I found her looking pale and worn.

"I have obeyed you," she said, with an attempt at smiling as pitiful as it was ineffectual. "What has happened? Why did you not want me to see the papers or talk with Mrs. Penrhyn?"

"Because I wished to be the first to tell you the secret of Leighton Gillespie's life. It was not what was suggested to you by the discrepancies you observed between his character and life. He is sane as any man, but—" it was hard to proceed, with those eyes of unspeakable longing looking straight into mine— "but he has had great sorrows to bear, great suspenses to endure, a deception to keep up, not altogether justifiable, perhaps, but yet one that was not without some excuse. His wife—Did you ever see his wife?"

"No," she faltered.

"—Did not perish in that disaster of five years ago, as everyone supposed; and it was she—"

"Oh!" came in a burst of sudden comprehension from Hope, as she sank down out of sight among the curtains by the window. But the next moment she was standing again, crying in low tones in which I caught a note of immeasurable relief, "I thank God! I thank God!" Then the sobs came.

I noticed that, once she had taken in this fact of his personal rectitude, all fear left her as to the truth of the more serious charge against him. Even after I had explained to her how he came by the phial of poison, and how it was through his agency it came to be in his father's house, no doubt came to mar her restored confidence in this her most cherished relative. She even admitted that, now this one unexplainable point in his character had been made clear to her, she felt ready to meet any accusations which might be raised against him. "Let them publish their suspicions!" she cried. "He can bear them and so can I; for now that he has been proven a true man, nothing else much matters. I may blush at hearing his name,—it will be years, I think, before I shall overcome that,—but it will be because I failed to see in his kindness to me the sympathetic interest of one whose heart has been made tender towards women by his wild longing after the wandering spirit whom he called his wife."

Then she asked where I had placed Mille-fleurs (a name so natural to Millicent Gillespie that no other was ever suggested by her friends); and, having been told where, said she would like to sit beside her until the time came to lay her in the garden of that little home from which all shadow was now cleared away save that of chastened sorrow.

As this was what Leighton Gillespie secretly wished, I promised to accompany her to New Jersey, and then, taking this pure-hearted girl by the hand, I asked:

"Have I performed my task well?"

Her answer was—but that is my secret. Small reason as it gave me for personal hope, I yet went from that house with my heart lightened of its heaviest load.

I did not read the papers myself that morning. I had little heart for a reporter's version of what had so thrilled me coming from Leighton's own lips. Merely satisfying myself that the latter was still in custody, I busied myself with what came up in my office, till the stroke of five released me to a free exercise of my own thoughts.

How much nearer were we to the solution of this mystery than we had been the morning following Mr. Gillespie's death? Not much; and while Hope and possibly myself felt that the band of suspicion had narrowed in its circle, and by the exclusion of Leighton, whom we could no longer look upon as guilty, left the question of culpability to be settled between the two remaining sons of the deceased stockbroker, to the world in general and to the readers of sensational journals which now flooded the city with accounts of the most sacred incidents of Leighton Gillespie's past life was still the man through whose agency the poison had entered the Gillespie house. Nor could we fail to see that the feeling called out by these tales of his domestic infelicities and the wild search in which most of his life had been passed had its reverse side for those people who read all stories of disinterested affection with doubt, and place no more faith in true religion than if the few bright spots made in the universal history of mankind by acts of unselfish devotion had no basis in fact, and were as imaginary as the dreams of poet or romancer.

That Leighton Gillespie had not been released after his conference with the District Attorney was proof that his way was not as clear before him as I had hoped. Yet I was positive that Mr. Gryce as well as Sweetwater shared my belief in his innocence; and while this was a comfort to me, I found my mind much exercised by the doubt as to what the next turn of the kaleidoscope would call up in this ever-changing case.

I had not seen Underhill in days, and I rather dreaded a chance meeting. He did not like Leighton, and would be the first to throw contempt upon any mercy being shown him on account of his faithful attachment to his disreputable wife. I seemed to hear the drawling query with which this favourite of the clubs would end any attempt I might make in this direction: "And so you think it probable that a man—a man, remember, with a child liable to flutter in and out of his room at all hours—would leave a phial of deadly poison on his dresser and never think of it again? Not much, old man. If he laid it down there, which I doubt, he took it up again. Don't waste your sympathy on a cad."

Yet I did; and to such an extent that I took a walk instead of going home and hearing these imaginary sentences uttered in articulated words. I walked up Madison Avenue, and, coming upon a store which had a reputation for an extra fine brand of cigars, I went in to buy one.

Have you ever greatly desired an event which your common sense told you was most unlikely to happen, and then suddenly seen it wrought out before you in the most unforeseen manner and by the most ordinary of means? From the first night of the tragedy with which these pages have been full, I had wished for an interview with the old butler, without witnesses, and as the result of a seeming chance. But I had never seen my way clear to this; and now, in this place and in this unexpected manner, I came upon him buying fruit at a grocer's counter.

I did not hesitate to approach him.

"How do you do, Hewson?" said I, with a kindly tap on his shoulder.

He turned slowly, gave me a look that was half an apology and half an appeal, then dropped his eyes.

"How do you do, sir?" said he.

"Been buying oranges for the family?" I went on. "Startling news, this! I mean the arrest of Mr. Gillespie's second son. I never thought of him as the guilty one, did you?"

The old butler did not break all up as I expected. He only shook his head, and, taking up the bundle which had just been handed him, remarked:

"We little know what's in the mind of the babies we dandle in our arms," and went feebly out.

I laid down a quarter, took a cigar from the case, forgot to light it, and sauntered into the street with it still in my hand. I felt thoroughly discouraged, and walked down the avenue in a sort of black mist formed of my own doubts and Hewson's calm acceptance of the guilt attributed to Leighton. But suddenly I stopped, put the cigar in my pocket, and exclaimed in vehement contradiction of my own uneasy thoughts: "Leighton Gillespie is as guiltless of his father's death as of other charges which have been made against him. I am ready to stake my own honour upon it," and went immediately to my apartments, without stopping, as I usually did, at Underhill's door.

I found a young man waiting for me in the vestibule. He had evidently been standing there for some time, for he no sooner heard my step than he gave a bound forward with the eager cry:

"It is I, sir,—Sweetwater."

He was a welcome visitor at that moment, and I was willing he should realise it.

"Come in; come in," I urged. "New developments, eh? Mr. Gillespie released, perhaps, or—"

"No," was his disappointing response as the door closed behind us and he sank into the chair I pushed forward. "Mr. Gillespie is still in detention and there are no new developments. But another day must not pass without them. I was witness to the sympathy you felt last night for the man who claimed the wretched being we saw before us for his wife; and, feeling a little soft-hearted towards him myself, I have come to ask you to lay your head with mine over this case in the hope that we two together may light upon some clue which will lead to his immediate enlargement. For I cannot believe him guilty; I just cannot. It was one of the others. But which one? I don't mean to eat or sleep till I find out."

"And Mr. Gryce?"

"He won't bother. Last night was too much for him, and he has gone home. The field is clear, sir, quite clear; and I mean to profit by it. Leighton Gillespie shall be freed in time to attend his wife's funeral or I will give up the detective business and go back to the carpenter's bench and my dear old mother in Sutherlandtown."

CHAPTER XXXI

SWEETWATER HAS AN IDEA

I was greatly interested. Taking out a box of cigars, I laid it before him on the table.

"Be free with them," said I. "If there is any help to be got out of smoke let us make use of it."

He eyed the cigars ruefully.

"Too bad," he murmured; "unfortunately, it does not work that way with me. Some people think better between whiffs, but smoking clouds my faculties, and I would be no friend to Mr. Gillespie if I took your cigars now. Free air and an undisturbed mind for Caleb Sweetwater when he settles down to work. Smoke yourself, sir; that won't affect me; but draw the box to your side of the table and give me a rebuking look if my hand goes out to it before this subject is settled."

I did as he requested, but not to the point of taking a cigar. I could think without its aid as well as he.

"Now, sir," he immediately began, "you were the first man to enter upon the scene of crime. May I ask if you will be so good as to relate afresh and circumstantially your whole experience with Mr. Gillespie? You cannot be too minute in your details. Somehow or somewhere we have missed the clue necessary to the clearing up of this case. You may be able to supply it. Will it bore you too much to try?"

"Not in the least. I am as anxious as yourself to get at the bottom of this business."

"Begin, then, sir. You won't mind my closing my eyes? I find it so much easier to identify myself with the situation when I see nothing about to distract me. And, sir, since I dread speaking when actively absorbed in this kind of work, will you pardon me if I simply raise my finger when I want a minute for reflection? I know I am a crank, and not much used to gentlemen's ways, but I appreciate kindness more than most folks, especially when it takes the form of respect paid to my whims."

I assured him I was only too ready to do anything which would serve to further the end we had in view; and all preliminaries being thus amicably settled he dropped his head into his hands and I began my tale in much the same language I have used in these pages. He listened without a movement while I spoke of Claire and of my entrance into the house, but his finger went up when I mentioned the appearance presented by Mr. Gillespie as he stood propping himself against the table in a condition of impending collapse.

"Was the house quiet?" he asked. "Did you hear no sneaking step in the halls or adjacent dining-room?"

"Not a step. I remember receiving the impression that this old gentleman and his grandchild were all alone in the house. One of the greatest surprises of my life was the discovery that there were servants in the basement and more than one member of the family on the floors above."

"A discovery which leads to our first argument, sir. We have taken it for granted (and certainly we were justified in doing so) that Mr. Gillespie knew whose hand poured out the poison he felt burning into his vitals. We have argued that it was this knowledge which led him to spend the final moments of his life in an extraordinary effort to settle the doubts of his favourite niece. But, sir, if he had had this knowledge, would he not have mentioned outright and without any circumlocution the name of the son he had finally settled upon as the guilty one, rather than have made use of the same vague phrase which had been his torment and hers, ever since the hour he told her of the shadowy hand he had detected hovering over his glass of medicine? With the remembrance in your mind of the few words he left behind him, are you ready to declare that you find in them any proof of his knowing then, any better than before, which of his three sons had mingled poison with his drink? And, sir,—you are a lawyer,— does it follow from any evidence we have since received that he even positively knew it was one of these three men? Might not his fears and the haunting memory of that former attempt have so worked upon his failing faculties that he took for granted it was one of his sons who had made this last effort at poisoning him?"

"It is possible," I admitted, "but—"

"You don't place much stress on the suggestion."

"No," said I, "I don't. Anxious as I am that each and all of these young men should be relieved from the appalling charge of parricide, I saw too great a display of anxiety on his part for the right delivery of what he believed to hold the last communication he had to make to his favourite niece, for me to think these final words of his contained nothing more definite than a repetition of his former vague surmise. He was facing immediate death, yet all his thought, all his fast-ebbing strength, were devoted to the effort of making her know that he had not been mistaken in his former conclusion: that it was one of his sons who sought his life, and that this son had now actually succeeded in poisoning him. That he did not proceed further and name which one, was due probably to a sudden loss of strength. That he meant to say more than he did is evident from the he which follows the four words we have been considering."

"True, true, but my argument holds; an argument which the difficulties of the case surely justify me in advancing. You say he would never have made such an effort to insure the safe delivery of words that were a mere repetition of a former statement. Yet what more were they in the unfinished condition in which we find them? Do you think he could have been blind to the fact that he had not succeeded in mentioning the name which alone could give value to his accusation, and make its safe delivery a matter of real moment to Miss Meredith? Surely, sir, you do not believe his wits were so far gone that he regarded himself as having made his suspicions clear in those five words: one of my sons he?"

"No, I do not. Yet who can tell. Bright as his eye was, his faculty of memory as well as of observation may have left him. Witness how he tore off the blank edge of the paper, instead of the words he wished to send."

"I know."

Sweetwater's tone was gloomy; a cloud seemed to have settled upon his newly risen hopes.

"Nevertheless," I now felt bound to admit, "I cannot quite bring myself to believe that he was so bewildered. On the contrary, I feel confident that he was in full possession of his faculties when he cast that dramatic glance upward, which, by a happy inspiration, I was led to interpret as meaning Hope. If we could penetrate this matter to its very core, I believe we should find the truth we seek either in those five words themselves or in the means he took of getting them to Miss Meredith. Have you ever thought, Sweetwater, that we have not given all the attention we should to the latter fact?"

"Yes, sir." His hands had fallen from his face, and he spoke with volubility. "It has struck you, I see, as oddly as it has us, that it was a very strange thing for him to send into the street for a messenger when he had one right at his hand."

"Claire, do you mean?"

"Yes."

"But Claire is a child; the slip of paper to which he attached such importance was unsealed and he dreaded its falling into wrong hands. Miss Meredith already knew his secret, but for him to proclaim openly that his death was due to the hatred or cupidity of one of his children would not be the act of a father who already, at the cost of so much misery to himself,—nay, as it proved, at the cost of his life,— had kept back from every ear save that of the one confidant of his misery, a knowledge of the fact that a previous attempt had been made upon his life."

"Yet to send into the street for a messenger! Why not send for one of the servants? Or why, if he knew which son he had cause to fear, did he not bid the child bring down one of the others?"

"Leighton was out, George was half drunk, and Alfred was two flights up. Besides, he might have thought that an alarm of this kind would prevent the delivery of the letter on which he laid such stress. Who knows what goes on in the mind of a man conscious of having but one minute in which to perform the most important act of his life?"

"True, true, sir; and yet there is something unnatural in his conduct, something I fail to understand. But I don't despair. I won't despair; we have only begun the recapitulation of details from which I hope so much; supposing we go on." And he sunk his head again in his hands.

I at once took up the thread of my relation at the point where I had dropped it.

"When I approached Mr. Gillespie I noted three things besides his tortured face and sinking figure. First, that the shade was pulled up over his desk; second, that a typewriter stood close to his hand; and third, that a pot of paste, knocked over by some previous movement on his part, lay near the typewriter, with its contents oozing over a sheet of unused paper. You ask me to mention all details and I have done so."

Dreamily he moved his finger, but whether in thanks or in an injunction for me to continue, I could not determine. I therefore remained still.

"I saw the paste," he murmured. And taking this as an intimation to proceed, I went on till I came to the moment when I pulled down the shade.

"You glanced out as you did that?" said he, lifting his finger as a signal for me to pause.

"Yes."

"And saw Mr. Rosenthal in his room in the neighbouring extension?"

"Yes."

"Standing how? With his back or his face to the window?"

"His back. He was sauntering about his room."

"So that settles one fact. He had not been looking into Mr. Gillespie's room at a critical moment. Had he seen that gentleman in a suffering condition or noted the curious incidents following your entrance, he would have been held to the spot by his curiosity, and you would have encountered his eager face staring down upon a scene of such uncommon interest."

"Very true. All he saw was the seemingly insignificant incident of Mr. Gillespie emptying the contents of a wine-glass out of his window."

As Sweetwater had no remark to make to this, I proceeded with my narrative, relating, with a careful attention to details, my journey upstairs, the words I had overheard at the door of Alfred's room, my first sight of Hope, and—I was proceeding to describe the results of my intrusion into the Gillespie attic, when I perceived that Sweetwater was no longer listening. His head, which he had raised from between his hands, was turned my way, but his eyes were looking into space and his whole body was quivering in intense excitement, such as I have seldom seen. As I paused, he came back to earth and jumped to his feet.

"Come," he cried. "Come with me to the Gillespie house. I have an idea. It may not stand the test, it may prove a fatuous one, but—"

The very hair on his forehead was bristling; the eagerness he tried to keep out of his voice showed itself in his eyes and in every jerking movement which he made.

"Come," he cried again; "it is not late. We will find the young gentlemen at home and perhaps—"

He added nothing to that significant "perhaps," but his repressed excitement had awakened mine, and my hat was on and I was following him down stairs before I realised that I had failed to turn out my gas.

As I wheeled about with the intention of rectifying this oversight, I encountered Underhill's languid figure loitering in his doorway. He accosted me with an easy:

"Halloo, Outhwaite!" Then, as he leaned close enough to whisper in my ear, he added, in an indescribable drawl, these unexpected words:

"I recognise your friend there. If you are piling up the evidence against poor Leighton Gillespie, you are doing wrong. No fellow with a heart like his ever put poison into his father's wine."

Which shows the folly of thinking you know a man's mind before he speaks it.

CHAPTER XXXII

WITH THE SHADE DOWN

Not many words passed between Sweetwater and myself on our way up the Avenue. He had his "idea" to brood upon, while I was engaged in turning over in my mind various vague conjectures rising out of the argument we had just indulged in. But before reaching the point of our destination, I ventured upon one question.

"Have you, during any of your investigations, public or private, learned which of the three sons of Mr. Gillespie is the greatest favourite with the old family servant, Hewson?"

"No; that is, yes. Why do you ask?"

"Because if it is not Leighton—"

"And it certainly is not."

"Then I advise you to direct your energies towards the one he is known to like best."

Sweetwater stopped short and surveyed me in very evident surprise before venturing upon the following remark:

"I should like to know just why you say that?"

I replied by relating my interview with the butler in the drug-store, and his easy acceptance of Leighton's guilt as implied in the arrest which had just taken place.

Sweetwater listened and moved on; but so quickly now I could hardly keep pace with him.

"If my idea has no will-o'-the-wisp uncertainty in it, and I have lighted upon a way out of this mystery, I will be made for life," he declared, as we reached the Gillespie house and he paused for a moment at the foot of the steps. "But there! I'm counting chickens—something which Mr. Gryce never approves of at any stage of the game." And rushing up the stoop, he rang the bell, while I waited below with my heart in my mouth, as they say.

Who would respond to the summons; and if we effected an entrance—which I felt to be a matter of some doubt—whom would we be likely to come upon in a visit of this nature? George? Alfred? I did not like to ask, and Sweetwater did not volunteer to inform me.

The opening of the door cut short my reflections as well as gave answer to my last-mentioned doubt. Old Hewson, and Hewson only, opened the door of this house; and whether this renewed encounter with his patient figure had something disappointing in it, or whether the solemn grandeur of the interior thus quietly disclosed to view produced an impression of family life that was more than painful under the circumstances, I experienced a recoil from the errand which had brought me there, and would have retreated if I had not recalled Hope's interest in this matter, and the joy it would give her to see Leighton Gillespie proved innocent of the crime for which he was at present held in custody.

Meantime, Sweetwater, with an air of perfect nonchalance admirably assumed, had stepped past Hewson into the house. Evidently he was accustomed to go in and out of the place at will, and though the old servant did not fail to show his indignation at this palpable infringement upon the family dignity, he did not abate a jot of his usual politeness or even watch the unwelcome intruder too closely in his passage down the hall.

But his complaisance did not extend to me. He gave me a look which demanded a response.

"Some formality of the law!" I whispered, hoping that the unaccustomed words would befog the old man sufficiently to cover my own embarrassment, and answer any doubts he might have as to the purpose of our errand there. And perhaps they did, for, with some muttered words, among which I heard this pathetic phrase, "There are so many of them!" he crept away and disappeared through the door leading into the dining-room. As he did so, I noted a man sitting on a settee pushed well into the corner near the study door. I did not know this man; I only noted that he sat there very quietly, and that the only movement he made at our approach was a slight raising and falling of his fingers on his crossed arms.

We were making for the study behind the stairs, and into this room Sweetwater, after unlocking it with a key he had taken from his pocket, now walked:

"Do you object to visiting this place again?" he asked, striking a match and reaching up to light the gas.

Of course I answered no, yet it was not quite a pleasant experience to stand there and watch the light flickering on his face, in a spot where I had last seen the one horrid spectacle of my life.

But when the cheerful flame had sprung up, and walls made familiar not by long seeing but close seeing had come into view, I was conscious simply of a strong desire to know why I had been brought to this room in such haste and secrecy, and what the "idea" was which had produced so marked an effect upon my singular companion.

He showed no immediate intention of enlightening me. He was engaged in casting a keen glance about him, a glance which seemingly took in every detail of the well-remembered room; then, as if satisfied that nothing had been disturbed since his last visit, he advanced to the window and pulled down the shade.

"We will not have the curious Mr. Rosenthal giving away our secrets," he dryly commented. "And this is our secret, is it not? You won't feel called upon to repeat outside what goes on between us in this room?"

"Certainly not."

The assurance seemed unnecessary, but I did not regret giving it when I saw how it relieved him of all doubt, and caused his eye to lighten and his manner to grow easy as he went on to say:

"So far as mortal calculation can go, this room has not been entered by anyone but the police or persons acting under the instructions of the police, since the hour when Mr. Gillespie was carried out of it. Consequently we have a right to expect all articles remaining here to be in the same condition as on that night. This, for instance."

He had taken out the typewriter from a closet built in one of the corners, and set it as he spoke down in its old place on the edge of the desk.

"Ah!" I burst forth. "Your idea is in connection with this typewriter!"

He frowned, or almost frowned, for he was an amiable fellow; then, giving me a pleading look, observed:

"I am young yet, Mr. Outhwaite, and it is very easy for me to deceive myself with imaginary results. You will therefore allow me a minute to myself, and if I find out that I have struck a false trail, or if my idea proves to be one I cannot sustain by facts, I'll sing out and we will consult as to our next move."

"Shall I step outside?" I asked.

But this he would not listen to.

"All I want," said he, "is for you to look the other way while I stoop over this typewriter."

I naturally felt disposed to humour him, and meanwhile he remained so still that I was confident he did not touch the instrument. But the cry which impetuously burst from him after a moment of intense stillness startled me so I can never forget it. It was something between a sob and a shout, and it was so suggestive of triumph that I could not forbear turning about and rushing up to the instrument over which he still stooped.

He greeted me with a look of delight and a rush of confused gestures.

"See, sir; oh, see! How I wish Mr. Gryce were here! Look at the top of that key, sir—the one with the words, 'Shift key' on it. Yes, that one; that! What is the matter with it? Tell me."

"The face of it is obscured. I can scarcely read the words. There is something on it. Something like—"

"Paste!" he cried. "The paste that ran out of the bottle and spread over the desk. You can still see unmistakable signs of it here and here" (pointing rapidly as he spoke), "for Mr. Gryce would not allow a woman in the room, and nothing has been cleaned since that night. The paste is but a dry crust now, but you must remember that it was moist when Mr. Gillespie stooped over the table, so that when his fingers got into it in his struggle to reach the typewriter, he readily transferred it to the keys. This will be apparent to you if you will scrutinise the exact keys he made use of in writing those last five words. Observe the one marked e; now this n, and now the o. There is but a trace of paste on some of them; but it is thick on the e, and thicker still on—what key, sir?"

"The one you first drew my attention to; the one marked 'Shift key.'"

"Just so. Now, do you know the use of the 'Shift key?'"

"I do not."

"You press it down when you wish the letter you are writing to be a capital. For instance, I wish to write the capital I. I hold down this 'Shift key' with one finger and strike the key marked i with another."

"Yes, but—"

"Oh, I know what you are going to say: 'No capital appears in the five words we are now considering.' True, sir, but does not this paste on the 'Shift key' show that he made an effort to write one; that a capital was in his mind even if it did not get on paper? In beginning any communication, one naturally starts with a capital, and you see, sir, that the space between this last hurriedly added phrase and the words of his unfinished letter is long enough to hold one. But the haste and agitation of this dying man were such that he did not put enough force into his stroke to bring an impression of this opening capital. If, therefore, we would read this communication intelligently, it is imperative upon us to supply this missing capital. Now, what letter do you think he meant to write there and did not?"

I blankly shook my head. My thoughts were in a great whirl.

"There is but one," he cried, "which would make any sense; the letter N, sir, the famous letter N. Supply that letter, sir; then tell me how those words would read. You know them well, or, stay, I have them here."

And Sweetwater spread before me a copy of the letter as it appeared after Mr. Gillespie had added the five words which had moulded the whole course of the investigation up to this point.

But this was an unnecessary precaution on his part. I knew the words by heart, and already had prefixed to them the capital N which he had just convinced me belonged there, as witness:

"one of my sons he"

"None of my sons he"

"Oh!" I cried, "what a difference!"

Young Sweetwater's face absolutely shone.

"Isn't there?" he cried. "I got that idea while you were talking about Miss Meredith. But that is not all. We are not through with our experiments yet. A letter prefixed is not enough. We need to affix a few. Can you supply them?"

I stared at him in amazement.

"'None of my sons he' fails to make good sense, Mr. Outhwaite. But look!"

Replacing the paper in the typewriter, he pressed a few keys, lifted the carriage, and drew me down to see. Imagine my amazement and the shock given to all my previous convictions when I saw written before me these words:

"None of my sons hewson."

CHAPTER XXXIII

IN WHICH WE CAN PARDON MR. GRYCE HIS UNFORTUNATE ILLNESS

"You didn't expect that? I thought I would surprise you, sir. Oh, I know what you want to say!" Sweetwater eagerly continued. "You miss the period and capital H which would show 'he' to be the beginning of a proper name. But, sir, Mr. Gillespie would not have been the failing man he was, if by this time he could think of capitals, much less periods. He was not even able to complete the word, though he evidently failed to realise this. 'None of my sons. Hewson' is what was in his mind; you may take my word for that. And now," he triumphantly concluded, after a short but satisfied contemplation of my face, "you can see why this dying man should expend his last energies in insuring the safe delivery of these words to the one person who knew his former dreadful suspicions. Shrinking as any father might from letting his sons know to what a fearful extent he had misjudged them, and dreading, as he doubtless had good reason to, some interference on the part of Hewson if he attempted to call any one in the house to his aid, he sent his little grandchild into the street—"

"But—"

"I know we are dealing with mere possibilities as yet, sir. But these possibilities are much more credible than the surmises in which we have hitherto indulged. I feel as if free air had entered my lungs for the first time since the inquest; and if I can refrain from yielding too much to the intoxication of it—"

"But," I again repeated, determined to have my say out before he had gone too far, "what motive can you ascribe to this poor old servant for a death which robbed him of a master he had served devotedly for years?"

"Motive be —!" cried Sweetwater, in some heat. But, with his usual good nature, he instantly begged my pardon, and his next words were uttered with more restraint. "Facts first, motives afterwards. What motive have we been able to find for the committal of this deed by any one of his sons? Yet each and all of them have been suspected and almost arraigned. Still," he concluded, "if you want a motive, search for it here," and he drew from his pocket a second folded paper, which he opened out before my eyes.

It was a copy of Mr. Gillespie's will.

"Ah!" I cried, in dim perception of what he meant.

"A thousand dollars," explained Sweetwater. "Not much in your eyes, but quite a fortune in his."

"And for so paltry a legacy you think that this man—"

Sweetwater's finger went to his lips. "Excuse me," said he, "but had we not better put back this typewriter on the shelf from which we took it? If I do not mistake, it will figure largely in the trial which I plainly see approaching."

I nodded, recognising the wisdom of the admonition thus given, and together we placed the typewriter back in the closet. Then he turned towards me with a new light in his small grey eye.

"And now, sir," he cried, "let me request you to stand back a trifle. I am going to finish this business."

Opening the door with a sudden jerk, he plunged into the hall. A shadow was just disappearing from the opposite doorway. With a shout to me to light up, he leaped across the hall into the dining-room. The next minute I heard a cry, then a low gurgle; then the match I had hastily struck flared up, and I beheld the detective holding down the butler and looking eagerly towards me for the expected light.

The man in the hall was by this time at my side, and between us we soon had three jets lit, illuminating two white faces: Sweetwater's pale with triumph, Hewson's blue-white from fear.

"Murderer! Poisoner of your benefactor and friend, I have you at last!" cried the struggling detective, watching how each terrible word he hurled blanched to a greater and greater degree the face he held pressed back for our inspection.

"You could see without faltering your master's sons, the boys you have dandled on your knee, fall one after the other under the shadow of public suspicion. Now we will see if you can show as much heroism on your own account. You are the man who drugged Mr. Gillespie's wine; and if the officer here will take you in charge for an hour or so, I will go down and procure a warrant for your arrest."

The attack was so sudden, and Sweetwater's manner one of such complete conviction, that the old man succumbed to it without a struggle.

"Mercy!" he moaned. "I was old—tired of work—a little home—a little freedom in my old age—a—a—"

I fled from the room. It seemed as if the walls must cave in upon us. For this, for this!

The sight of a half-dozen frightened faces in the hall restored my self-possession. The servants had come up from below and stood crowding and jostling each other just as they had done three weeks before. At the sight of Hewson's cowering figure they began to moan and cry.

"Be quiet there!" exhorted Sweetwater, advancing upon them with the courage born of his triumphant success. "The old man whom you have doubtless thought the best-hearted and most reliable of you all has just confessed to the crime which has desolated this house and all but ruined the three young gentlemen, your masters. Cry away if you want to, but cry quietly and without giving the least alarm, for the good news has not gone upstairs yet, and this gentleman, who was the first to announce Mr. Gillespie's death to his sons, naturally would like the satisfaction of telling them that his murderer has been found. I have no doubt that Mr. George and his brother are to be found above."

"They be, sir, they be," spoke up a voice.

Sweetwater, whose divination of my wishes struck me as remarkable, stepped aside at this, and, waiting for me to pass him, followed me to the floor above with a step so light he seemed to be buoyed up by wings.

As on a former memorable occasion, I stopped at George's door first. The knock I gave was followed by a rather surly invitation to enter. Excusing his un-graciousness in consideration of the fact that his visitors of late had not been entirely those of his own choice and consequently far from welcome, I pushed open the door without any other exhibition of feeling than an apologetic smile.

A scene of disorder confronted me; the disorder of an idle man who feels that with the withdrawal of all women from the house he had lost all incentive to neatness, perhaps to decency. In its midst, and lolling on a table over which lay spread some cards he was pushing about with idle fingers, sat George, much the worse for liquor, and by just that much short of being the handsome man he was intended to be by nature.

At sight of me he rose, and, propping himself forward on the table, looked the inquiry he was probably unable to formulate in words. I answered as if he had spoken:

"You must pardon my intrusion, Mr. Gillespie. I have come to bring you very good news."

"What news?"

"News of your brother's speedy release. News of your father's murderer, who, though an inmate of his house, does not bear the name of Gillespie. It is your butler, Hewson—"

With a shout he threw out his hands, and then sank panting and with drooped head into the chair mercifully at hand to receive him.

"I have always sworn that Leighton was innocent," he cried out with unexpected vehemence. "In public and private, declared that—he could—no more—have done—that thing—"

Sweetwater slipped from the room and I quietly followed, shutting the door softly behind me.

We went directly above; and this time found the room we wished to visit, open. As the face of its natural occupant could be plainly seen from where we stood, we gratified our curiosity by a momentary contemplation of it. Like his brother, Alfred Gillespie was sitting at a table, but he was neither flushed with wine nor engaged in idle revery. On the contrary, he was very busy writing letters. But he was not satisfied with his work. He looked restless and disturbed, and, in the minute or two we stood there watching him, tore up the wretched scrawls he had just indited, with a groan indicative not only of impatience, but deep, almost heartrending anguish. On his pale brow and in his attenuated frame few signs remained of the once luxurious Alfred, and when, after a second attempt at expressing himself, he made a dash at the unfinished letter and, crumpling it to nothing in his hand, threw it into the fire, I turned to Sweetwater and whispered:

"Cut this misery short."

The young detective nodded, and with a clearing of his throat, meant, I am sure, as a warning, he advanced and entered the room, into which I rapidly followed him. Without pausing for any greeting from the astonished Alfred, he at once presented me in the following manner:

"Mr. Gillespie, will you allow me the honour of presenting Mr. Outhwaite, who has come to offer you his hearty congratulations?"

"Congratulations!" I don't know whether I was more moved by the sarcasm or the despair expressed in this repetition of the word, which must have fallen with strange effect on Alfred Gillespie's ear. "For what, may I ask?"

"For the speedy lifting of the cloud which has darkened this house; for the free and honourable return of your brother from his present place of detention, and the incarceration in his stead of the old man, Hewson, who has just confessed to the crime of having poisoned your father."

"Hewson! Old Hewson!" Alfred rose with a wild laugh that was not unlike a curse. "You are playing with me! You are—"

"No," I interposed, with a decision he could not but recognise. "Far from it, Mr. Gillespie. What the detective says is true. Hewson acknowledges the whole thing. He wanted a little home, knew that a legacy awaited him at your father's death, and wished to hasten his enjoyment of it. Your father recognised him as his poisoner when too late. He tried to communicate the fact to Miss Meredith in the five words: 'None of my sons. Hewson,' but his strength failed him, and he only succeeded in impressing on the paper the unfinished words: 'one of my sons he.' The detective will explain."

"Ah!" was his troubled response, as he sank back into the seat from which he had risen. Then as he met our eyes fixed sympathetically upon him, he dropped his head upon his arms, crying brokenly: "Don't look at me! Don't look at me! All this misery and shame! And it was Hewson! Oh, Hope! Hope!"

We left him. It was all we could do. As we stepped down together into the lower hall, Sweetwater remarked to me, with one of his rare smiles:

"If you know of anyone to whom this unexpected clearing of the Gillespie name will be especially gratifying, you are at liberty now to make the good news known. I'm off for police headquarters, there to begin those proceedings which will release Leighton Gillespie in time to meet the body of his wife at Communipaw."

CHAPTER XXXIV

"IT WAS THE SHOCK!"

Later, Hewson made a fuller confession. In it, he explained how he first came to meditate the crime which he afterwards carried out with such diabolic persistence.

He had never indulged himself in dishonest longings, never allowed himself to dream of any other life than that of daily work in the household of which he had for so many years been a member, until the day he was called into his master's study on some errand or other which led him to the desk. A memorandum was lying there, and as he had his glasses on, he could not help seeing his own name among a list of others, with the figures $1000 against it. Now, it was no secret in the house that his master was at this very time engaged in drawing up his will. Indeed, the lawyer had been there that very morning. Consequently, Hewson immediately drew the inference that these figures represented the amount he was to receive upon his master's death, and though at the moment he experienced nothing but gratitude for the good-will thus shown, the knowledge of what he might expect under certain circumstances slowly roused in him strange ambitions and new desires, which afterwards resolved themselves into longings which gave him no rest day or night.

The relief from daily routine,—a little home in a country place where he could raise vegetables and flowers,—a quiet smoke in the twilight on a porch all his own,—all this would be paradise to the tired old man, and as he dwelt upon its charms he became impatient at his master's robust health, and began to note the difference in their years—which, alas! were entirely in his master's favour; and to think— yes, to think—that though it would cause him regret—naturally so—to see that master's health give way, it would not be so hard as this endless counting of years nothing but disease could annul; that, in short, a lifetime of service devoted to Mr. Gillespie and his sons had become as nothing in the light of his new desires, and when the usually healthy broker was finally seized with some complaint which laid him on his back, these desires grew into hopes which it was useless for him to smother, for he was now determined to have his little fortune whether or no, and have it before he was himself too old to miss its full enjoyment.

Meanwhile, he was much in the confidence of the family. He heard his master's symptoms discussed, and learned while waiting on table that Mr. Gillespie was being given small doses of a certain poison as medicine; doses which it would be dangerous to increase. He could go through all his duties with the utmost precision without ceasing to take in such a conversation; and when in the course of time he heard that Mr. Gillespie was improving and would soon be quite well, he allowed himself to dwell upon the tempter's whispered suggestion that three more little drops from a bottle constantly in use by his master's bedside would remedy all this, and in a safe and seemingly natural way end the one existence which stood between him and the money he now regarded as his own.

The carrying out of this thought was easy. He knew that his master was now well enough to be left alone at night, likewise to help himself to his own medicine after it was once prepared for him. One had only to steal into the room in the early hours of the night, and, with careful manipulation of bottle and glass, increase that dose before the time came for the sick man to want it. Hewson was accustomed to noiseless actions; he could even handle glass without a sound, having been trained in quiet ways by the very man who, in such an unexpected manner, was now destined to fall a victim to these very precautions. He therefore did not fear waking Mr. Gillespie; he only feared finding him already awake.

But even this possibility lost its terrors when he considered that to make himself quite safe he had but to utter the low-whispered Father! with which the young gentlemen were accustomed to approach the sick-bed at night. If Mr. Gillespie heard and answered, he would know the moment badly chosen and steal away. While, if no answer came, he had but to proceed as the devil and his own dark instincts prompted.

Night came, and he went through his part, as he supposed, successfully; but in the morning he missed the alarm he had a right to expect, and soon learned that Mr. Gillespie had accidentally overthrown the glass of medicine which had been so carefully prepared for him. Worse than this, he saw the bottle of poison emptied clean out, and heard that Mr. Gillespie's medicine was to be changed to one quite harmless.

What did this mean, and how could he now hope to carry out the scheme he was more than ever resolved upon? For a while he felt quite discouraged, and drooped a little over his work, which was becoming hourly more irksome. He began to hate the man who had upset the glass which, if drank, would have insured him an immediate enjoyment of his little fortune; and even to cherish the same feeling towards Mr. Gillespie's three sons, to whose wants he catered and who were all young enough to wait for their fortunes, while he, now nearly four-score, could not. That is, he hated the two eldest; but Alfred—well, he didn't quite hate Alfred; indeed, he almost loved him, loved him well enough to be glad that he, as well as himself, would profit by the old man's death, if only some new way could be found of bringing it safely about.

Meanwhile, he found as many errands to his master's rooms as possible, especially when the doctor was there; and, being regarded as a piece of household furniture rather than a living, breathing, and determined man, these two rarely made an end to their talk or changed their topic on account of his presence. And so it was he heard them often discuss poisons, and was able to gather up one or two items in regard to these dangerous drugs which otherwise he might have missed. Among other things he learned that an acid smelling like bitter almonds killed quickly and without much pain; but he failed to take in that this very smell was calculated to give away its presence. Brooding over this happy discovery, he cast about in his mind how he could prepare a drink likely to please his master without awakening his distrust. For weeks he thought it over, testing and trying various concoctions. Finally he hit on one which he prepared under Mr. Gillespie's eye and partially under his directions, and which was so strongly spiced that his master did not detect, or at least made no objection, to the flavouring of bitter almonds which he was careful to put into it. Indeed, Mr. Gillespie grew to like it, and, for a reason now readily to be understood, seemed to prefer anything brought him by his old servant to the finest of wines poured out for him by his sons.

Having thus provided a means for disguising the poison when the opportunity came for administering it, he cast about how he could procure the necessary drug without risk to himself. Ignorant as he was in most matters, he knew that he could not walk into a drug-store and buy so deadly a poison without rousing suspicion. So, as I have said before, he waited. But not long. Will begets way, or, truer yet, the devil prepares the way for him who is willing to walk in it.

One morning he came upon a phial in Mr. Leighton's room whose very appearance strangely affected him. It was small; it held a dark liquid; and it had a wicked look strangely attractive to him. He took the phial up; he smelt it. Bitter almonds! Greatly excited and somewhat shaken, he set it down again. How had Mr. Leighton come by this? What did he want of it, and why was it left standing in this open way on his bureau? Was it for medicinal purposes like the other? Probably; but it seemed stronger, very strong indeed; it seemed strong enough to kill a man. Catching it up, he carried it away.

"If any inquiries are made, I'll say I knocked it over and broke it." But Hewson didn't think any inquiries would be made. Mr. Gillespie's sudden death would make all such little matters forgotten.

Having in this unexpected way secured the very poison he most desired, Hewson poured into the sink all but the few drops he had heard constituted a fatal dose. Then he put the phial away in a tea-cup and waited his opportunity. It was not long in coming. That evening he prepared the drink as usual for Mr. Gillespie, and, while waiting for that gentleman to call for it, saw Mr. George come into the dining-room and take away the bottle of sherry, and afterwards Mr. Alfred, who hunted about for his pencil. Later, he heard Mr. Leighton come downstairs, but he did not wait to see what that gentleman wanted, for his own work in the butler's pantry was now done, and he thought it better to show himself in the kitchen. But he was suddenly called up by the dining-room bell. Mr. Leighton wished a glass of sherry for his father. This was an unexpected order, and for the moment set him quite aback. For if Mr. Gillespie drank sherry now, he would not want his spiced drink later. However, he put a good face on the matter and got out the wine, which he handed to Mr. Leighton, who poured out a glassful and carried it in to his father. A moment later he heard the front door close. Leighton had gone out to one of his numerous meetings, and Mr. Gillespie was left alone.

Somehow the old servant had an irresistible desire to see how his master looked at this moment. There had been loud words between that master and Mr. Leighton before the latter had left, and he wanted to see how his master had borne it—wanted to see—well, he hardly knew what; but he went to the dining-room door and, finding the opposite one open, peered in.

Mr. Gillespie was standing just where his son had doubtless left him, gazing intently into the wine-glass which he held, untasted, in his hand. His face was wan and troubled. Suddenly he moved and, glancing behind him, like a man bound on some guilty errand, but not looking far enough into the distance to see Hewson watching him from the depths of the dimly lighted room on the other side of the hall, he hurried to the window, and, raising, first the shade and then the sash, flung out the contents of the glass into the back-yard. This done, he uttered a sigh, which spoke of some great inward trouble, and, reclosing the window, carried back the empty glass to the dining-room, from which Hewson had, by this time, slipped in guilty confusion.

Not understanding Mr. Gillespie's sudden distaste for the wine he had ordered, but determined to profit by what struck him as a very happy chance, Hewson put his own concoction on a tray, and, creeping to the buffet, took the phial out of the tea-cup in which he had concealed it, and emptied its contents into the glass he carried. Then not liking to put the phial back, he thrust it into his vest-pocket, mouth up (the cork having slipped from his hand and rolled away in the darkness). He was willing to be heard now, and was stepping briskly around the room, when Mr. Gillespie called out:

"Who's that? Is it Hewson?"

"It is, sir," was the demure reply. "I came up to make you that drink you like so well; but Mr. Leighton said you preferred sherry."

"Yes, yes; but I like your drink, too. Brew it and bring it in to me. I seem to be unusually thirsty to-night."

Without a quiver, without a conscious sense of doing anything greatly out of the common, this tried old servant brought him the glass which he knew would end all earthly relations between them. He even waited until he saw it emptied, then he took it out again and immediately washed it.

Why he felt this precaution necessary he hardly knew, unless it was to pass away the moment of suspense. He never dreamed for a minute that there was anything special for him to fear. Were not men dropping dead every day in counting-houses or in the streets? And why not this man? That the police would be called in or that so quiet a death would be treated as a crime, had never occurred to him. He had never read murder cases much; indeed, had never read anything much; he only knew he wanted his master to die, and that the quickest way to bring this about was to give him a dose of very strong poison. Yet after he had done this, he felt some nervousness, not over what he had done, but its seemingly slow results. He had expected Mr. Gillespie to fall at once, perhaps before he was, himself, well out of the room, and Mr. Gillespie did not fall. Hewson had had time to wash the glass, put it away, go down into the kitchen again, and come back, without hearing the heavy thud for which his ears were strained. Was his affair to fail again? Had the dark and pungent liquor been harmless, and was it decreed that he was to go back to the old life with no hopes of a change or relief? He was so worked up by this thought that he crept into the dining-room again and was making for the hall door to take another peep into the study, when his foot encountered a small object on the floor. Yielding to his usual methodical habits, he stooped and picked up what proved to be Alfred's pencil. This he mechanically dropped into his pocket, then he went on.

He found his master reeling over the study floor in the first consciousness, perhaps, of his alarming condition. He seemed to be trying to find the door, but as Hewson drew nearer (fascinated, perhaps, by the sight of suffering of which he himself had been the cause), Mr. Gillespie suddenly paused in this effort, and, meeting Hewson's eyes, threw up his arms and made for his desk, upon which he fell in a way which assured his anxious watcher that the last minutes of his quondam master were at hand.[A]

[Footnote A: It was at this moment probably, and not till this moment, that Mr. Gillespie recognized his real murderer. Of the tumult thus awakened in heart and brain, who can judge!]

As he had no wish to watch his sufferings, he made another journey downstairs and showed himself in the servants' hall just as little Claire broke away from her nurse and rushed, laughing loudly, up to her grandfather.

This convinced him that his own comings and goings had been so natural that they had not even been noticed by his fellow-servants. He saw that they had been playing a merry game with the child, and that not one of them had had an eye for him or his unaccustomed nervousness. This gave him courage, and soon, very soon now, they all had reason for nervousness. The long-delayed alarm was heard at last; strangers came into the house; the police followed, and this old reprobate, who had remained serene amidst all the turmoil, realised that there was more to fear in the matter than had ever struck his mind. With this fear came not only a desire to hide his own guilt, but the requisite cunning for doing so. He realised that he must get rid of the phial before he was searched, and, being left a minute to himself in the dining-room, he took it out of his side vest-pocket, and, shaking out the pencil which had slipped into it, he thrust it under the clock as being the one article not likely to be moved. It was a heavy lift for his old arms, and his elbows shook as he guided it back into place. The consequence was that he knocked over the glass which Mr. Gillespie had set down on the mantel-shelf a few minutes before; but though the clatter which it made attracted attention and the broken pieces of this glass were carefully examined, nothing was discovered from them, the glass having held nothing but sherry. Not so with poor Alfred's pencil, the end of which had rested in the last drop of poison remaining in the phial. The odour of prussic acid thus communicated to it came near bringing his favourite young master into jeopardy. But something, Hewson hardly knew what, intervened to save him, and all was going on well, or as well as could be expected after the suspicions expressed by Mr. Gillespie against his sons, when this young demon in the shape of a detective flung himself at the old butler's throat and, without telling him why or by what means he had learned it, accused him of being his master's poisoner.

"It was the shock! the shock!" the miserable wretch wailed out. "Had I had more time to think, I would have known that he had no proof against me; that it was all guess-work, and that I would be a fool to fear that. But it is too late now. I have said it, and I stand by it. Only I wish I could have seen the thousand dollars for which I killed my master lying for one instant in my hand. I would willingly go without the cottage, go without the evening pipe in the sight of hills and meadows, just to realise the sensation of holding all that money and knowing that it was mine."

CHAPTER XXXV

ROSES

One more scene, and this narration of my life's most stirring episode will have reached its conclusion.

It was a memorable scene to me. It took place in the parlours of the little cottage in New Jersey on the day we laid Mille-fleurs away to rest.

The burial had taken place, the guests had departed, and only the members of the family remained to close up the cottage, now more than ever precious in Leighton's eyes. George and Alfred, with an assumption of brotherly feeling they probably thought due the occasion, had stepped out together to see that everything was ready for Hope's departure, and, from the window where I stood, I could see—arrant spy that I was—the nonchalant air with which either turned a wary eye upon the other as Hope's voice was heard above, speaking to little Claire. They evidently still looked upon each other as the possible object of her preference, no suspicion having reached them of the tragic secret which had made this young girl's heart inaccessible to them both. I, who knew it, and had my own place in the tragedy to which they had been blind, did not watch them long, Leighton being the more interesting figure at that moment, as, standing on his desolate hearthstone, he allowed his eyes to wander for the last time, perhaps, over the beauties of the bijou dwelling which, exquisite as it was, had been as powerless as his love to hold his roving wife in check.

He was waiting for Hope, and as this thought, with its suggestion of another and longer waiting struck my mind, a pang seized me which it took all my self-possession to hide. Waiting for—Hope! Hope, who had sat that day with his child crushed close against her breast, and a look on her face which angels might view with pity, but which I—

Ah! she was coming! I turned my face away, not that I had anything to dread from this meeting, but that I felt as if I could not bear at this moment to see the shadow veiling his melancholy countenance lift, were it ever so lightly, at the sound of the step that was shaking my own heart. But I immediately glanced back; uncertainty was worse than knowledge; and, glancing back, saw Hope, and Hope only.

She was standing in the open doorway with her arms full of roses—roses which she had brought from New York, and which she now held out towards Leighton, with a smile I hardly think he saw, so much was his attention fixed upon the flowers.

"What are these for?" he asked, advancing towards her and touching the great roses with a trembling hand.

"They are for her," said Hope, in a low tone; "for my cousin Millicent. I could not bear to have her lie with only her husband's tokens on her breast, as if she had no—no—"

He caught her to his heart. Moved to the very soul, he kissed her on the lips; then he took the flowers.

As he passed out, she tottered pale and almost swooning to where I stood trembling with my own emotions. Lifting her face, with its candid eyes and quivering lips, she faltered between her sobs:

"Have patience with me! I see now that he has never loved me and never will. Had so much as the possibility been in his breast, he could not have kissed me like that to-day."

It was not on George's arm, or Alfred's, or even Leighton's that she passed out of that little house into the new life she was to share some day with me.

A long time after those flowers had withered on Mille-fleurs' peaceful breast, Leighton said to me, with his hand on the head of his child:

"I shall never marry again, Outhwaite. To train this child up to be my pride as she is now my joy, will fill my life as full of happiness as is necessary to me now. And, Outhwaite, she is a quiet child,—" he stopped—I knew what thought had stayed him,—"a quiet and a loving child. Yesterday she sat for a full hour with her arms about my neck and her cheek pressed to mine, listening while I talked to her of things a child usually cares but little about. This is balm for many a hurt, Outhwaite, and if it is given to her mother to look down upon us two—"

A smile, the rarest I had ever seen, finished the sentence. Seeing it, and noting how it irradiated features which once bore the stamp of deepest melancholy, I could never again look upon Leighton Gillespie as an unhappy man.

Anna Katharine Green – A Concise Bibliography

The Leavenworth Case (1878)
A Strange Disappearance (1880)
The Sword of Damocles: A Story of New York Life (1881)
The Defence of the Bride, and other Poems (1882)
X Y Z: A Detective Story (1883)
Hand and Ring (1883)
The Mill Mystery (1886)
7 to 12: A Detective Story (1887)
Risifi's Daughter, A Drama (1887)
Behind Closed Doors (1888)
Forsaken Inn (1890)
A Matter of Millions (1891)

The Old Stone House and Other Stories (1891)
Cynthia Wakeham's Money (1892)
Marked "Personal" (1893)
Miss Hurd: An Enigma (1894)
The Doctor, His Wife, and the Clock (1895)
Doctor Izard (1895)
That Affair Next Door (1897)
Lost Man's Lane: A Second Episode in the Life of Amelia Butterworth (1898)
Agatha Webb (1899)
The Circular Study (1900)
A Difficult Problem (1900)
One of my Sons (1901)
The Filigree Ball: Being a Full and True Account of the Solution of the Mystery Concerning the Jeffrey-Moore Affair (1903)
The Amethyst Box (1905)
The House in the Mist (1905)
The Millionaire Baby (1905)
The Chief Legatee' (1906)
The Woman in the Alcove (1906)
The Mayor's Wife (1907)
The House of the Whispering Pines (1910)
Three Thousand Dollars (1910)
Initials Only (1911)
Masterpieces of Mystery (1913)
Dark Hollow (1914)
The Golden Slipper, and Other Problems for Violet Strange (1915)
To the Minute; Scarlet and Black: Two Tales of Life's Perplexities (1916)
The Mystery of the Hasty Arrow (1917)
The Step on the Stair (1923)